THE BOOK OF ANSWERS

A Rev. Thomas Book Mystery

Darrow Woods

reluctant sleuth press

For those who really like apples.

*"If I were once to settle down
and be satisfied with the surface of life,
with its divisions and its clichés,
it would be time to call in the undertaker,
except that in the monastery
we do without the ministrations of an embalmer."*

THOMAS MERTON (CHOOSING TO LOVE THE WORLD)

CONTENTS

FOREWORD

Saint Mungo's Church is a fictional congregation. I borrowed the location, and some architectural features from an actual church in Bronte Village, Oakville, Ontario. The events and people were all created for this story, and their behaviours, for good and for bad, are products of my imagination. They do, however, have stories about a ghost in that church, and about someone who lived for a while, secretly, in their belfry.

The story of the Anglican rector in Oakville who got lost in a snowstorm, and the one about the Methodist pastor and his wife interred in the wall of a church in Port Rowan, are rooted in actual history.

While the events of this novel are fiction, the seed of the story was planted decades ago, when I first heard rumours of a well-loved pastor, who actually did disappear over night, and was never heard of again.

THE BOOK OF ANSWERS

A Rev. Thomas Book Mystery

1

Zeke the cadaver dog raised his big head as if he'd just thought of a question. He paused his zig-zag search pattern, to turn and face me and his handler. His loud bark sent a shock through me, even though I'd watched him open his jaws to let loose with it.

The producers of "The Ghost Toucher" claimed they were testing a theory that dogs like Zeke are guided by the spirits of the dead. Zeke and his handler were brought in to sniff out the ghost of Saint Mungo's Church. I thought it was a ploy to jazz up an otherwise boring location shoot.

My assignment was to be the generic minister type in a dark suit and clerical collar who'd say to the camera, "I've heard the wild rumors, of course, but haven't seen anything like what you're looking for…"

That's the line I'd stick with if asked. I sure wouldn't tell them what I'd seen just before the dog barked.

Annika, the handler said, "Good dog, Zeke. You're such a good dog."

She knelt to unclip Zeke's black nylon leash from his safety orange Search and Rescue harness.

"Bones, Zeke. Find the bones!"

Annika tucked the leash in a pocket of her khaki tactical vest as she rose to stand.

She said, "That bark was his first tell Reverend Tom. He may have something."

The sable-coated German Shepherd bounded up the aisle towards the front of the Saint Mungo's sanctuary, leaving paw-prints pressed deep into the crimson carpet. He cleared the three steps up to the chancel platform in a powerful leap, landed under the dark oak communion table, and skidded between its legs. Zeke's nails clicked and scratched at the polished wood flooring as he scrambled for footing.

I turned to face the dog-handler, who had all of my six feet of height, and a bit more in her tactical boots. I met her eyes, which were amber.

"Annika, is he really searching for bones?"

"That's just his go-word. Zeke's trained to find bones, blood, and partial or complete human remains."

Those last words chilled me, despite Annika's bright smile, and the withering heat. The production crew had set up a bank of huge carbon-arc spots. They shone down from the rear balcony, lighting the church up like a high-end car dealership, and roasting us like convenience store hot-dogs.

All the sanctuary windows are stained glass. You'd never know that outside it was a cold and grey morning. A late winter blizzard that left folks from Arkansas to Quebec plowing and digging had also blasted Oakville. I'd felt lucky to get from my car to the church's side door without tumbling on the slick ice.

Zeke regained his traction on the hardwood floor and dashed towards an oak door set in the wall beside the organ keyboard. He nosed it open and stood peering down the back stairs.

His body vibrating, Zeke turned back towards Annika and opened his jaws for another harsh bark, which echoed through the sanctuary.

"That's his second tell," Annika explained. "He wants to get down to the basement."

Annika's long blonde hair lifted as she ran to her dog. Her thick-soled boots thudded on the hardwood floor. A holstered phone and a long black flashlight bounced against her hip.

Reaching the doorway, she squatted near Zeke and dug into a vest pocket for a treat. The German Shepherd licked it from her open palm.

"Good dog, Zeke. Bones?"

Zeke took his cue and dove down the back stairs. Annika was right behind him.

I headed toward the chancel steps, halting when I heard, "You need to let us through, Reverend Tom!"

I pivoted in time to avoid Kat Daniels, the assistant director, waving her aluminum clipboard as if she were swatting flies, and me, out of her path.

Hassan the camera operator was close at Kat's fashionable heels. His muscled frame made the video rig strapped to his shoulder look small. As he sidestepped to pass us, I backed out of his way until I felt the hard edge of a pew against my rear end.

Kat ran after the camera operator, shouting orders.

"Go! Go! We need this shot. Get downstairs and see what the dog's found."

2

Zeke the cadaver dog stood guard at the entrance to the old boiler room, the last door at the far end of the basement hallway. Annika knelt close to him, patting his back.

Annika said, "You are a good dog."

Hassan aimed the big lens of his video rig over Annika's shoulder. Kat was beside the camera operator, hugging the metal clipboard close to her chest.

Hassan sniffed, and said, "What the hell is that?"

Something sweet and rotten emanated from the dark windowless room. I moved closer, pushing down the urge to gag.

Annika said, "Zeke picked up the scent before we did and followed it down here."

Kat said. "Let's get lights on in there. We need the shot of whatever he's found."

"Annika," I said, "What's happening?"

Annika rubbed Zeke's neck and turned to look back over her shoulder.

"We have to call 911 and limit access. I know that smell."

I looked at Kat. "You heard her. We shouldn't go in."

Kat waved her clipboard for emphasis as she said, "She's working for me not you, and neither of you have authority here. Ed's the pastor. You're just his part-time assistant. You need to get out of our way!"

Kat grew up around this church. The clipboard was new, but she'd started telling me what to do twenty years earlier, when I was here as the student minister.

I'd been put in charge of the Christmas pageant. She'd been thin as a whisper but loud as thunder. A nine-year-old girl with salon styled blonde curls. Tight little fists balled on the hips of her princess dress. Stamping her tiny high heels and proclaiming, "Since my mommy and daddy are in heaven, you need to make me boss of the angels."

Grown up Kat still had the same haunted pale blue eyes. I knew she had personal reasons for arranging this ghost-hunt. I couldn't see how they connected to whatever we'd find in the boiler room.

I said, "Kat, we can't..."

Annika said, "Zeke seems to agree with Kat. He wants to finish his work."

The big dog stood alert; nose pointed at the dark room.

"Can you..." I began. "Will he..."

"He's trained for this. He won't disturb a crime scene."

I nodded and reached in the doorway for the light switch.

The stench hit us full force as we followed Zeke in. I had nothing to cover my nose and mouth.

The big dog stopped short of a dark puddle spreading fast on the tiled floor. His body was an arrow aimed at the exterior wall, which was pockmarked with clusters of drill holes, each oozing black fluid.

Water-soaked plaster melted away from the wall. It splatted in fat clumps on a classroom-sized whiteboard which lay flat on the murky tiles. It was a match to the shiny new whiteboards now hung on the other walls. Thin lines of plaster dust streaked down the wall below their frames like gritty tears.

"Someone went to town with their drill," I said, "looking for anchor spots."

Annika said, "Something's pushing at the drywall from the other side. See how fast those cracks are spreading?"

Kat said, "Hassan you getting this?"

A section of wall as tall as the camera man and wide as his outstretched arms bulged out then burst towards us. Sodden slabs of plaster smacked the wet floor, splashing Zeke and Annika.

Hassan turned away from the spray to protect his lens. Kat wasn't as quick. Her blouse and clipboard were scatter shot with greasy drops. I was out of range.

Even when his shoulders and chest were spattered, Zeke never flinched. Annika knelt beside him, ignoring the fetid fluid soaking the padded knees of her tactical pants.

"Stand down, Zeke. You are a good dog."

Zeke dropped to his haunches. He turned his head to Annika, who proffered a treat. Before he could tongue it from her outstretched palm there was a loud whoosh.

A murky plastic wrapped mass, large as a man, pushed out of the black hole and crashed on the remnants of plasterboard. The head end landed short of Zeke, sending up another dirty splash. He shook off a spray of dark droplets.

"Good dog, Zeke. Let's get out of here."

A slow dark stream bled out of the wound in the wall. A slurry of gravel and grey snow spilled on the checkerboard tiles.

There was a human form under those layers of plastic sheeting.

Kat asked, "Can we get Zeke back in here? I need a shot of him with the corpse."

Annika leaned in the doorway to shake her head. "We're done here. Zeke needs drying off."

Icy water soaked through my shoes.

"Kat, I don't think…"

Kat ignored me. "Go wide as you can on the big dark hole. It's like some weird crypt."

The boiler room was flooding. The mess flowed into the hallway. The basement reeked with a miasma of decay.

"Okay, Hassan, now back to the body…"

"Kat, please," I said. "Stop now. This is not what you came here for today."

Kat opened her mouth but said nothing.

Hassan looked to Kat and then me. Lowering his camera, he left the room.

I turned to Kat, and said, "Whoever that was mattered

to someone."

After a moment, Kat asked, "Who could have done this?"

All traces of the bossy little angel were gone.

3

I pulled the boiler room door shut with more force than needed. The slam echoed in the empty basement hallway.

I was angry that a person's body had been wrapped and tossed like a roll of old carpet.

I wondered how I could have worked here 20 years ago, and now, and never question the persistent mustiness in the basement.

I felt guilty for leaving the body alone in that cold wet room, but also because I'd been so relieved when the 911 operator advised, "Touch nothing, get out, and secure the scene."

My energetic closing of the door had not stanched the murky flow from the boiler room. I stepped away from the spreading dark puddle.

Despite the stench I breathed deep and tried to settle. I prayed for peace for the dead man. It looked like a man. Peace for those of us who'd just seen his corpse, and for those who must still wonder what happened to him.

My phone buzzed. It was Michael Powers, chair of the church property committee.

"I was going to call," I said. "We have a… situation."

"I heard. I'll be there soon. Tell Kat to stick around. The investigator may want her footage. Say hello to Annika and Zeke. We've worked together. She's good people."

"Annika went home… she said Zeke needed a bath. We traded contact information."

"You did? Good for you, Tom. Like I said, she's all right."

Until his retirement a year ago Michael was a detective with the Halton Regional Police.

"I thought… the police might need it."

"They'll know how to find her," Michael said, a smile in his voice. "Now you do too. How about Kat? She still there?"

"She and her crew are out in the production van. I think the smell got to them."

"Can't blame them," Michael said. "I never got used to it."

I moved further from the stench. Muscle memory brought me to a door down the hall that bore a brass plate engraved with 'In memory of Douglas Beacham, Church Sexton: 1967-2013'.

"How do you know what's happened? I just called it in."

I pushed on the heavy door and stepped into another dark windowless space. Without thinking, I knew just where to reach and grab for the hanging light's pull-cord.

"I'm not totally out of the loop," Michael said. "It sounds like you're on the move. What're you doing now?"

"Checking on something," I said. "Talk to you soon."

"I'm on my way, partner."

The basement workroom was Doug's domain for decades. A heart attack took him while he'd been upstairs, cleaning the sanctuary. The board ordered the memorial plaque for the door, and the space became an informal shrine. I hadn't been in this room since I came back to Saint Mungo's.

Shadows shifted as the single bare bulb swung a short arc. The room hadn't changed since the last lunch hour I'd shared a sandwich here with Doug twenty years ago.

Hand tools hung in painted outlines on the pegboard. Neatly ordered caddies on the workbench held arsenals of screwdrivers, drill bits and chisels.

Place of pride on an otherwise empty wall went to a framed pen and ink rendering of the exterior of the Saint Mungo's building.

A battleship grey metal shelving unit dominated the wall opposite the door. Hand-printed masking tape labels on the edge of each shelf assigned spots to jars of nails and bags of polishing rags. Doug told me the army drilled into him the value of things having their place.

His room still had a muscular, chemical scent. Varnish and paint, solvents and oil. Work was done here.

One handmade label on the shelf read 'dark walnut stain, desk in minister's study 1989'. I shook the pint can, and felt liquid slosh, even after thirty years. I returned it to its home, and saw an empty space beside it, labelled 'wood polish'.

Just before Zeke barked his first tell, I'd had a moment when I thought I'd seen my old lunch companion, who's been dead for years, on the chancel steps, at the front of the sanctuary. I'd thought I must've suffered heat-stroke from the movie lights or been spooked by all the stories about the ghost of Saint Mungos.

But then I'd smelled lemon oil.

I had the same spray can under my kitchen sink. Even after two decades I still thought of Doug whenever I used it.

It was that tangy scent that lured me away from the plastic wrapped sadness in the old boiler room. Like a search dog, I followed the hint of that smell to Doug's workroom. I wanted to nose around before the crime scene crew descended with their yellow tape and rules.

In the light of the single hanging bulb, I spotted a shadowy shape on the top shelf, with no label marking its spot. It made me wonder.

I climbed on a wooden stool, to get a closer look. The stool rocked, and I heard the soft tap of its shorter leg when I shifted my weight. Then another sound, like distant footsteps.

"You come back to help me, Doug?" It sounded foolish as I said it.

The workroom door swung inward. A shower of light poured in, as well as the fetid smell of death. The door closing hardware squealed. Without thinking, I turned and faced the full brightness of the hanging bulb.

Turning from the intense light, I asked again, "Doug, is that you?"

Stretching an arm towards the shelving unit, I slid my

hand across the top deck. The tips of my fingers found the cool hard edge of something but only managed to push it away. I leaned in further, rested a forearm on the shelf and stretched my other hand towards the mystery object.

"Not even close, partner."

It was Michael, the ex-cop, current chair of the property committee, and a good friend.

I strained to reach a little further, grabbing at what felt like a metal box. The wooden stool rocked under my feet. I leaned harder into the top shelf for balance. The shelving unit tilted out from the wall, and toward me.

I balanced on the rickety stool, half hanging from the mass of metal teetering towards me.

Michael asked, "Tom, what are you doing up there?"

Reasonable question, I thought. I felt Michael apply his weight to steady the stool.

"I may have something," I said. "Might be important."

"Careful, partner."

I reached into the darkness. My fingers gained purchase, then a tenuous grip on a sharp corner of the metal box. I inched it closer.

The shelving unit lurched further. I had a quick flash of all that metal crashing on us. I grasped at the shelf, but the structure toppled, and I felt like it was all coming down.

"Michael, look out!"

There was a clattering as items skittered to the floor. My eyes followed a spray can rolling off the top deck. Yellow plastic shards flew when the cap shattered on hard tile. I heard a pressurized hiss, and lemon scent wafted up.

Michael braced against the shelving unit, shoving it hard against the wall.

The stool rocked under my feet. I gripped the top shelf with both hands, to keep from falling. A flat tin box slid off the shelf, bounced off my chest, and hit the floor with a thud.

Michael offered his hand. "Partner, let's get you down and see what you've got there."

4

Michael placed the battered tin box on the church administrator's desk, centering it between her telephone console and a brass-framed photo of Brigid, her Irish Setter. He shifted his weight in her office chair.

"Why'd you look for it?"

The desk was pointed at a wall of windows, which offered a gatekeeper's view of the church's office entrance, and the rear parking lot. We'd escaped upstairs to watch for the arrival of the crime scene team, away from the horrid smell in the basement. I sat opposite Michael in one of the visitor's chairs.

The box I'd found in Doug's workroom was the shape and size of a cake pan. The sliding lid was scraped and dented and splattered with paint.

"Doug taught high school shop," I told Michael. "This could have been a class project."

"You're avoiding my question."

"I tried to make a pencil box in grade eight shop," I said, "but could never get the solder to stick."

"Trick was to use your iron to heat the tin, then hold the solder close enough to the tin to melt, and let it flow on to where you painted the flux," Michael said. "But stop changing the subject. How did you know to look?"

"I have an idea about what's inside." I said, reaching for Doug's box.

I set the lid aside, careful not to scratch the desktop, and lifted out a hefty rectangular object wrapped in one of Doug's polishing cloths. I dropped the cheesecloth on the desk top, to reveal a black leather-bound book. A thin gold ribbon held a place about mid-way through the pages.

"Interesting," Michael said.

The writing on the flyleaf was in the same meticulous hand as the masking tape labels in Doug's workroom. I read it aloud for Michael.

"This fine volume was a generous, unwarranted, and unexpected gift from the Reverend Stephen Peretz, who seems to feel I will profit by the regular, if not daily exercise of filling its pages with my shallow thoughts and meagre observations. Douglas Beacham, December 26, 1988."

"Did you know he kept a journal?"

I passed the book to Michael.

"In my student days I hung out in his work room. A few times, I saw this out on his table. He'd close it up when I came in."

Michael turned pages. "You going to read it?"

"I think I'm meant to."

Michael's eyebrows pulled closer together. He set the journal on the desktop, squaring it with the edge of the tin box. He folded the polishing cloth and placed it on the journal.

"So, really Tom, how did you know to look for it?"

Michael and I met a little over two years ago. At the hospice, at three in the morning. My daughter was curled up in the recliner beside my wife's bed, and they were both breathing slow and even. I slipped out to stretch my legs, and top-up the coffee I didn't actually want, and knew I wouldn't drink.

A bear of a man in a dark blue uniform, complete with Kevlar vest and holstered side-arm strode into the family lounge. The turquoise plastic jug was like a tea party toy in his hands.

"Know where I can find ice chips for my Mum?"

There'd followed many nights of us bent over opposite sides of the jig-saw table in the lounge, trading pieces of an English garden puzzle we never finished, and not needing to talk. Then came the morning I stretched my arms wide to hold this broad-chested man as he shook with sobs.

My wife Carrie lasted a little longer than Marjorie Powers, and she insisted I say yes when Michael asked me to do his mum's funeral. Two weeks later Michael brought his sister to Saint Mungo's for Carrie's service, and he's been around ever since.

"You're a good friend, Michael."

"That doesn't get you off the hook, partner."

"Hook?"

"You were literally climbing the walls in his old workroom. My gut, which is considerable, says you must have had a reason."

I looked at Michael. "I wasn't climbing…" The words I tried out in my head sounded lame.

"Kat's crew was shooting video for The Ghost Toucher," Michael prompted.

"You know about that?"

"Kat talked to me about running power cable for those big spotlights. I've heard about the ghost of Saint Mungo's."

"What do you make of them… the ghost stories?"

Michael kept a straight face. Was that from all those years as a cop?

"You experienced something, and you're worried I won't believe you."

I let out a breath. "I saw Doug. He was kneeling on the chancel steps, polishing the communion table. I know how this sounds."

I know how it would sound if someone told me the story.

Michael asked, "Was that something you ever saw him do?"

He seemed to be keeping an open mind.

"Yes, but this was more like a waking dream than a memory. His hair was dark, not the grey I remember, and he looked fit."

"How did it feel to see him?"

"Great question. Like I was intruding. Like I was a cathedral tourist snapping photos while the faithful light candles and say their prayers."

Michael smiled. "That's poetic, partner. Did he speak to you?"

"He never turned our way. Not even when Zeke, the search dog stopped in front of the chancel steps, barked, then ran right through the spot where I'd just seen Doug kneeling."

"Story is he died on those steps, slumped over when his heart failed," Michael said. "What about your other senses?"

"Michael, you sound like you could work for The Ghost Toucher. Have you dealt with this kind of thing before?"

"Try to remember. Did you hear anything unusual, or notice a change in temperature?"

"I was a little dazed. It was hot in the sanctuary. I'd made the mistake of looking straight into the big movie lights and did not really trust my eyes... or my head."

"What prompted you to search the workroom, a place you hadn't gone in how long?"

"Lemon oil. I caught a whiff of Doug's furniture polish. I thought that even if I couldn't trust what I was seeing..."

"You thought smelling was believing?"

"Something like that."

"You often see, or smell things like this?"

"I've always had strange dreams, but at night. Seeing weird things in my waking hours started around the time I met you."

"Hey!" He was grinning, which helped.

"That's not what I mean. When we were at the hospice for Carrie and your mum, I used to see... like wisps of smoke from candles that weren't there."

"You never said."

"We'd just met. Didn't want you to think..."

"No, that actually makes sense to me," Michael said. He looked past me, and I turned, wondering if the police had arrived. The parking lot was empty.

"What do you mean?"

"Some of Mum's Scottish kin had what they called 'second sight.' They saw things others didn't."

"And… you never said," I said, smiling.

"Like you said, not the easiest thing to talk about."

"Carrie was way more open than me, especially in those last weeks. She said receive any experience, waking or asleep. Take it like it was a gift, not a problem to be solved."

"She sounds like Mum. I wish they could have met. They were both stuck in their beds… just down the hall from each other." Michael's eyes shifted again. "Here they come."

An unmarked cruiser cut fresh tracks in the snow-covered lot. I nodded towards Doug's journal.

"Do we need to tell them about this?"

Michael shut his eyes, and his face pulled tight. He gave his head a shake, to release the tension.

"You're worried they'll think you're a few sandwiches short of a picnic if you say you saw a ghost, who sent you to find a book."

"Pretty much. That, and they might take it before I can read it."

Michael tried on his "serious" cop look, then smiled. "You found the journal in a different room, in the building where you work. If it had been in the wall, with the body…"

I said, "It may have nothing to do with any of this."

He nodded. "Or there may be something in there. Go ahead and read it. But let me know if Doug has a story to tell."

5

"Virgil's the creepy one with the eyes who scared my intern last summer, yeah? Why do they keep him around?"

I rolled my shoulders and pressed hard into the back of the heated leather seat. I felt a crack and a release of tension. Funerals are the only time I ride in such comfort.

Gwen picked me up in her funeral car for a 1 pm graveside service. It was a relief to leave behind the crime scene tape and the fetid smell infiltrating the church.

"That's the thing," I said. "Virgil was supposed to be there early to clear the snow, make it safe for the video crew. The crew brought in by his twin sister Kat."

I pictured Virgil as a child, shadowing behind Kat, hunched down to match her height and scanning the surroundings with vigilant eyes.

"That is weird," Gwen said. "But if he's so useless, why keep him on?"

"The twins were raised by their great aunt Attie Beacham. She thought Virgil should work at the church and she usually gets what she wants."

Gwen said, "My aunties are like that."

I grinned. "I think you're at least as ornery as they are."

We accelerated round the curve of the Bronte ramp, on to the QEW, and up to speed. Tall ridges of dirty snow were scraped up high against the barriers on both sides of the expressway.

"I don't take them on," Gwen said. "I'm going to need them on my side."

Gwen guided us into the middle lane. Ahead, a pair of plow trucks scattered salt and sand on freshly scraped lanes of the Queen Elizabeth Way, the main artery for the Golden Horseshoe. Even this late in the day, a coagulation of commuter cars rolled thick and slow toward the city.

"You haven't talked to your mom yet?"

"She knows Richard and me are split and I've moved into your basement, but…"

"You haven't told her about Jill."

"She thinks you and I will end up together, and I don't correct her."

"That explains the way your mom and aunties were smiling at me at dinner last Sunday. I wondered if I had something on my teeth."

"You probably did. And they like you anyway."

Gwen gunned the sedan to claim the outside left lane ahead of a red Lexus. She overtook the sander trucks, pulling well ahead of the clot of cars caught behind them.

"You'll find a way through," I said. "Your mom's one of the most open-hearted people I know."

I love Sunday dinners at Mama Jessie's house. They start after church and carry on late enough for all the in-laws and out-laws and hangers on like me to eat in shifts. The aunties haul in big foil pans of chicken and goat curry, rice and peas, salt fish and cabbage, and savory patties.

"Your mum hugged her big arms around Hope those first days after Carrie died," I said. "She's been good to us."

"Yeah," Gwen said, "but she's old school."

"And she loves you."

"She believes people like me are ungodly. Back home they still call us sodomites, and the constabulary look the other way when sisters are raped, or worse."

"I've not heard any of that from her. Besides, she's lived in Canada longer than Jamaica."

Gwen shook her head. "She'd never say it around you."

I moved to something less upsetting. The smell of death.

"What do you know about cleaning up a crime scene?"

Gwen said, "I know a guy."

"Of course, you do."

"Rod and I were at Humber together. He fell into trauma scene cleaning on the side. Now it's his full-time gig. Has his own company, calls it Remains of the Day."

I laughed. "That's pretty good."

"They know anything about the body? It wasn't Ed, your missing senior pastor?

Gwen slowed minimally as she veered onto the exit ramp. I gripped the handhold.

"Don't see how it could be," I said. "Whoever he was, the poor soul was in the wall a long time."

Gwen asked "Was there a smell before?"

"It was always musty. I told Ed no one would want to sit in that room, and his plan to make it another teaching space was crazy."

Speaking of crazy, I remembered from my time as a hospital chaplain that smelling things that aren't there can indicate neurological issues.

Gwen braked to veer onto the exit ramp. I gripped the handhold as the big sedan rocked into the curve. She looked over at me.

"Hey, you okay?"

"Everyone's asking me about smells today," I said. "Like you're worried I had a stroke or something. Maybe I am losing it."

Gwen said, "Losing what?"

She caught the green light and we rolled straight across Southdown to Sheridan Way.

"When I saw Doug's ghost or whatever," I said, "I smelled lemon oil. When he disappeared, so did the lemons. No one else seemed to notice. Not even Annika's dog, Zeke."

"Annika," Gwen said. "You light up a little when you talk about her."

That startled me. "Um…"

"Never mind. We'll come back to your dog lady. There's nothing wrong with you Tom. My Auntie Rosie's an Obeah woman. She says the spirits come to help us make something right. They help us see what needs to be seen."

"I didn't know that about Rosie," I said. "What's your mother think of that?"

"Don't you mention it to my mum. Her church crowd bashes the Obeah as bad as they do people like me. There's a saying on the island. In the light of day, folks preach against him, but in the dark of night, they run to the Obeah man."

My cheeks flushed, heat spreading to my ears and scalp, and the back of my neck. We humans are so quick to judge, to condemn, to dismiss people. I bad-mouthed Virgil for not clearing the snow around the church but had not thought to ask why he hadn't made it to work.

Gwen braked, waiting on a bright orange Mercedes SUV in the oncoming lane to turn before she followed it south on Clarkson.

"If you had money for a Mercedes," Gwen said, "would you go for that colour? It's a big pumpkin on wheels. A Cinderella truck."

Gwen showed all her teeth again, in that broad smile that had always seemed to say, life is hard, but we can have a laugh.

"If the pumpkin had seats as posh as this car," I said, "I couldn't care less about the colour."

"Speaking of fairy-tale princesses, tell me about the lovely Annika."

I held up my buzzing phone. "This is probably Hope."

"You're saved for now." Gwen declared. "Give that child my love. But we'll talk about your dog lady later, yeah?"

6

Hope's picture lit up the screen on my phone. She has her mother's eyes.

"Hi sweetie," I said.

Gwen slowed the funeral car for a turn, and we rolled through stone gateposts guarding the cemetery entrance. The iron gates were buried in snowbanks on each side of the driveway.

Hope said, "Daddy, what's going on?"

"I'm with Gwen, doing a burial."

Gwen pulled in ahead of the funeral coach, two more sedans, and a silver utility van. The custom license plates all started with MB, for Morrison Brothers.

"Someone on my floor texted me," Hope said. "They saw online about a dead body at an Oakville church. Was it Saint Mungo's? Was it someone we know? Are you okay?"

That didn't take long.

I gazed out the car window. The light was strange this morning. Wan and indirect. Spindly shadows of ancient maple, oak and elm traced across the taller headstones and monuments. Wind-blown snow was high against some of the stones. A few bare trees supported dark leafy clumps of empty nests in the crooks of limbs.

The blizzard quashed any hope of spring weather. I didn't want Hope's Easter break overshadowed by another sad death.

Hope said, "Dad, can you hear me? Was it someone we know?"

"Sorry, I hear you," I said. "The police just got into it. Whoever it was died long ago."

The grey light of the winter sky strained my eyes. I blinked and focused on the glossy faux wood of the funeral car's dashboard.

Hope's voice was washed away in static.

I said, "Sweetie, where are you? It's hard to hear you."

Gwen's door opened and I was chilled by wintry air as she mouthed, "I'll be right back."

The Cadillac chimed until Gwen closed her door.

"…Atlanta airport," Hope said, "Air Canada put me on stand-by. I could fly Delta to Detroit tomorrow and work on getting from there to Toronto or Buffalo. I'd have to buy another ticket. Is that okay?"

"That's why you have the credit card," I said. "Good for you to figure it out."

Hope doesn't take money for granted, even though there'd been a big payout on the whole life policy Carrie started when she joined the nurse's union.

"Dad, how are you doing?"

"I'm good. We're about to start the graveside service. Gwen says hi."

The sedan chimed as Gwen opened her door and rocked as she sat. She pointed at my phone.

"How's my girl doing? She on her way?"

Hope said, "Tell her I want to see her and Mama Jessie while I'm home."

Gwen smiled and nodded.

I said, "She heard you, and she wants that too."

I looked to Gwen and said, "She's still in Atlanta, but she's got a plan."

"Dad, I know you have to go, but tell me for real. Are you okay?"

I took a breath before speaking.

"Hope, I'm as good as we can be, this time of year. We'll talk more when you get here. I love you."

7

A red Toyota Corolla, grimy with road salt, rolled through the cemetery gate and stopped beside Gwen's car.

Gwen waved to the driver, a fortyish looking woman with ash brown hair pulled tight in a bun, and sad eyes. "That's Ella Sayers. It's her mother who passed."

I powered my seat back as Gwen lowered the window on my side. She spoke across the gap to the woman in the Toyota.

"Ms. Sayers, everything is prepared. Would you like to follow me?"

She said, "Let's just get this done. I need to get back to work."

Gwen pulled ahead to open a space for the red Toyota. The funeral car's tires crunched slowly through ice and snow as Gwen led the procession. On both sides of the lane rows of headstones poked up through drifted snow.

Gwen said, "She's having a time."

"That's how she was on the phone," I said. "Didn't want to meet to plan things or talk about her mother."

Dirty red-brown tire tracks in the snow marked where they'd backed out the front-end loader. The cemetery crew placed plywood sheets around the hole in the frozen earth and laid green plastic carpet over the wood. It was for safer footing but always made me think of miniature golf.

Gwen said, "She was all business when we met. Her mother had pre-planned, and specified a Protestant officiant. The original arranger's notes were still in the file, and they'd penciled in A.B.C. You know, Anything but Catholic."

"So much of my ministry is helping people get over hurtful history."

Gwen patted my arm. "Part of why we love you, Tom. It's also why I asked you to help, even though you're supposed to be off this week."

Gwen was a student intern at Morrison Brothers when we first met. I walked in the back office to pick up a clergy record as an older, white, male staffer schooled her about the need to control her hair. Back then, she'd kept it in shoulder length tight twists.

"With respect, Mr. Morrison, do you see who's up there?" Gwen pointed to the photos of the deceased on the schedule board. "They look a lot more like me than you."

Morrison brought his hands up, like a Brooks Brothers Jesus calming the waters, and said, "At Morrison Brothers we require a certain… professional look, Ms. Bailey. That's all I'm saying."

"Did you read their announcements? Nuala Clark was a Bay Street lawyer, Dr. Williams an orthopedic surgeon, and Henrietta Brown was a clerk at the provincial legislature for 27 years. Is that "professional" enough for you?" She even made the air quotes with her fingers.

Later that day, as she drove us to a cemetery, I saw Gwen's broad smile for the first time when she declared, "I do weary of the rule of old white men. No offense!"

She was the one in charge on this chilly afternoon.

To the right of the grave, loose soil and frozen clods of dark brown earth spilled out from under a green tarp. Where the dirty tracks met the cemetery lane, a discrete sign read "Morrison Brothers."

Down the road, two men sat in an idling pickup truck. They'd wait until Gwen gave the nod to fill in the hole.

Gwen said, "I'll get things going. We're using interns and new hires as pall bearers today. Good experience for them. You stay warm in the car until we need you, yeah?"

Ella Sayers stood alone on the path to her mother's grave. Above us there was a break in the clouds.

Sunlight glinted off a polished aluminum rail of the

casket lowering device. I looked up from that unexpected brightness to see a small blonde girl dancing on the mini-golf carpet. I'd just been talking with Hope. Was that why I saw or daydreamed this little one?

The dancer seemed about five years old. She wore a fuzzy red wool poncho trimmed in white fur. She circled the dark hole into which Mrs. Sayers's remains would descend.

Gwen rapped on the car window with her gloved knuckle. It always felt odd to have her open my door but it's the Morrison Brothers way. The Cadillac chimed as I climbed out.

The little dancer moved to the beat of the door chime. The curled ends of her long blonde hair bobbed with each step. The smooth leather soles of her shiny black shoes slipped a little on the frosted green carpet. She smiled broadly as she circled the grave, leaving no tracks I could see.

Gwen said, "Ms. Sayers, this is Reverend Book."

She was about halfway between my height of six feet, and Gwen's five feet. Close up, her eyes looked tired. Strands of ash brown hair pushed out from under a blue and white Maple Leafs toque.

"Ms. Sayers. Hello."

Our breaths made clouds in the cold air.

"Reverend Book, thank you for doing this."

"It's Tom. I asked before, but is there anything I should say about your mother?"

Her jaw stiffened. "Can we just please start?"

I turned to Gwen. "Ms. Bailey?"

Gwen nodded to Pat, another senior staffer, who stood between the grave and the funeral coach with a squad of junior staffers.

Pat was as wide and solid as the stone posts at the cemetery entrance. He swung open the rear door of the funeral coach and rolled the casket out a third of the way. The pallbearers were paired by descending height. They wore matching charcoal topcoats and standard issue Morrison Brothers ear warmers. They stepped in to grip the carry handles on either side of the casket.

Four of the six were women and three were persons of colour. I saw this as a sign of Gwen's influence at one of the stuffiest family firms in a very conservative industry. One pallbearer had hair fixed in tight braids at least as long as Gwen used to keep hers.

A slight lift of Gwen's two gloved palms, and the six pallbearers moved as one. I fell in beside Gwen as we trod in unison toward the grave.

We followed muddy tracks in the snow from the road to the grave. I snuck a peek over my shoulder and saw Ella Sayers lagging.

I turned to face her mother's resting place. As I stepped up on the golf green carpet to the right of the grave, the little blonde dancer gamboled towards me. Her blue eyes were luminous.

The little girl seemed startled to see me. She stopped short, skidding on the slick, frosted surface. Her arms flew out in anticipation of a fall. I stepped towards her, and leaned forward, reaching out to catch her. The little one halted her forward slide and regained balance, just before those woolly white mittens would have met my hands.

On the other side of the grave, Gwen cleared her throat, and with the slightest nod to me, signaled the approach of the casket.

I turned my head and saw Pat huffing clouds behind me.

I stepped aside for the young staffers carrying the casket.

I strode to the head of the grave, moving through the spot where I'd last seen the little dancer. All that remained was the memory of the clarity of those pale blue eyes.

If Aunt Rosie the Obeah woman has it right, what was this spirit trying to tell me? If it's not a guiding spirit, then what's happening to me? I tried to remember what my wife would have said. Be open, accept, receive.

Pat's crew set Mrs. Sayers's casket on the cross bands of the lowering device. The canvas straps tightened and audibly strained but held. The pallbearers stepped back from the grave.

I took a centring breath as I reached in my coat for my notes. I looked to Ella Sayers, the lone mourner at her mother's grave. She met my gaze for the first time, as I began to speak.

"We are here to say farewell to Mrs. Wanda Mae Sayers. With faith and hope we entrust her to God's loving care. We want that for her as much as we want that for every soul who's ever lived, and for ourselves when it's time. Her body will be laid to rest in this place but those we love do not perish with their body. We are part of a bigger story, and there is more to us, more to everything, than we can usually see."

8

"Eric Halliday, was that your handiwork in the old boiler room?"

"Reverend Tom, are you asking if I hid that poor soul's body in the wall?"

Eric carried himself like the old-school banker he once was. His checked flannel shirt and pressed khakis fit neatly on his small frame. He kept his white hair freshly trimmed, like he was ready to go back to the branch tomorrow, even though he's been retired longer than I've been working.

"No, I meant the new whiteboards, and all those drill holes on the outside wall... but are you trying to tell me something?"

"We had some trouble with the last one. The whiteboards were on Deborah's muffin list."

Our church administrator leaves out a tin of fresh baking topped with a post-it note for the old boys coffee and fix-it club.

Eric's one of her favourites. He came in early to help Michael and I set up for an emergency council meeting in the Christian Education wing. The scene of crime techs had taken charge of the basement and cordoned off most of the main building.

At fifty-eight, Michael is the youngest of the old boys. He wore loose fitting jeans and a navy t-shirt with the logo of his restaurant, 'Amazing Sandwich Powers' stretched over his broad chest. It's a police shield engraved with the outline of a B.L.T.

"Eric... help me with this?"

Michael's large hands rested on the top corners of one end of an ancient steel-cased television cinch-strapped to a tall cart. It might have come from my high school's A-V room, back in the last century.

Gamely cracking his knuckles, Eric pulled his shoulders back so he stood his full height of five feet, four inches. He stretched thin arms upwards to grip the bottom corners at his end with blue-veined hands.

"Ready when you are, young feller."

After high school Michael chose police college over a football scholarship to Ohio State. He was still formidable.

Michael and Eric's friendship reminded me of Penn and Teller. It was their size difference, and the pure delight they took in each other.

During the week this room was used by a co-op day care. I dropped a pile of tot-sized carpet squares near the junior tables and chairs we'd just stacked against the wall.

The old boys pushed the media cart into a back corner, obscuring a Happy the Squirrel poster.

I said, "Careful guys the cart is top-heavy. A wheel jams and the whole thing could tip."

A mess of shiny DVD's and clunky black VHS tapes clattered from the cart's bottom shelf to the tiled floor. My eyes were drawn to primary-coloured sleeves for 'The Adventures of Punky the Beaver' and 'Buddy the Truck's Good Day'.

"Eric," Michael asked, "Does anybody use this anymore? Does it even work?"

"It's from the church library," Eric said. "Some of these DVD's look like old worship services. Kat Daniels used to video on Sundays as part of a course at Sheridan College."

I said, "That had to be before I came back to Saint Mungo's."

Eric said, "Reverend Ed likes his face on television. He said once he was in broadcasting before going into ministry. He helped Kat do her college project here, took her under his wing."

Michael said, "Which makes it even odder he didn't show for Kat's video shoot."

"I was thinking the same," Eric said. "Reverend Tom,

I'll sort through these old videos. See what's worth keeping. You may want to watch a few, get some pointers…"

"Maybe, Eric. At my last church more people watched online than came on Sunday."

"My grand-kids all watch the YouTube on their phone. Don't use a tv. We should junk this before it topples over on someone. It's a lawsuit waiting to happen."

A shrill voice cut through our good humour.

"Who's suing who, Eric Halliday?"

Attie Beacham sailed in. Four and a half feet tall, most of her wrapped in a battleship grey winter coat. White hair pulled up in a bun that seemed to tug at her forehead. Firm jaw and a glare that could melt icebergs.

Attie's searchlight eyes scanned the room as she lined up her shot. "Reverend Book why aren't things ready?"

Eric fired back before I could duck.

"Virgil should have set this up. No one's seen him today. The snowy steps and icy sidewalks still haven't been cleared or salted."

He sent another across Attie's bow.

"What exactly does your great nephew do around here anyway?"

"Eric Halliday we are not here to talk about Virgil," Attie warned.

"I'm just saying…"

"I know very well what you were just saying."

Michael seemed to search the nursery walls for a way out of this conversation. Happy the Squirrel waved from behind the old television, high up in his Praline Tree. Next poster over, an ark-full of animal families grinned under a cartoon rainbow. Across the room, Jesus and the Super Disciples smiled back.

I shook my head but Eric ignored the ceasefire signal.

"My treasurer's report shows revenue is trending down. We'd save money if we cut the caretaker's position and hired a cleaning service."

Attie steamed over to Eric. Stabbing a finger up at his

face, she said, "I donate enough to cover Virgil, Reverend Book here, and a large portion of the exorbitant salary we pay that Edward Wilder. Out of touch since Friday, and I don't hear you complaining about him…"

"Attie you are the only one who ever calls him Edward."

Betty Torrance-Martens, chair of the Saint Mungo's council came through the door. She was in her early sixties. Her salt and pepper hair was in a loose ponytail that bounced with her steps. She carried a pottery plate, a pillar candle, and a black-bound notebook. The denim backpack slung over one shoulder added to her youthful air.

Betty said, "Let's give Ivy and the table some space."

Ivy Torrance-Martens moved with graceful ease while wielding an eight-foot table. The thick plywood top and the metal folding legs make those tables beastly heavy.

Ivy is a decade younger than her partner. Her short black hair has just a hint of silver. She is shorter and wider than Betty and solidly muscled.

Ivy set the long edge of the table-top on the hardwood floor. With elegant precision, she snapped open the legs and locked them.

I said, "You make that look so easy."

Corded muscle tightened in Ivy's forearms as she flipped the table. It landed upright with a thunk.

"Throwing pots at the wheel develops the upper body. I also haul fifty-pound boxes of clay for my art classes. I'm used to it."

"Ivy can shoulder more than twice her own weight," Betty added. "I don't feel guilty when she leaves me just the candle and minute book to carry."

"Thanks everyone," I said, "for helping us get ready."

Betty surveyed the nursery, nodding first at me then at Michael, Eric and Attie.

"Thank you for coming on short notice. Sorry we're last to get here."

Ivy added, "We came straight from an open house at

the centre. It went well despite the weather."

They wore white polos with the Town of Oakville crest over the heart. Betty taught fitness classes until they made her manager.

Ivy must have been at her potter's wheel today. The splattered clay on her hands looked like dried blood.

"Please help yourselves to a chair from the stack in the hall," Betty said.

I pulled in a chair for Attie, who ignored me. She had her sights on Eric.

"Virgil works hard to keep this place looking good. He does it in memory of his great uncle, my Douglas, who worked tirelessly for all those years, and never asked for a penny…"

Michael cut her off.

"Mrs. Beacham, Reverend Tom has worked all day. After filling in for Reverend Wilder yesterday, at the last minute. He's with us again tonight when he's supposed to be on vacation."

The corners of my mouth pulled towards a smile. I coughed and raised a hand for cover.

Betty said, "Maybe we should start. There's much to discuss."

Ivy slid her earthenware plate to the middle of the table and placed the pillar candle.

Betty struck a match, touched flame to wick, and said, "Let's all breathe. Reverend Tom can offer a prayer and then we can get to work."

The candle flame grew, and there was a little more light.

"We have much to pray about," I said, "but I don't have many words."

"Then you'll keep it short." Attie let loose from her end of the table. She was on the edge of her chair, arms tight across the front of her down-filled coat. Michael had turned the heat down to limit the spread of the smell from the old boiler room.

"As Betty suggested, let's take a breath and remember

we are not alone. I'll say a few words at the end."

A thin wisp rose off the wick of the tall white candle. I wondered, not for the first time, why Attie Beacham always had it in for ministers while her late husband always got along with them. In Ed's absence, I was squarely on her radar.

Betty and Ivy sat across from me, heads bowed and eyes closed. Eric was at the end of the long table, back straight, staring openly at Attie, who met his gaze from the opposite side.

Michael was on my left, a welcome buffer between me and Attie.

I reeled in my wandering mind. The council needed me as a non-anxious presence. I closed my eyes, settled my breathing and prayed out loud.

"God help us listen more than we speak and have the courage to live with hard questions. We are grateful for those digging us out from the blizzard. We pray for those who knew and loved the person whose remains were found this morning. We pray for the well-being of Reverend Ed Wilder…"

"Does that mean it wasn't Edward in the wall?"

I smiled. Attie'd done well to hold back as long as she had.

Betty said, "Maybe we can start there. Michael what can you tell us?"

"This is all preliminary, and unofficial. My contact says the remains of a man approximately 30-50 years of age were hidden behind that wall for years, possibly decades."

I'd already heard all of this. For the council's benefit I asked, "How did he… the body get there?"

Michael said, "There used to be a boiler in that room. There's an old coal bin set in the ground outside that wall."

Eric said, "I forgot about that. We filled in the chute and paved over it when we put in the gas furnaces. That's a long time ago."

Attie asked. "If it isn't Edward Wilder, where is he?"

"I talked with a detective sergeant named Lawrence Kitchen," Betty began, "Nice young man. His mother comes to

Tuesday morning Pilates."

Michael said, "Lawrence is a solid guy. Good cop. What did he say about Reverend Wilder?"

This was also for the council. Michael knew all about Betty's interview with Detective Kitchen.

Betty said, "The detective sergeant said they've obviously noted the timing of the body being found and Ed being out of touch. He feels at this point there is no reason to connect the two."

Eric slid his chair back and ducked low. There was a clamour when he popped up with a load of video tapes, discs, and cases, and dropped them on the table.

"Sorry! Thought I'd sort these while we talk. Will the police look for Ed? Or do they have to wait 48 hours or something?"

"That's from American cop shows," Michael said. "In Canada there's no waiting period."

Betty said, "The detective asked if this was unusual for Ed. I had to admit it's happened before."

Attie turned to me. "My Virgil says Reverend Wilder disappears all the time and the rest of you cover for him."

Michael said, "When a person steps out of their normal routine it sets off bells. In Ed's case the Halton police are interested but it's not a high priority."

Attie slapped the table, rattling the candle on its plate.

"He was supposed to be at the video shoot. Kat was beside herself."

I said, "That did seem out of character."

Betty said, "I think so too. But the detective said they have to balance legitimate concern against Ed's right to privacy."

"We dealt with this all the time," Michael said, "when I was on the job. It's not illegal for an adult to take a break from their life. It happens more than you know. Without clear reason to suspect Ed's in danger, or a danger to others, they won't act."

Attie said, "What about those shady types Edward's dealing with on the development deal? I don't care for that

Kazinski."

I'd wondered how long it be before Attie got to the Bell Tower proposal. Brad Kazinski runs several local businesses from his office in a payday loan store down the street. He'd come knocking with a scheme to build 15-storeys of high-end condos. He'd tear down most of the church but leave the Bell Tower and the sanctuary for our use. Ed had maneuvered around Attie, chatting up the other trustees. I saw merit in the idea but had managed to stay out of it.

Betty said, "It's early days. We're not committed to anything."

Ivy looked up from her minute book. "It's just so Oakville to be lured by the almighty dollar."

"My Douglas poured so much time and sweat into this place," Attie lamented. "He'd rise up out of the grave if he knew what Edward and that Kazinski are plotting."

The room quieted at Attie's mention of Doug's grave.

Ivy dropped her pen, laced the fingers of her strong hands and clasped them tight.

It wouldn't help Attie's mood if I told the board I'd visited Doug's hallowed workroom and retrieved his private journal. Not to mention seeing his ghost.

I said, "It may be an over-statement to suggest Reverend Wilder is working with Mr. Kazinski. He's been exploring possibilities."

"Virgil saw the drawings," Attie said. "They want to tear down my... this beautiful church. My family paid for this whole wing including this ridiculous, childish room we're sitting in. I'll not stand for it!"

Ivy stiffened at the mention of tearing the church down. As she clenched her fingers flakes of red clay shed on the open page of her minute book.

Ivy looked up from her notes. Her eyes landed on Attie then shifted away.

"You all know I've been a big supporter of Reverend Wilder," Ivy said. "But lately... it seems he's been doing things more for himself."

Eric closed a plastic case with a sharp snap. All eyes went to his end of the table. The stack of tapes in front of him seemed awkward and huge beside the slim pile of silver DVD's.

Eric held up a garish yellow tape case. "This one's called Happy the Squirrel Cleans Up. Speaking of cleaning up… Attie, why did Virgil see the developer's plans before this council?"

Attie leaned forward to fix her steel grey eyes on Eric.

Betty spoke before Attie could launch her salvo.

"I think there are more pressing matters."

"Like what?" Attie asked.

"Let's get back to tracking down Reverend Ed," Betty said. "Michael since you're chair of property I was hoping you and Tom could drop in at the manse."

I turned to Michael. We'd seen this coming.

"The church owns the manse but Ed's the legal tenant." Michael said. "He has the same rights as any renter. Tom going with me doesn't make it any less a violation."

Our first manse was a high-gabled two-storey gothic beside the church in a New Brunswick mill town. One Monday afternoon after a shopping trip to Moncton we walked in the side door and found four grey-haired men in the parlour, seated around our coffee table for a trustee's meeting.

I dropped the groceries with a thunk on the linoleum floor and was about to tear a strip off the intruders, when Carrie gave me the eye, and sent me upstairs with Hope still asleep in her car seat. While I put the baby down for the rest of her nap, Carrie brought the old boys a tray of tea and cookies.

I said, "Betty, I'm with Michael when it comes to entering Ed's house without permission. He's a very private man."

Betty pressed. "We're worried about Ed and I hoped we could at least rule out him being sick or worse."

At the Irving Falls manse, while the trustees munched and slurped away Carrie called someone to come and change the locks. She had the new keys in her hand before they invited me into my parlour to end their meeting with a prayer.

I relished the memory of my wife's wide grin as she ushered them out, saying, "Come back soon!"

"So, Tom, what do you think? Will you and Michael take a look?"

Startled back to the present, I said, "Let me think about it."

"Okay." Betty said. "Let's talk about the church building. Michael?"

"Scene of Crime is working down there. Which is why we're meeting here in Brown Hall. When they release the space, we'll need special help. Way beyond regular cleaning."

"Sounds expensive." Eric had pushed aside the video collection. He held up a copy of his treasurer's report.

"Insurance will likely help," Michael said. "We don't have a choice. The residue must be dealt with properly."

"So, the main building?" I began.

"They'll probably finish in a day or two. But we won't want to be there if we can help it."

"Why?" Eric asked.

"They need to fully excavate the coal bin to search for trace evidence. That'll stir up even more of the decomp odour."

"That smell!" Eric exclaimed. "Like a butcher shop dumpster in July. Michael and I went down for a peek. He introduced me to some of the investigators. Nice fellas…"

Attie snapped, "The parking lot full of police vehicles and yellow tape across the sanctuary doors looks terrible. Can't we have that all cleared away? It's Holy Week. What will people think?"

Michael gave Attie his 'Inspector Powers' look.

"They'll think something tragic happened and it's being duly investigated."

"Can't you do something? Show your badge and ask them to be more discreet?"

"Mrs. Beacham my old badge was stamped retired and sits in a box on my dresser. I'm not one of those ex-coppers who flashes the brass for favours. And it's not the badge that matters. That's more American television. Active sworn officers carry a warrant card which represents their lawful authority. I turned that in when I retired."

Betty looked ready to push on. My throat tightened as I realized what was next. I opened the topic for discussion.

"As Attie said, it's Holy Week. If the police can release the main building, we'll have Good Friday and our Easter Sunday services to think about."

Betty met my eyes. "This is a hard time of year for you, and Hope."

Ivy's words were quiet and careful. "We all loved Carrie."

Eric cleared his throat. "She was like a daughter to Joanie and me. You know that."

The throb began in both temples and pushed inward to meet behind my eyes. Not pain. More a physical expression of latent grief, a limitless natural energy in my inner world. Tapped in raw form it could fuel centuries of sorrow every day.

I pushed the tip of my ring finger into the bridge of my nose. The next two fingers rested over my eye while my thumb rubbed my temple. Carrie taught me, her small hand over mine, when she could still lift her arms.

Something tiny and hard popped, like when you're flying and the plane takes a sudden drop. I blinked; grateful I could focus.

Carrie died on Good Friday, two years ago.

Everyone around this table except Attie had been to the hospice while Carrie was still up to seeing people.

Carrie had boarded with Eric and his wife Joan when she was training at the Oakville Hospital. They invited her to Saint Mungo's. Before long she sang in the choir beside Betty who'd introduced her to me, the new student minister.

Betty brought me back to the question of Holy Week.

"We know you took this week off to be with Hope for her spring break, and Reverend Ed was supposed to…"

"If Ed doesn't turn up," I said, "I can take those services."

Betty released a breath. "That helps a lot, Tom. Will Hope make it back?"

"She's trying."

Ivy glanced up. "I hope it works out. But things don't always go as we hope."

Betty said, "But we hope, anyway."

"Well, my hope is the sanctuary won't smell like death for Good Friday." Attie declared. "If the basement needs special cleaning, I'll pay for it myself. Make it like it never happened."

Michael squared his pile of notes. "Someone already tried that, Mrs. Beacham. That poor man's remains were sealed up and hidden away for a long time."

Attie gave him a hard look. "Some things are better left buried, don't you think?"

9

I'd waited all day to dig into Doug's journal. I started in by looking for what he wrote about me. I couldn't help myself.

I've heard our new student minister preach twice now, and for a young man, the (soon-to-be) Reverend Book seems a very deep thinker, unwilling to take anything at face value. I knew fellows like him while I was at teacher's college, after the war. Able to thoroughly analyze a situation and speak clearly in ways that helped others see the "light." That is not to suggest Tom brings an uncomfortable or overbearing zeal. He doesn't push himself or his ideas on people. He raises questions I find worth considering.

He spoke yesterday morning about free will, and the limits of God's power. These lines stuck: "If I have to choose between a God who pulls all the strings, and controls everything, like some cosmic micro-manager, and who is therefore responsible for every devastating storm or earthquake, and the pain and havoc they cause, or a God who is limited in power, and can't stop wars or hurricanes, child abuse or brain tumors, but is all loving, and who sorrows when people suffer, I choose the God of love." (For the record, I did not recall all of that. I found his script in the pulpit.)

I had no memory of that sermon, but that's not unusual. I don't remember what I said on Sunday, and I'd recycled an old Palm Sunday sermon when Betty called at the last minute.

I couldn't imagine at the tender age of twenty-five I'd had much to say about human suffering. Ask me now, after Carrie's struggle, and what it did to all of us.

Doug had me hooked, so settled into my leather recliner, Jazz FM low on the stereo, I carried on reading.

I have been spending less time here at the church, and I

admit, I miss the solitude. The simple quiet.

Attie and I have moved into Ralph and Lila's grandiose East Oakville house, to care for Dido's children. Attie instructed her lawyer to initiate the process to legally adopt them.

Only once did I broach with Attie that we could move the children into our modest bungalow in Bronte. It's more than enough house for four people. Attie would not hear of it.

Lila has absented herself almost totally from her grandchildren's lives. She has some arrangement with Attie about the house, details of which they have not shared with me. Lila has bought a unit in the new, adults only condo building beside Saint Mungo's. From her new place, she literally looks down on the church, which I find funny, and sad at the same.

The double burden of her daughter Dido's suicide, and her husband's ongoing dissolution, and gradual but inevitable demise by alcohol seem to have exhausted Lila's capacity to be positive about anything. She does not speak of Ralph Daniels, and I have not had the nerve to ask after him. While he is certainly footing the bill for the new condo, it is equally certain he is not living there with Lila.

Virgil reminds me of a boy I saw outside a boarded-up bakery in Nijmegen after the liberation of Holland. Thin and wary. He has this way of meeting your eyes full on, and still not revealing anything of his inner self.

Kat is more social but has also learned (perhaps from Lila) to be manipulative and demanding. I fear they both need more than we can give. Virgil seems especially stricken by his mother's death, and Lila's emotional retreat. She no longer permits them to call her "Grandma."

I attempt to sympathize with Lila, but she has become so closed-hearted. She seems to operate only from the rat-like bit of brain dedicated to preservation of her small self.

The other day I attempted to make conversation about the coming of winter, and preparations that need doing around the church. There was a time she'd have been as concerned as Attie about how appearances are kept up at Saint Mungo's. But Lila was having none of it, and went on instead about some advice she'd received from her new lawyer.

"Trent told me to book a mid-morning appointment for the Mercedes over the border in Buffalo. Apparently, there are reputable shops accustomed to dealing with a certain clientele from Canada. They supply and install snow tires and store the summer ones at a reasonable cost."

I found her sense of entitlement abrasive as 40 grit sandpaper but held my tongue. After all, we've just moved into a six bedroom "colonial" in East Oakville. (The literalist in me says colonial is exactly the right word.)

"Trent says they're full service, so I can also have the vehicle winterized, the oil changed, and they will even drive me to the Galleria Mall. I can enjoy a tasty little lunch and get in some shopping. When I cross back over to Canada, I will have something small to declare at customs, and no incriminating summer tires in my trunk. I avoid the duty on the new tires and have a pleasant day to myself in the bargain."

Lila reported these words of legal counsel with great excitement. She feels that her Trent understands the needs of a person like her. This would appear to be accurate.

"This clever young man has quite a future ahead of him," Lila assured me. "I was referred to him by a woman at bridge club. She said Trent was quite helpful when she needed some additional medication between prescriptions. He was very understanding and so accommodating she didn't mind paying a little extra."

It does not seem to worry my sister-in-law that her lawyer has the ethics of a rabid coyote. Trent sounds like the black-market operators during the war, finding ways around rules and decency, loyal only to their own avarice.

She asked me, "When are you going to get rid of that old rattletrap you drive? Surely, with your teacher's salary, you can afford something more respectable."

I drive a Ford Windstar minivan. They built it here in Oakville, and I think there's something to be said for that, despite the pretensions of Lila and her Mercedes-driving ilk. When I haul lumber and paint for the church, or more recently, the 7-year-old twins and all their necessaries, I am glad to have my old rattletrap. I am considerably more relaxed about their inevitable spills on the seats, than Lila was, when they occupied the back seat of her Mercedes S420. (Heaven help me, I have committed to memory the model number of her vanity car!)

Reverend Paul, thankfully, seems not so much above the issues of wealth and worldly status, as disinterested in them. I recently overheard a conversation at the back of the church. When asked what kind of car he drove, he answered, without missing a beat, "Em, a blue one." I liked his answer, so very much.

I am also grateful as I observe the effect his calm and quiet manner is having on the atmosphere around the church, after all the tumult.

The unanswered questions about the sudden disappearance of Rev. Stephen Peretz seem to be less pressing, perhaps because his wife, Wendy, is no longer on the scene. I have not inquired after her, of course, but I do pick up snippets as I push my broom about the church.

The most credible theory I've heard is she may have gone back to Vancouver, to be with family.

Ivy has returned to her former place in the choir. She'd been absent for quite some time after Wendy Peretz's departure. They had been quite close, for a time before Rev. Stephen's... abrupt disappearance from the scene.

Attie has, in her words 'taken a leave from her duties in the choir' so she can sit with Virgil and Kat in church, and see they make it down to Sunday School, which she believes does them some good.

The church's music ministry seems likely to survive Lila's temporary absence. There's a new voice in the soprano section. A young woman who boards with Eric and Joan Halliday has been out to the last few Thursday night rehearsals. She has a sweet clear voice, and I've heard she will be asked to take a solo in the weeks to come. Carrie is a nursing student at McMaster, doing her practical work at Oakville Trafalgar Memorial Hospital.

I was not sure what to make of Ivy's reappearance, but she seems to have matured, and I notice she makes an effort to be kind to young Carrie. Betty has taken them both under her wing.

I wondered what Doug wasn't saying about the abrupt disappearance of the minister before Paul, but I got distracted by his mention of Carrie.

It roused the memory of my first glimpse of my future wife, standing confident in the Saint Mungo's choir loft.

She did get that solo, on the first Sunday in Advent, the start of the pre-Christmas season. I remember every word, every note. Her voice rang out bright, and true.

"When God is a child
there's joy in our song.
The last shall be first
and the weak shall be strong,
and none shall be afraid."

Paul Bennett, my supervising pastor, and I had been sitting in the minister's chairs on the chancel platform. He saw me swivel around for Carrie's solo.

"She brightens things around here, doesn't she?"

10

"You said there's more to each of us than we know and people we love do not perish."

Ella Sayers voice cracked as she repeated my line from her mother's graveside service almost word for word.

She paused to sip her coffee.

"You weren't just saying words. It seemed to really mean something to you."

"It's something I hold on to," I said. "It helps me when I close my eyes at night."

"It was good for me to hear that." Ella cleared her throat and drank some coffee. "I loved… I love my mother."

A loud "Omigod!" flared up from the booth next to ours, followed by a stage whispered "Shush!"

A surge of adolescent laughter filled the dining space at my friend Michael Power's retirement project, a small sandwich shop.

Ella had claimed the last open booth. The other three were crammed with students in the male and female variants of the Colborne College uniform. Collared white shirts, navy ties and dark blue jackets emblazoned with the school crest. According to my mother, who taught there for almost 30 years, it's required dress when they venture off-campus, to remind students they represent the dignity of the elite private school.

"Looks like the Colborne kids have discovered Amazing Sandwich Powers." I said, wondering what Michael thought of his place turning into a teen hangout.

The gaggle of students had marked territory with designer book bags plunked down on placemats and navy-blue pea-coats thrown over chairs.

"I suggested here because it's handy. Gwen said you're down the street at The Cash Box."

"I do the books. But on busy days, like the end of the month, or before a holiday like Easter I help out front."

The dark roast aroma from Ella's mug was enticing. I scanned the room for Michael's sister and her carafe.

Bonnie appeared beside our booth with a thick-handled mug of coffee that matched the one in front of Ella. She's a shorter version of her brother the former linebacker, and almost as wide. Her grey hair was pulled back in a ponytail secured with a Union Jack scrunchie that matched the tattered flag on her Sex Pistols t-shirt.

"It's decaf, Tom. You've probably had at least two cups of the real stuff already."

"Thanks Bonnie. This is Ella."

"We met." Bonnie said, smiling, "And before you ask, Tom, you still can't have cream. You need more time on your treadmill. Your clerical shirt looks a little tight."

"At least my shirt is from this decade." I smiled, and said, "Bonnie has strong opinions about my diet, and I don't argue."

Bonnie nodded at me, and said, "He doesn't get one, but I've got some nice fresh butter tarts on the cooling rack. Can I bring you one? On the house."

"That's very kind, but…" Ella looked over at a student with long blonde hair making a show of tossing a ball of waxed paper in the general direction of the trash receptacle, to the raucous amusement of the Colborne crowd. "… you've got lots going on here."

Bonnie raised an eyebrow at the young crowd and winked at us. "Don't worry about them. I'll be back in a tick with your tart, while it's still warm."

On her way to the kitchen, Bonnie had a quiet word with the student with the poor aim. As Bonnie slipped behind the counter, the student bent to put their trash in its place.

"She likes to mess with you." Ella said.

"She's a little rough on the outside, but…"

"You matter to her."

"I met Bonnie and her brother while their mom and my wife were both patients at the hospice."

The dining area became quiet but for the bustle of the now very polite high school students gathering bags and coats, saying "thank you" to Bonnie. There was a blast of brisk wind as they headed out the door.

Not for the first time, I wished Michael would invest in a sound system. Last time I'd suggested it he'd said if I wanted smooth jazz and cloth napkins I'd have to go over to condo row in Burlington.

When the last student pulled the door closed behind them Bonnie approached our booth bearing a single butter tart on a small white plate. She gave me her serious look as she set the tart and a pastry box on Ella's side of the table.

"The tarts are on the house," Bonnie said. "The coffees go on Tom's tab."

"Thanks, Bonnie," Ella said. "This is very kind."

"Come by anytime." Bonnie patted my shoulder. "You don't have to bring him."

Bonnie stepped away to clear the now-vacant booths.

I said, "Tell me about your mother."

Ella set down her coffee mug. She looked up for a moment, as if sifting memories.

"She was a tough old broad. Before the dementia, and the rest of it, she'd sit in the Port Credit Legion and let the old farts buy her draft beer. Her words for them, not mine. She liked Dancing with the Stars, and her soaps. Especially Corrie… Coronation Street. She smoked too much, loved her scratch tickets, and never missed Tuesday night bingo."

Ella stared at me, as if waiting for my reaction.

I said, "Your mom sounds like my grandmother."

"Really?"

"My Nan smoked two packs a day and always said she was quitting. My Dad's mother. She had this plastic filter thing that was supposed to wean her off. It never did. Alzheimer's quit for her. She just forgot about smoking and most other things. Before that she loved her lottery tickets and was at the legion 'til closing three nights a week."

I don't know why I told Ella so much, but it seemed to help her relax.

"When I was little Mom played her Louis Armstrong records and we'd read those little square Beatrix Potter books. My favourite was Mrs. Tiggy-Winkle the Hedgehog. She'd make us weak tea with lots of milk and sugar and we'd sit up in her bed, and she'd read me to sleep. That was when she could be home."

I felt the familiar tightening behind my eyes. I sipped from the large white mug. The decaf had an edge and needed cream.

"I have a daughter. Hope. She used to love picnics in bed when she was young. She'd say the best place in the world was between mommy and daddy."

Ella set her mug to one side. She leaned in close and spoke in a softer tone.

"Wanda Mae… my mom, wasn't a typical mother, like on Happy Days or One Day at a Time. I grew up mostly with my aunt Judy while mom worked on cruise ships in the Caribbean. They called it hospitality. She danced and sang in the ship-board revues, but she made her real money after the shows were over… it was a hard life. Does that shock you?"

"I don't shock easy. And I don't judge."

"That's what the funeral director told me. She said I could trust you, but I wasn't sure until I heard you at the cemetery."

"It feels like you want to tell me something."

"I told you about my mom, because I want you to understand."

"It sounds like she loved you and did the best she knew how."

"She was in a life that once you're in, it's hard to get out of. She wanted better for me."

"Are you okay? Is there something you need help with?"

"No… I mean yes, I'm okay. But I wanted to tell you about my boss and your boss."

With no idea where this was going, I just nodded. When I don't know what else to do, I can listen.

"Like I said, I work at The Cash Box, just down the street, towards the Sobeys mall."

"Uh hunh."

"A lot more happens there than cashing cheques. More money comes in the side door than ever goes out over the front counter."

"I don't know if I'm the one you should be telling. But my friend Michael, Bonnie's brother, used to be with the police…"

"The cops are already sniffing around. Grow up like I did, and you can tell."

"So, what do you think is going on?"

"Ever take a close look at The Cash Box? You said you know where it is."

I said, "It's that single-storey cement-block building beside Petcetera. Bars on the side windows, and steel doors on the side and back. It's friendlier in front, with the bright lights and the happy face with dollar signs for eyes, but it looks like a jail."

"More like a vault. Runners from the drug and sex business in Burlington and Oakville bring in loads of cash. It's counted and stored at The Cash Box."

"Are you part of this?"

"No, I do the books for the legit business. But they trust me because of who my mom was. I've seen what happens in the back."

"So what do you want me to know?"

"My boss Brad Kazinski has something going with your boss, the other minister."

"You mean Ed? Ed Wilder?"

"Not as tall as you. Dark hair. Dresses better than you, no offense. Suits that cost more than my car. Always smiling without meaning it. Like he's selling timeshares in Orlando."

"That… sounds like him," I admitted. "Are they friends? Ed knows a lot of people."

"I hope he doesn't know a lot of people like Brad. Do you know about his family?" Ella used the word family like it should be in quotes and italics.

"I've heard rumours. Bronte's a small neighbourhood, in a small town."

"Brad's job is to clean up their image. Move their money into respectable businesses."

"What does that have to do with Ed Wilder?"

"I don't know exactly. But last week, the Thursday before the storm they were in Brad's office and they got loud. I heard one of them yell "You need to fix this. We don't need more complications!"

"Who said that?"

"Hard to tell. They sound the same, especially behind a closed door."

"What do you think they were talking about?"

"I have no idea Tom, but a few minutes later they both stormed out, and they each looked angry enough to hurt someone."

I lifted my mug to sip, but the coffee was bitter and cold.

11

"You find anything interesting in Doug's journal?"

Michael lowered his bulk into the passenger seat of my Suzuki Swift. There were creaks of protest as my little car rocked on its 10-year-old suspension.

"I read some stuff he wrote about me when I first came to Saint Mungo's. It brought up memories. I also have a better understanding of why Kat and Virgil are both so... broken."

"Lot of that going around," Michael noted.

I was parked in front of the Saint Mungo's manse. The church-owned residence was a three-bedroom bungalow on yet another stretch being overtaken by developers. Its cheerful yellow wood siding looked dated amid the dark brick and smooth stucco of the starter mansions.

"After their mother died, their grandmother, Attie's sister Lila, washed her hands of them. She made a deal with Attie to take over their care, in exchange for that big house in East Oakville."

"Anything more in there about Stephen Peretz, the pastor who gave Doug the journal?"

"I just read something about his wife leaving town after he disappeared. Oh... is that who..."

"Scene of crime techs found his wallet in a water-tight bag floating in the coal chute."

"I don't know why I didn't think of him right away. There was talk their marriage was in trouble and she'd hooked up with someone else. He was at Saint Mungo's before Paul Bennett. Paul was my supervisor."

"When they ran his driver's license the system said it was the last one issued."

"When Paul came to Saint Mungo's he had to do a lot of mopping up. Stephen Peretz disappeared over night. No one seemed to know where he went. I wouldn't have thought to look behind a basement wall."

"That happen often in your line of work?"

"I really hope not."

"How about a minister disappearing over night?"

"I never heard anything like it. From what Paul said the congregation was more relieved than worried. There'd been screaming matches that year that almost split the church over the issue of gay ordination. They just wanted things to settle down."

"Sounds like a mess."

"It was not an easy time to be a minister."

"So Tom when's the easy time?"

"I appreciate your pushing back with Attie at the meeting, but you don't have to..."

"You know I've got your back, always. There's something sour in Attie and she takes it out on you," Michael shook his head. "Even while we're dealing with a dead body and searching for the senior pastor."

"It comes with the territory. I know you took a lot of crap from people who don't like cops."

"Yeah, but I could arrest them," Michael laughed, "or shoot them."

We climbed out of the car. Despite the wintry air neither of us bothered with hat or gloves. Ice and snow crunched as we moved towards the house.

A lofty maple dominated the manse's front yard even stripped as it was of leaves. Bare branches left thin shadows on the snowy lawn as well as my little salt-stained car and the steel-grey Ford Taurus parked a car length behind it. It looked like one of the unmarked cars that filled the church parking lot these days.

I looked to Michael, and asked, "You still drive a cruiser?"

"I attended at way too many accident scenes to drive a little tin box like yours."

"I like my car," I said, then cleared my throat. "Carrie said it kept her humble and made her drive careful."

Michael shifted gears. "Someone just cleared this driveway. Their snow-blower needs work. Look here. It's leaking oil."

"Maybe a neighbour?"

Michael gestured towards the street. "The neighbours did their driveways earlier. You can see where the wind has softened the edges. Let's look inside."

Not for the first time, I thought Michael must have been a great detective.

"You make it all seem so… elementary."

"Years of practice partner. Years of practice."

The inlaid brick path from the driveway to the house had also been freshly cleared. Naked branches of the tall maple were reflected in the bay windows on either side of the front entry. Three days of the Globe and Mail lay on the doorstep, sheathed in clear blue plastic, and dusted with snow.

I knocked on the door.

"Nice suit, Michael." I'd got used to seeing him in jeans and T-shirts from his restaurant.

"It's always good to dress up when you plan to trespass in a good neighbourhood."

"Is it still trespassing when you have this?" I waved a key chain, and said, "Betty left it for me, with another note reminding me we agreed to this."

"It's trespassing unless the tenant has consented, which Reverend Ed hasn't. Let's just do the walk-through, clear the rooms, so we can tell Betty there was nothing to see."

The front foyer was as I remembered. An open space that used to serve as a buffer between the domestic busy-ness of the kitchen on the right and the reserved quiet of the living room on the left. Paul Bennett and his mother Mavis called it their parlour.

My eyes were drawn to the gas fireplace on the far left outside wall, framed on both sides by built-in shelves crafted of dark oak.

None of Paul's books or his mother's remained. A massive flat screen television now hung above the mantle. The shelves held the requisite black boxes for sound and picture and orderly rows of DVD movies and music CDs.

A wall once graced by what Paul called "a few small, but quite good paintings" was now home to an over-sized framed poster of the black steel of the Eiffel tower, shot looking up from the ground. On either side, smaller frames held tourist shop prints of the Bronte Harbour lighthouse.

Michael said, "Not much here."

I nodded. "Paul and his mother had cozy armchairs set in front of the fireplace. There's no dining room so they put their big table right about here, handy to the kitchen."

The old kitchen had been gutted and redone. It was fitted with glossy black glass-front cabinets, most of which were empty, and ultra-modern stainless-steel appliances. A stark white breakfast table stood tall near the side door. Matching stools were pushed under it.

Michael opened one side of the massive refrigerator. The glass shelves were pristine.

He asked, "Whose fridge stays this clean?'

Michael swept an arm around like a show-room model. "It's like a page from an IKEA catalogue. Doesn't look like it gets used."

"I think Ed eats out a lot." I said. "When Paul and his mother lived here we'd sit for hours after supper. I'd ramble on and on, and he'd listen me into making sense."

"Useful talent," Michael said, grinning.

Michael stepped back into the living room, tilting his head to scan titles on the shelves of DVD cases.

"Your colleague favours the works of Jim Carrey. The Mask. The Truman Show. Bruce Almighty. Not a fan myself. He always comes across as frantic and trying way too hard."

I nodded. "Ed's a bit that way himself. That's very insightful, detective."

"Paul on the other hand, sounds like my first training officer. A real mentor. Taught me more than how to talk to the citizens and write reports."

I studied the polished brass of the gas fireplace. In Paul's time it burned wood. I used to imagine it was the coal grate in a tutor's rooms in a college at Cambridge.

One Sunday evening twenty years ago, we'd sat heavily in the armchairs near the fire, allowing the roast beef and Yorkshire pudding to settle. I asked Paul how long he'd stay at Saint Mungo's.

Paul gestured towards the kitchen, and I followed the gaze of his clear blue eyes to the sight of his mother, apron over her Sunday dress, washing up at the kitchen sink. She was already in her early eighties.

"We've lived so many places. This has become home. She has her bridge ladies, our Blue Jays seasons tickets, and just a short walk for the shopping. She says she plans to die here."

Paul's calm acceptance of his mother's mortality had unsettled my younger self.

"And you, Tom? I'd wondered if you've any new thoughts about your own future…"

"Carrie and I've been seeing a lot of each other," I admitted.

Paul leaned forward to shift a log with the fireplace poker. Sparks went up the flue, and the dormant fire erupted with bright new flames.

"Something you weren't anticipating during this internship year."

It was easier to watch the fire than meet his eyes. At seminary we'd read case studies about the damage caused when ministers crossed that line with parishioners.

"I thought I'd put that part of life on hold. And now I think I need to be careful."

Paul said, "A lot of our colleagues lead lonely lives

despite the many social opportunities and obligations. If you are blessed to find someone with whom you can build something real and life-giving, I encourage you to explore it, rejoice in it."

"It's comfortable with Carrie. We talk a lot."

"That's good. Have you shared your ethical qualms?"

"A little, after someone from the choir saw us out for a walk, I didn't want to spook her. It feels early to get into the steps they taught us in the professional boundaries seminar."

"As in advising your parishioner they have to look to someone else as their pastor, if you become romantically involved." Paul chuckled. "I don't mean to make light of your concern, but I was just imagining being on the receiving end."

"It's a lot. I didn't want her to think I was presuming…"

"Tom, you're a good lad, and yes, it might feel a little cart before the horse. I think you can sense if Carrie is truly attracted to you, and not some complicated projection. My own instinct is she's not likely looking to you to fill the God-space in her life. At least not beyond what we always seek in a relationship with another human."

"I'm really not sure where it's going with her."

Paul nodded. "If you told me you were sure, I'd offer different counsel."

"So you think it's okay for us to see each other?"

Paul's blue eyes sparkled. "I'm delighted for you both."

"But what about pastors not dating parishioners?"

"It's generally a good rule of thumb. But Tom, you are a student minister, and not exactly the pastor. You carry some of the burden and blessings of the role but not in the same way as if you were here in solo ministry. Carrie's been accepted as part of the family, but she is not actually a member of the congregation. And you'll both leave Saint Mungo's within the year."

"That's true. I'll be back at school, and Carrie will be graduating, looking for a nursing job, probably in the Maritimes, where she grew up."

"Ah, so you have been looking to the future…"

Michael interrupted my thoughts. "Ready to check the

house?"

"I am," I said, staring at the dark oak mantle. "I wonder if Ed knows about this."

"What?"

"This wasn't always a manse. Paul and his mother bought it when they came to Oakville. He retired when she died, and he gifted the house to Saint Mungo's."

"I'd never heard that."

"Mavis was a fascinating woman. And very private."

I pointed to the fireplace and surrounding cabinetry.

"This was all custom work. Mavis had them build in what she called her hidey-hole. She popped it open once to show me a photo of Paul as a child, looking very much like Little Lord Fauntleroy."

Michael said, "I think I'd like to see that."

"The picture of Paul in short pants, or the hidey-hole?"

Michael laughed. "Yes, to both."

I pressed under the mantle as Mavis had shown me. A mechanical click. I grinned like I'd solved a Rubik's Cube. A section of the dark oak opened to reveal the secret drawer.

My joy vanished when I saw the contents. A letter-size envelope stuffed with cash, a file folder labelled 'Bell Tower' and a ziploc bag full to bursting with grey-green pills.

"If that's what I think," Michael said, "we can't leave that bag here. It's a controlled substance. I have to turn it in. The rest is suspicious, just by circumstance."

I said, "How will you explain our being here?"

"I'll sort that later. Let's finish this up." Michael pointed. "I'll head upstairs."

He saved me from having to poke around in my colleague's bedroom.

"I'll take the basement," I said.

"This house is a back-split," Michael said. "There'll be a crawl space below us, running the full width of the house."

I nodded agreement. "Mavis used it for storage. How did you know?"

"I was undercover in a real estate firm for 20 months."

"I didn't know you were undercover,"

"That's kind of how undercover works."

"Was that here in Oakville?"

"No, but not far from here. When this house was built… about 60 years ago I'd say, builders would dig you a full basement for an extra five hundred bucks. That used to be a lot of money and most new home-owners didn't see the need."

I thought of the enormous houses taking over this block.

"They had different ideas about what was enough."

"You see anything else weird, give me shout," Michael instructed. "Don't touch it."

I gave only a cursory glance to the family room. I remembered it as the space where Mavis hosted three tables of bridge ladies once a month. It was empty except for a futon couch below the rear basement window.

The downstairs bathroom had the same unused feeling as the showroom kitchen above.

Ed was divorced and never mentioned his ex-wife. Did they have children? I knew so little about a man I'd worked with for over two years.

Michael called out, "Doing okay down there?"

"I'm good. Heading to the crawl space."

An overflowing hamper in the laundry room was the first sign of human habitation. A squat gas furnace filled the corner nearest the crawl space. The blower cycled on, causing the duct work to vibrate.

I remembered going on hands and knees to get under the ducts, to pull out card tables and folding chairs for Mavis. My knees were 20 years younger then.

A faint red light pulsed from deep in the crawl space.

I called up to Michael, "Going in to check something."

I couldn't find a light switch, so I struggled in the dark, scraping the knees of my suit pants on rough concrete. The intermittent red glow gave me something to head toward.

My eyes adjusted to the gloom, and I made out the shape of a power bar dangling from an outlet mounted on a floor joist. The light I'd followed came from the illumined switch. The power bar swung toward me, smacking the bridge of my nose, as the whole house shook.

A loud thump knocked the breath out of me and popped my ears. A strong wind knocked me down. I felt heat coming at me.

I wanted out. The only choice was back the way I'd come. I aimed toward the laundry room and pushed into waves of heat. Foul smoke engulfed me. The temperature rose as I crawled on hands and knees.

Fear fueled my efforts to move faster and I forgot the low hanging duct work. Something jagged and evil clawed at the top of my head.

I gasped at the sharp and sudden pain until a numbing shock set in. I felt blood pump out of the gash in my scalp and drip down my forehead. I wiped warm stickiness away from my eyes. This motion pushed my head back and I knocked my skull against a floor joist.

"Shit! Ow!" It registered that I'd been deafened by the blast that caused the heat and smoke.

I called out, "Michael! You okay?"

Thumping over my head told me Michael or someone else was moving around upstairs.

I crawled further and emerged from under the duct work. Oily smoke burned my eyes and nasal passages but in the laundry room I could at least rise from all fours. Ragged wool threads stuck to wet flesh at both my knees. The pant legs and my skin had been scraped raw.

I coughed hard, felt the sting deep in my lungs, and only then had the sense to not breathe in the fumes. I knocked over the laundry bin as I groped for a towel to cover my face. Smoke blinded me. My eyes teared, my ears rang, and my lungs demanded fresh air. I felt along the wall for the way out. I wrapped the towel over the knob, pulled the door open, and stepped into the hall.

Thick black clouds issued from the family room and billowed up the stairwell. Waves of intense heat pushed me forward as I stumbled up the stairs.

At the main floor landing I toweled blood and grimy tears from my stinging eyes. Lowering the towel, I made out Michael coming at me fast through the dark cloud, crouched low as if he was squaring off against a defensive line.

I tried calling out and took in more hot smoke. My throat and chest burned. My lungs forced out a searing cough. A wave of deep drowsiness washed over me.

Michael's shoulder hit me hard in the belly, forcing out the remaining air as he hefted me in a firefighter's carry. He pivoted towards the front door, and we were out of the smoke-engulfed house.

Wintry wind sucked the heat from my body. I fought to breathe. The world spun as I bounced on Michael's hard muscled back.

Michael took us down the driveway and out to the street side of his grey Ford Taurus. He keyed his remote, pulled open a door and flopped me down on the back seat.

"Don't try to get up, partner. Breathe slow and steady."

I think that's what he said while I gasped, and worried I might pass out.

Michael dropped into the driver's seat, started the engine and cranked the heat.

"I need to call this in."

I croaked, "What's happening?"

Before Michael could answer, another blast shook the car.

Michael yelled, "Stay down!"

Ignoring him, I raised myself enough to peek my head over the back of front seat and peer out the windshield, which had been obscured with ashy ice, and blown snow.

I ducked instinctively when the bay windows on each side of the manse's front door exploded outward. I leaned back until the rear bench caught me.

Shards of glass hailed down on drifted snow. Dark smoke pushed out into the cold.

I gasped, "You okay?" The effort of speech led to more coughing, and I felt light-headed.

Michael turned and said, "I'm good, you?"

I nodded, and said, "But sleepy... dizzy... can't catch breath..."

I coughed, and my ears popped. I leaned forward to tell him not to worry, but Michael was working his phone. He tapped in a few more digits than 9-1-1.

Whoever Michael dialed did not keep him waiting.

"It's Powers. Yes, I require assistance. I need a patrol supervisor, fire, and ambulance. Ping my GPS for location. I'm on Hixon, between Bronte and Jones. They'll see it. Multiple explosions, heavy smoke and fire in a two-storey detached. No occupants. Advise fire they'll need foam, hazmat and breathers."

I followed Michael's gaze to the black smoke billowing up through the bare branches of the maple tree.

Michael nodded to the voice on the phone. "Yes. Large quantity of opioids, my guess is fentanyl found on scene."

I heard sirens. We were just blocks from the Bronte Fire Station.

"No, I'm fine... good." Michael reported. "Yes. Advise paramedics I will administer naloxone on scene. Their patient is Book, Thomas."

Michael smacked open the glove compartment and pulled out a small blue plastic box. It was labelled with an O.P.P. shield, a first aid cross, and "Narcan" in bold letters.

Michael smiled and said to the phone, "No, not a suspect."

A black pickup frosted with road salt rolled by slow. I heard a low rumble in the truck's exhaust. I wondered if the driver was curious about the fire or wanted to help. The rumble grew louder as the truck sped past Michael's car.

The truck's rear gate was down. A cargo net was tied

across the opening. Through the holes in the flapping orange plastic, I saw a familiar rusty red machine on small rubber tires.

I pointed.

"You see that truck?"

Michael nodded and mouthed, "Got it."

Michael continued on his phone. "No... no weapons evident. No suspects present. Advise search for vehicle leaving the scene. Late model Ford F-150, black. Snowblower in back. Ontario plate..."

The sirens grew close and whined out in several tones.

I said, "I think that was Virgil's truck. I recognize the snowblower."

Michael put the Taurus in gear and gave it some gas. He pulled around my little car and down the street.

"Are we going to follow him?"

"No. We're getting out of the way."

Flashing red lights, the wailing of a siren, and the bold deep honk of a pumper truck's horn announced the arrival of the firefighters.

Michael shifted the car into park. He turned to me and ordered, "Lay down, I have to give you a shot."

12

"You're in better shape than the folks we usually pick up at the hospital," Gwen said. "But not much."

The joke was undone by the look on her face. As Gwen says about talking with her mother, not every smile is a laugh.

"Climb in," Gwen said, as she started the funeral car.

My legs were stiff, and my scraped knees stung as I lowered myself into the black sedan. I fingered the recline button, and the magical control that caused heat to radiate through the seat. I groaned with relief, and gratitude. The short walk through the sliding glass doors and out into the cold had left me weak and shivering.

"I'm glad you didn't make me lie in the back of a transport van."

Gwen steered away from Emergency, following the exit lane towards Hospital Gate. She paused at the red light then hit the gas for a quick right onto Dundas Street, just ahead of a rusted brown Dodge pickup pulling a horse trailer. There was ice on the corner, and the Cadillac's rear end slid out wide. A warning beep issued from the dash.

Gwen muttered, "Be quiet, you."

Was she was telling me or the car?

The sun was low in the grey sky. I checked my Nike running watch, which bore a fresh, deep scratch across its crystal face. Almost six, which explained the heavy traffic.

The watch was a Christmas gift from my mother, the first time I trained for a marathon.

Mom taught history. When we were kids she turned every car ride into a lesson. I could hear her saying, "Eighteen-wheelers and commuter SUV's have replaced farmer's wagons and the carriages of military officers, but this stretch of the old Governor's Road has been busy since the British built it for their army."

Gwen's heavy silence was a warning she was building steam. She'd soon let it off. She steered a hard left to Bronte Road.

The sun sank behind us, giving up for the day. Gwen drove southeast towards Lake Ontario. The headlights coming at us felt bright. I rubbed at my eyes.

Gwen asked, "So are we going home?"

"I need to get my car."

She turned to face me. The space between her eyebrows narrowed, like it does. "You think you're okay to drive? Didn't you say you'd been drugged?"

"My blood work was negative for opioids. They took care of my head and swabbed out my scraped knees. Gave me another shot for…"

"I'll give you a shot," Gwen interrupted. "You had a head wound. And you smell of smoke."

Gwen gave me her look, up and down.

"Your pants are shredded at the knees, that's blood on your jacket and shirt, and they checked for drug poisoning because you were in respiratory distress. You want to drive tonight?"

The lines went all tight around Gwen's eyes like on Mama Jessie's face when she feared one of her nestlings was flitting too far from home.

"Gwen, I'm fine."

The boulevards on either side of Bronte Road were buried under road-soiled snow. The high ridges seemed grey and alien to me, under the glare of streetlights and passing cars.

"It's like the moon." Did I say that out loud?

I ran fingertips over the fresh bald spot on the back of my head. They'd snipped and shaved, then popped in staples to seal the gash from the ductwork.

The lines on Gwen's face softened. "What?"

"When I was little my brother JP and I climbed the snow mountains. We pretended we were in space."

Gwen's expression softened. "You're in space now. Why did Ed have those drugs?"

"No idea. The firefighters wore haz-mat gear in case there was more we didn't find."

"How much smoke did you breathe in?"

"They said I was fine. Michael had a kit in his car. He took mouth swabs and injected us both even before the paramedics got there. I'm good."

I rubbed my arm at the memory of Michael's jab. It was like an epi-pen and left a bruise.

"Naloxone. I just ordered kits for our prep rooms. We had a seminar. With the synthetics like fentanyl, you inhale it or get it on you, and it can stop your breathing. How's Michael?"

"Better than me. They checked his blood and treated him for smoke inhalation. He needed to stop by the police station, which is why I called you."

"You talk to Hope? Tell her you were out playing Robin to Michael's Batman?"

"I texted her to say we're okay. She'd recognize the house if she saw the story online."

We emerged from under the QEW bridge, and my eyes were assailed by the aggressive brightness of the car dealerships on the service road.

Gwen asked, "Do they know what happened?"

"Someone snuck behind the house. They broke a basement window, poured gasoline on a futon couch, and threw in the can. They also tossed in a propane tank from the back deck barbecue. All it took was a match."

"Lot of damage?"

"Horrible black smoke from the futon mattress. The propane tank exploded. The blast blew out windows and propelled shards of metal into the walls of the family room. There's foam everywhere from the fire crew. I saw it on Michael's phone while we waited for blood work."

"How'd he get the video?"

"Police had a team in as soon as the fire captain said it was safe."

"We're almost at the manse," Gwen said, "but we could just head home, get your car tomorrow. We can pick up some Thai for supper, yeah?"

"That sounds good, and I am hungry, but I've got something on."

"Like what?"

Her eyebrows scrunched up again. I paused to choose my words.

We passed the Bronte fire station, and Gwen slowed the big sedan for the left at Hixon. The street showed no signs of the afternoon's excitement. The snowplow had come through, scraping over the tracks of emergency vehicles.

Gwen asked, "What's more important than supper and a good night's rest?"

Commuter cars dripped salt on their driveways. The strange blue light of flat screen televisions pulsed out of picture windows.

"I called Betty about the manse. When she heard I was okay she asked me to a meeting at Attie's house. Attie wants us to talk Kat into calling off the next video shoot at the church."

Gwen turned the wheel hard and stopped the car in front of the manse.

Yellow crime scene tape stretched across the driveway. Unfinished plywood was tacked over shattered windows.

I wondered what the folks in the starter mansions thought about their neighbour.

"You were almost blown up." Gwen declared. "There should be down time for that. And you're supposed to be on vacation."

"You'd think so, but..."

The Cadillac's horn honked loud as Gwen slapped the steering wheel with both palms.

She jerked her hands away from the wheel and looked

up and down the street.

"Why do you let that Betty push you? Am I the only woman you can tell no?"

"You asked me to do the Sayers funeral. On my vacation. I didn't say no."

"That's different."

"How?"

Gwen pointed at the manse. Streetlight glare made shadows in the oversized boot-prints and hose trails left in the snowy front yard.

"It's that Betty's fault you were here today almost getting blown up or poisoned. The last thing you need tonight is to play referee at a church lady catfight."

I stifled a laugh. "You're not wrong. But I grew up hearing Mom's stories of Attie terrorizing the Colborne staff. I'd like to spare Betty some of that if I can."

Gwen eased off the brake and the Cadillac rolled toward the only other car on the road. My little tan hatch-back sat in front of one of the super-sized houses half a block from the manse.

The plow had left my car in a furrow of icy snow that rose above the tires.

"How much does Ms. Betty remind you of your mom?"

"Betty is happily married and doesn't have Alzheimer's."

"Still, she's old enough to be your mother and you seem to jump when she calls."

Gwen shook her head and put the car in park. She hit the trunk release and opened her door. Cold night air rushed in.

"I've got a shovel in the trunk. I'll clear the snow. See if your little go-kart will start."

I popped my seat belt. Pain spiked in both knees as I clambered out.

"Michael called it a tin box. I love that car."

"Yeah, I know. It was Carrie's. But it's still a little go-kart. Let's get you out of that snowbank, so you can head out into the dark night, in search of more trouble."

13

"You can't back out now." Kat declared. "With respect, Ms. Torrance-Martens…"

Kat rocked forward on her chair, a cream and gold wingback paired with the one beside her, where her great-aunt, Attie Beacham was enthroned. Kat's bare feet pressed into the pile of a Persian rug woven in rich blues. She clutched a matching throw pillow in her lap.

"Kat please, it's Betty."

Kat pulled an errant thread from the pillow.

"Okay Betty… But you were always Miss Torrance. That was before you married Ivy. I thought… I hoped she'd be here tonight. She would understand how much this matters to me."

A formal portrait over the fireplace revealed the source of Attie's intimidating features. The faces of Cyril and Mabel Brown scowled down on Attie and Kat, and Betty and I with equal disdain. I recognized Attie's parents from similar grim images engraved above their names on the plaque outside Saint Mungo's education wing. They were the reason it was Brown Hall.

I felt confident Cyril and Mabel would have deemed it improper for a young woman to entertain in anything so casual as yoga pants and an over-sized top.

A clumsy neon chalk drawing of a feline face, and the words 'Odious Kat Productions' were printed on her black sweatshirt. Kat's blonde hair fell over her shoulders to frame the logo.

"I know this is important to you," Betty said. "But this is a hard time for Saint Mungo's."

"With respect… Betty. We have a contract. The

production company paid the church extremely well for two location days. You need to let us do our work."

I sat opposite Kat. When she leaned forward, the artfully torn collar of her sweatshirt, exposed more than I cared to view, or be seen observing. Each time she bowed I turned my gaze to photos on the shelves flanking the fireplace.

The closest cluster was dedicated to the Daniels family. The largest was a studio portrait of Attie's sister Lila with her husband Ralph and a swaddled infant that had to be Dido. Ralph's tie was cinched tight and he was red in the face. Lila looked as stern as every woman in her clan, but I might be influenced by what I'd read in Doug's journal.

There was an elegant click as Betty placed her china cup in its gold trimmed saucer. She set them on a small mahogany pedestal table. The sound and movement drew my attention back from the photos.

Betty met Kat's gaze, and said in a soft tone, "I understand this is important to you." She then looked to Attie. "Thank you so much for tea."

Attie gave a regal nod, and a small wave. Betty's signal to move things along.

From where I sat, the carved legs of Attie's chair seemed a fraction taller than the others. Attie wore a matching teal jacket and skirt that could have come from the Margaret Thatcher collection. She'd even donned pearls.

Betty leaned towards Kat.

"At this point we can't promise access to the main building. The police investigation continues, and the deep cleaning afterwards will take time."

I felt under-dressed even though I'd stopped at home for my back-up funeral suit. I ran a hand over my head, smoothing down the hairs they'd snipped short at the hospital. I was sure they pointed straight up. My fingers went to the spot they'd shaved for the staples.

"My crew is scheduled." Kat's voice rose in pitch. "Equipment is rented. I've even booked Annika and her search dog."

Kat folded her throw pillow and pressed the halves together.

Attie cracked a frown.

Kat caught her look and unfolded the pillow on her lap.

"We won't need inside, except for bathroom access, and power. If that's a problem, I'll have a generator, and a porta-potty brought in."

Attie flinched when Kat said potty. Not very East Oakville.

In her high school graduation photo, in a place of honour to the right of the fireplace, Kat appeared privileged, poised and perfectly coiffed. Virgil looked sad and sullen in his photo, facing the lens with dim, hooded eyes.

Had the police tracked him down?

"Kat," Betty asked, "couldn't you postpone your shoot until after Easter? Just a few days…"

Kat had expected Ivy to be here, and she had a point. I was used to seeing Betty and Ivy as a matched pair, usually sporting jeans and uniform polo shirts from the rec centre. They even wore them Sundays, under their choir gowns.

For tonight's command performance Betty'd upgraded to black dress slacks, a white silk blouse and a collarless leather-trimmed tweed jacket. With her salt and pepper hair in a bun for the occasion, she might pass for one of Attie's neighbours, or perhaps her accountant.

I wondered if Ivy's absence was a strategy to appease Attie. Her being the first out lesbian at Saint Mungo's hadn't sat well with Attie.

Kat glanced at her phone. "It's almost eight o'clock. It's too late to cancel things."

Betty looked to me.

"Reverend Tom, don't you think it would be better to put things on hold?"

I drained the tepid dregs from my teacup, remembering Gwen's claim that I can't say no to a woman. She's told me before it's a mother thing. She's one to talk.

"To be honest," I said, "I'm not sure how it would make a difference."

My next mistake was allowing my gaze to follow the guttural sound that came from Attie, breaking the silence she'd kept since leading me into her parlour. Her steel grey eyes met mine, and I saw that I'd lost any goodwill I might've gained.

"This… minister may not be sure, but I am!"

Attie snatched the pillow from Kat's lap.

Kat laced the fingers of her now-empty hands in her lap, leaned back, and met her great aunt's eyes with her own steely look.

Attie tucked the pillow behind her and asked Kat, "How do you think it will look?"

Kat shifted in her chair.

"How will what look?"

"You know very well what I mean," Attie replied. "The body in Saint Mungo's basement was the big story on last night's news, complete with garish footage of police cars flashing their ridiculous lights in front of our church."

"That's what happens when a body is found," Kat said. "People want the story."

Attie looked my way. "Then today sirens wail and smoke billows and the media swarms in front of the manse."

Did she actually blame me for something that could have killed Michael and I?

"It's time to let things settle. Another spectacle at the church would not be proper."

"That's what you're worried about? Propriety? Not about the poor man buried in the wall?"

"I worry about appearances. No one else seems to." She glared at me, again.

Gwen was right. I should have stayed home. We'd be eating pad thai right now. With our feet up, watching Netflix.

I looked again at the collected family photos. Had these people ever been happy?

A simple pewter frame held a shot of Dido Daniels as a teen mother. Her cut-off shorts and cropped Nirvana t-shirt must have scandalized Attie and Lila. She stood behind Virgil and Kat, who were suspended in a pair of toddler swings.

The twins wore matching red and blue striped outfits, and their faces shone with joyous smiles. Dido leaned in with a hand on each child's back as if she was pushing them away.

"Aunt Attie," Kat said, "you know what this project means to me. I put myself out there."

There was a light touch on my hand. I turned to see Betty mouth, "We should go."

I nodded my full agreement.

Attie missed this exchange or ignored it.

"Really Kat, the last thing we need is more people slowing down as they drive by, to gawk and wonder what new scandal has befallen our poor church."

"I studied film production for four years and have spent most of my workdays fetching coffee. This time I'm the assistant director!"

Betty rose from her chair, and said, "Attie, I want to thank you for your hospitality."

I stole a look at the photo next to the swing set shot. Mounted in an elegant carved cherry wood frame, the subject was a young girl caught in mid-spin, in a dance recital. Her blonde hair was pulled tight in a bejeweled ballerina's bun. Was it Dido? The innocent joy in her clear blue eyes reminded me of the little one I'd seen dance around a grave.

Kat said. "This began with the stories about Uncle Doug. Don't you wonder if they're true?"

Attie's face went white, then red. "You know I have no use for that ghost talk."

I turned to Kat. "As Betty said, it may be time to call it a night."

"That, Reverend Book," Attie declared, "is the most... no, the only helpful thing you've said. Good night, everyone."

Attie sailed out of the parlour before I could negotiate

out of my chair. My knees protested, and I suppressed a groan as I stood.

Kat said, "We won't see her again tonight. She's headed up to her royal chambers."

Betty ended an uncomfortable silence. "Ivy just texted. She's out front."

We followed Kat out to the foyer.

I helped Betty with her coat, then stepped back as she deftly slipped out of her flats, and into her boots.

Betty tucked her shoes into her handbag, and came out with a small manila envelope, which she passed to me.

"It's from the pile of videos Eric sorted. He said you should watch it."

"I doubt it'll be tonight."

I tucked the envelope in a pocket of my overcoat, which still smelled smoky from the fire at the manse.

"That's understandable. You must be exhausted. Thanks for coming."

There was a rush of frigid air as Kat opened the front door.

"Oh!" Kat said, "Ivy. Come in. I didn't know you were waiting there."

Ivy knocked her boot against the edge of the landing, releasing a tread-marked clot of snow.

"No, I'd just track this in. Don't want to make a mess in Attie's fine house."

Ivy looked snug enough in her bright red Canada Goose parka, but to be polite I asked: "Are you okay out there?"

"I'm good, Reverend Tom."

Ivy's breath hung in the wintry air. Only the bangs of her black hair showed under a dark shearling hunter's cap. She had the ear flaps pulled down, against the cold. In this light it was hard to make out her face.

"Well, I'm cold now," Kat said. She backed away from the doorway and grabbed a long grey cardigan from a hook behind her.

"Ivy, I so wish you'd been here," Kat said, pulling the sweater tight around herself.

Ivy turned to me, and said, "Be good to her. She's been through so much."

Betty stepped out into the chill night.

"Take my arm as we walk," Ivy said. There's black ice, and I don't want you falling. Attie needs a railing here. Doesn't have to be fancy, like the rest of this place."

"Kat, it was good to see you," Betty said. "Please thank your great-aunt for her hospitality."

"I will."

Ivy led Betty towards her Toyota Tundra pickup, which idled on the circular drive.

"Good night, Kat. Thank you, Tom."

Their movement activated a security light. In the yellow glare, I saw one of the chrome bars on the truck's front grille was cracked. There was an oval shadow where the Toyota emblem belonged.

Ivy was particular about her possessions. I once referred to her truck as purple. With surprising ferocity, she'd said, "I'm an artist. Colours are my language. It's not purple, it's black currant."

Kat pushed the heavy door closed, and turned to face me. She shivered, and sobbed, and stood just a little too close. "Reverend Tom, I need you to tell me the truth. Did Virgil do something to Ed?"

14

"Kat, why would Virgil harm Rev. Wilder?"

Wielding a chef-worthy serrated blade, Kat carved generous slices from a crusty french loaf. The sweet yeasty scent conversed with my grumbling stomach, which was calling out for more than the Tim Horton's muffin I'd grabbed at the hospital.

Kat set a platter of spiral cut maple ham on the white marble top of the kitchen island, alongside a block of aged cheddar and a tub of butter. "Choose your mustard from the fridge door."

Did they have Grey Poupon? My kitchen had store brand yellow mustard, and whatever takeout packets landed in the junk drawer.

Kat still wore the oversized grey cardigan she'd wrapped tight around her against the cold. While leading me to the kitchen with the promise of a sandwich, she'd wiped at her tears on her sleeve. The mascara smears under her eyes made her look both fierce and vulnerable.

"Tell me about Virgil," I asked. "Why are you worried?"

"He acts like my big protector." Kat poured milk in a copper pot and set it on the stove. She lit the gas beneath it.

"He's your brother." I remembered the photo of the twins on the toddler swings. They'd lost their mother not long after. "You've been through a lot."

"Can you do the sandwiches?" She peeled gold foil from a bar of Cadbury Royal Dark. "This was my mother's favourite."

She diced the slab of chocolate, lifted the cutting board, and plowed thin shards into a small glass bowl with the knife edge.

I built and plated the sandwiches. "Anything else to do?"

"Add chocolate." Kat handed me the glass bowl. I shook in dark flakes, which melted as she whisked the steaming milk. "If I stop stirring the milk will scald."

"I should make it this way for Hope." I said. "It smells incredible."

Kat poured in table cream.

"My mom would make this when she was sad or scared. Grandma Lila always had good chocolate. That was before…"

"Is that why Virgil… why he looks out for you?"

Kat killed the flame and lifted the pot. "When my mom… when she died, that was when Grandma Lila moved out. Auntie Attie and Uncle Doug came here to take care of us. Virgil was never the same."

"I never met your mom. It couldn't have been easy for any of you."

I thought of Doug's take on Lila's deal with Attie. Adopt the kids, get a big house.

Kat poured cocoa into large mugs. Rich aroma rose with the steam.

"Virgil worries he'll lose me." She pointed to a white ceramic crock on the kitchen island, that held cooking implements. "Hand me that grater?"

I gave her the tool. "You've both lost a lot."

"I don't remember Grandpa Ralph. Aunt Attie says he drank himself to death." She pulled a cinnamon stick from a glass canister. "You want some on top?"

I nodded. "And your grandmother?"

"We see Lila at Christmas, and usually in July. She has to come back from Sarasota every six months for her health insurance."

Kat rubbed the cinnamon stick across the grater.

"I'm sorry it's been this way. You and Virgil did nothing to deserve it."

"Mom was lovely, but like Aunt Attie says, she was

flakier than a snowstorm. Ow!" Kat caught a knuckle on the grater. "Shit!"

I said, "Let's get cold water on that."

Kat held her hand under the stream from the chrome kitchen tap.

"Don't worry, there's no blood in your hot chocolate."

I smiled. "I bet it stings."

"Would you grab a band-aid from under the sink?"

"Of course." I backed up against the kitchen island and knelt to search for the box.

"Looks like you've had some first aid of your own. The back of your head."

I rose and opened the kit on the island counter.

"Looks worse than it is."

Kat laid her hand flat on the countertop.

"Was that from today at the manse?"

I ignored her query.

"Let's get some antibiotic cream on there."

Carrie was the nurse, but she'd let me assist when she patched up Hope's scrapes over the years.

"Two of these small ones will do. The abrasions are below the knuckle, so they won't stop you bending your fingers."

"Reverend Tom, what happened at the manse? Did my brother do something to Ed?"

I gestured to the stools at the end of the kitchen island.

"Let's sit. I'm hungry."

The conversation might go better without eye contact. Some of my best talks with Hope have been on long car rides when she can stare out her window.

"I want to know what happened at the manse."

"There was a fire and an explosion. It's a mess."

"You were there, with Michael Powers from the church council. The one with the restaurant, who used to be a cop. I saw you in his car when I drove by."

"Kat, why were you there?"

"I was looking for Ed… for Reverend Wilder."

"You want to say more about that?"

I bit through the crust and took in a mouthful. The maple ham was sweet, the butter salty. My stomach was happy.

"I've been worried since Monday. He said he'd be there for my shoot. I think Virgil…"

"You keep saying you think Virgil did something. Do you know where he is?"

Kat blew across the surface of her cocoa, then sipped.

"He doesn't live here anymore."

"There are people who want to talk to him."

"He's in trouble. I knew it."

"Kat, why do you think Virgil would be in trouble?"

She pushed her plate away. "He saw us. Ed and me."

I set my sandwich down, with reluctance, and turned to face Kat.

"Maybe you should tell me what's going on."

"Ed and I are… seeing each other." Kat pulled the long sweater tight around her.

"We were in the lady's parlour. We thought we were alone in the building."

I took a breath and nodded.

"When was this?"

"Saturday night."

"Ed and I were on that old horsehair sofa, and we were… Virgil just walked in on us. Ed locked the door, but…"

"Virgil has all the keys."

I tried not to picture the scene.

"He yelled 'you're just like Mom.' I asked what he meant but he just came at us. Ed stood and tried to pull up his slacks. He said, 'Virgil, we can talk about this'."

I shifted on my stool and worked to keep a neutral face.

Kat continued. "Virgil pulled out his phone and snapped photos…"

I raised my eyes toward the kitchen ceiling. "Does your aunt…"

"She can't hear anything." Kat shook her head. "She'll

be up in her sitting room, with her big tv up loud and the door shut."

"No, I mean, does she know about you and…"

"No way. She would kill him." Kat flashed a sly smile. "She hates ministers. No offense, but she says you're a necessary evil."

"So I've heard."

"Ed grabbed at Virgil's phone, but his feet were tangled in his pants. Virgil backed away and kept on clicking. He said, 'I can't believe you Eddie.' By this time I'd put myself back together and just wanted out."

I nodded. "I wouldn't want to be there either."

"Virgil said, 'I'm going to tell her. She warned me about you. I'm sending her a picture.'"

"Send a picture?" I asked, "To who?"

"Ed stepped towards Virgil, tried to grab the phone. He tripped and fell forward. I tried to catch him, break his fall, but I wasn't fast enough. Virgil just stood there and watched as Ed went down. I couldn't believe it."

I took a warming swallow from my mug, against the creeping chill I felt. "What happened then?"

Kat closed her eyes. "It was awful. Ed caught his forehead on the edge of that ugly old coffee table, and he was knocked out. I said, 'Help me get him up,' but Virgil just turned and walked away. He slammed the parlour door."

"Um." I felt sick, and heavy with exhaustion. Ed is twice her age and is supposed to be her minister. Kat's not much older than my Hope.

"I rolled Ed on his side, made sure he was breathing. I fixed his pants, kind of tucked everything in. I didn't want anyone else to see him that way. Can you understand that?"

"You were trying to help."

"I could feel a phone in his pocket. It must have been on vibrate. It was getting a bunch of texts. I was going to use it to call 911, but then Ed woke up."

"Was he okay?"

Kat's eyes went wide with the memory. I saw the vulnerability of that little girl in the toddler swing.

"He threw up on that old Persian rug, which was awful. But that seemed to be what he needed. I thought he'd be okay. The gash on his forehead had stopped bleeding."

"What happened after that?"

"Ed told me he'd see me in the morning. He said I shouldn't worry; he'd fix it with Virgil. He looked at his phone, and swore out loud, which wasn't like him, and told me he had to go see someone."

"Did he say who?"

"Ed doesn't tell me about his work. He's very... private."

"What did you do then?"

"I had calls to make about the morning shoot, so I went home. I haven't heard from Ed since."

"What about Virgil?"

"My brother hasn't talked to me. He ignores my texts. He was supposed to open the church for me and the crew. But I think he's been following me."

I left most of my sandwich, and a brown smear of mustard on the plate. My appetite had fled. What I'd eaten was a lump in my gut.

"Kat, are you worried he'll do something to you?"

"He'd never hurt me, but he's being even weirder than usual. You know he's always been a little..."

"I've known both of you since you were kids, but never really connected with Virgil. I'm sorry about that."

I brought my plate to the sink and reached for the tap. Kat waved me away.

"I'll clean up."

"Thanks for the food."

"You looked like you could use it. Thanks for talking, and for listening. Especially after I was such a bitch at the shoot."

"Does Virgil have anyone to talk to?"

"Aunt Attie unless she's in a mood, like now. Or Ivy. She looks out for us."

I moved towards the front hallway, and my winter coat.

"I need to get home. It's been a day."

"I get that. Thanks again, Reverend Tom."

"What you disclosed about you and Reverend Wilder..." I pulled on my coat. "Aside from how awful it must have been when Virgil walked in..." I dug in my pocket for my keys, while I searched for words. "There are ethical boundaries in the church, and..."

"You think he's taking advantage of me."

"Honestly, yes."

"We're adults."

"Yes. But it's more complicated than that."

"My whole life has been complicated Reverend Tom. But I'm tired and like you said, it's been a day."

"Can we talk again?"

"Can it wait until we find Ed? I'm worried about him."

Kat stood in the doorway as I stepped out into the cold. Her big sweater hung below her knees. I saw a fierce woman and a lonely child, at the same time.

15

Snow squeaked underfoot as I plodded to the car, feeling my way along for patches of ice I knew were under-foot. Surgical gauze stretched tight when I bent my bandaged knees and adhesive tape tugged at a hundred short hairs.

The phone in my pocket buzzed. Like Ed's, only I'd kept my pants on. He's old enough to be Kat's father. She's a wounded soul, with a family like the cast of a bad TV movie. He's supposed to be her minister. There are lines you don't cross.

I varied the length of my stride to change the duration of each pang in my knees. This grim exercise offered the illusion of control over at least one discomfort.

What the hell was Ed thinking?

The sharp twinges also distracted me from fatigue. I bent to lower myself into the car. The seat was cold and hard. The windows were frosted from the inside. The warm luxury of Gwen's funeral car was an ice age ago. I turned the key. The starter whined until the little engine caught.

The ancient Suzuki Swift's cabin warmed up faster if the car was in motion. When Carrie was still taking shifts at the hospital, I'd start the car and take it around the block.

The blower rattled on full. I hit the rear defrost and sat back in the frozen seat.

The phone showed a text from Gwen.

"U ok? U looked wiped b4. Still say U shoulda stayed home. I'm off to bed."

I typed, "You weren't wrong," and went back to staring at the frosted windshield.

Seeing through a glass darkly summed up these last two days.

The body on the boiler room floor. The little girl frolicking around a grave. The cache of drugs and money. Shattered window glass pelting a snowy yard. The black truck racing away. The fear in Kat's eyes when she asked if Virgil hurt Ed.

Warmish air melted fist-sized peek-holes close to the dashboard. I glimpsed the driveway, yellow under the security lights.

Kat's story rocked me more than the manse explosion. Since I'd come back to Saint Mungo's Ed had skated around personal topics, slick as the hidden ice on Attie's walkway.

The windshield cleared enough for me to see my way home. I turned the noisy heater fan down and switched on the headlights.

The plow had left a foot-high ridge of dirty snow chunks across the driveway.

The dashboard clock blinked 10:07. It felt later.

I shifted into drive, glanced at the silent street and pressed on the gas. Spinning front wheels threw ice pellets up into the wheel-wells. The undercarriage caught on packed snow before the tires regained purchase and pulled the car out onto the pavement.

There were many days after Carrie died when it took all I had to push through the numbness to simulate regular life. Even so, I should have tried to find common ground with Ed.

I could hear my father's slurred, too-loud voice saying, "The should'ves will kill you, boy. Don't waste your time on 'em."

I should've braked earlier as I came to the four-way stop. The tires slid on black ice and took the Suzuki a car length out into the intersection. I was startled by sudden sense of peril. I only breathed again when I was certain there were no other cars. Veins pulsed hard in that swollen place where they'd stapled my scalp.

I lowered my window. Cold air shocked my face and pushed back the weariness. I needed to get home.

I turned on to Lakeshore Road. The pricey shops of the downtown core were locked up tight for the night. I sailed through the flashing green of three intersections.

A sander truck approached from the other direction. Glaring head lamps stung my eyes. The noise and fumes as the big diesel stormed past prompted me to crank up the window.

Hoping music would clear my head, I pushed in a CD. The Bruce Cockburn mix had been in the player since the last time Carrie rode in this car. The guitar and drums of "Coldest Night of the Year" kicked in.

The familiar brick and stone bulk of Colborne College was on the left. Sharp black spikes jutting out of the snow were all I could see of the wrought iron fence fronting the campus. My brother and I could've gone for free under the family plan, but my father stopped that dead.

With his third after-supper beer in hand my father had declared, "They'd know you as the teacher's kids and worse, as the charity cases."

"Tom and JP wouldn't be the only ones," Mom had argued. "Many of the staff enroll their kids."

"Still, they'd always be the poor cousins. Marco from the plant, his oldest won a scholarship. Full ride, except no freakin' way could they afford the extras. Formal parties. Fancy dress clothes. And get this… Tony's whole biology class, except him, went to the Galapagos for March break. The bloody Galapagos Islands. Can you freakin' imagine?"

The bright lights of the college guard shack were my cue to slow for the "T" intersection where Lakeshore met the end of 4th Line. I applied the brake with care, wary of black ice at this corner. As the car slid to a stop, the cd player reached Lovers in a Dangerous Time.

There was a huge engine roar, and my little car shuddered. The air was pierced by a metallic squeal as a big black something… sideswiped me. It scraped along my driver's side door, which at that moment seemed thin as tin foil, and tore off the mirror.

Brake lights flashed red as a black pickup swerved hard and made a 90 degree turn ahead of me. Spinning tires flung ice and gravel as the driver slammed the gas to accelerate up 4th Line, then veered left on to Rebecca Street. The exhaust rumble faded as the truck sped out of sight.

Had Virgil followed me from Attie's house? I hadn't noticed headlights. He could have been rolling dark behind me. But why?

The traffic light turned green. I hit the red triangular button on the dash for the hazard lights, shut down the music, and put the Suzuki in park. I was still for a moment, listening to the reliable beat of the safety blinkers. I took a deep breath, feeling it strain against the tightness in my chest, and let it out slow.

I shivered with fear and felt sparks of anger, but such intensity was hard to sustain. A heavy blanket of weariness muffled everything except the desire to be home.

I dismissed my suspicion of Virgil. There were lots of black trucks and, as my father often said, "plenty of assholes to go around."

I saw no vehicles ahead of me. My tired eyes failed to focus on the rear-view mirror. I blinked to clear my vision, turned my head to look out the back window and felt tears on my cheek.

Time to check the damage. I pulled up on the latch. The door caught before it was free of the frame. I shouldered it hard. Frigid air rushed at me when the door popped, like I'd been hit by a truck again.

I stepped out, leery of ice. No other cars in sight. I left the door open a fraction. I feared it jamming shut and locking me out in the cold.

The door was buckled in and had a streak of black paint smeared into the salt-stained surface, as if my little car had been scratched by a beast with dirty claws.

The side mirror cowling had bounced and rolled just ahead of the Suzuki. It lay cracked open like a small skull. Shiny bits of glass glinted in the dirty snow where they'd been ground under the big truck's tires. I tossed the mirror on the back seat.

The door squealed as I tugged it mostly shut. When the light cycled to green, I killed the hazard lights, and drove west along Lakeshore Road.

I distracted myself thinking of those who'd trod the path skirting the lake for generations before the British parceled out their traditional territory. My mother raised my brother and me on stories of the forest people. Travelling as they did, on foot under the cover of the trees, appealed to me right then.

The plow had been on my street since I'd been home to change clothes. There was a windrow across my driveway, another mountain range in miniature. I gave my battered a little car more gas, and the front tires chewed through their last obstacle of the night.

I pulled in behind Gwen's funeral car, which gleamed under the yard light.

I limped up my front steps, which sparkled with tiny crystals. Gwen must have cleared and salted them before she turned in. I worked the door with quiet care. My housemate could already be asleep downstairs.

Gwen had left the hall light on, so I was greeted by the print I'd hung in the foyer. "Family of Birds" by Norval Morrisseau. My mom gave it to Carrie when Hope was born, and I loved coming home to it.

Bird Mother and Father stand with their offspring, all long beaks and big bright eyes looking up to the sky. They are held close in the unbroken embrace of a circle.

Morrisseau survived the Indian residential school system but it ravaged him. My mother based an upper year Canadian history course on his life and work. The course theme, and her motivation for teaching, came back to me. "If we look close enough, we generally find our current problems have deep roots in the past."

16

My bed was too empty for sleep. I tapped the remote for the jazz station and nestled into the leather recliner. Carrie's quilt still held her scent.

I keep the music low. Gwen's not a jazz fan and she needs to be out the door before 7 most mornings.

A poet said we each have a world asleep within, which most wake to but rarely glimpse and barely recall. Most of us loll away a third of our lives unconscious, with little to show for it.

Since my wife's death I've learned to relish my dreams.

In this dream my fingertips hovered over the shaved spot on my scalp. I probed with care to not re-open the wound. I was looking for the staples. Carrie would want to see them. She's a nurse. She never wore one of those little white caps except for her graduation photo.

I was in a strange room with grey stone walls, but sitting on my mom's very familiar, horrible burgundy couch, its cheap nylon upholstery scratchy as dish scrub pads.

The week she found the courage to leave my father, Mom signed up to pay $58 dollars a month for this terrible couch, two matching chairs, a tiny box of a television and a VCR.

The volunteer movers were two gangly upper years from Mom's senior history class. They'd tried, bless them, but her old brown chesterfield couldn't make the turn down the narrow stairwell to that musty basement suite. We weren't going back to my father's house so it was left at the curb, and gone before morning.

I reached over the bad couch and pointed to a scarred spot. The fabric grabbed my arm hairs like velcro.

I said, "JP once held a lighter close to the panel here on

the back where he thought Mom wouldn't notice. He wanted to know whether it would burn first or melt. The smell made me sick."

Her dark brown eyes met mine. This was why I dreamed.

Carrie asked, "Was it awful? The staples, I mean, not the burning couch smell."

"I thought they'd hurt more. The tetanus shot was worse."

She laughed. "You were always afraid of needles."

"If I can find the staples, I'll pull them out myself when it's time. The nurse said the skin pushes them up as it heals and lots of patients do it themselves. Or maybe you could..."

"You know I can't," Carrie said.

She sounded sad.

Then I felt trapped and hot like I was back in the fire at manse. My scalp wound throbbed. I kicked off the quilt and lay uncovered on my leather recliner. I felt there should be steam rising off me. Or smoke.

I opened just the one eye a slit. The only light in my front room was the faint yellow glow of the stereo dial.

My will hovered in that liminal zone where I could choose to wake, or dive back in and maybe see her again. I closed my eye as "Quiet Nights and Quiet Stars" flowed from the radio. Carrie loved this version by Diana Krall.

The warmth of her hand. We lay side by side on the hospital bed the rental guys set up where she could look out the picture window.

"Touch there. The sutures are gone, but it feels like they left little bumps under the skin."

"No one will see them when your hair grows back. And it's already started."

The pre-op nurse told us they'd shave only where they'd cut the skin flap, but Carrie said, "Take it all!"

The new growth of tiny dark hairs was velvet soft.

Carrie squeezed her small hand over mine and said, "I

won't go through this again, no matter what."

Dark smoke threatened to swallow me. I sped-crawled towards the light of the laundry room. It was the only way out. Prickles of heat stung my face. Rough concrete tore at my pants, and my skin. My bare knees were gritty with dust and wet with blood.

The smell of lemons brought me back to the grey stone room.

"What's that about lemons?"

Carrie pulled the quilt up around us. It was the one Eric and Joanie gave her. Joanie did every stitch herself, in a falling leaf pattern Carrie loved.

"The sanctuary was so bright and hot from the movie lights. I didn't even want to be at the video shoot. But she was kind, and said she knew you from school."

"You mean Annika." Carrie's voice was gentle.

"Gwen calls her the dog lady. Zeke found a dead body in the church basement. The air was so cold when it fell out of the wall."

When Carrie came home after her surgery she couldn't get warm enough. I pushed the hospital bed closer to our gas fireplace, but she'd still ask me to pile the big quilt over two blankets when she slept.

"I like the leaves," Carrie would say.

A low rumble shook me out of my dream. I plummeted towards waking. My gut knew that dark vibration.

Through the gap in the picture window drapes I saw the salt-stained black pickup that had sideswiped my car, idling in front of my house.

An electric shudder spiked down my spine. I used the remote to power off the stereo, the only light in the room. In the dark, I slid my fingers over the smooth leather of the recliner and searched for my cellphone.

17

"You should've called it in when you were sideswiped," Michael said. "They might've got'em. It's a quiet night."

With quiet stars? Even half awake, I bristled at being scolded with a should've.

"I was past tired," I explained. " It's just the side mirror, and the door is a bit... crunched."

When it happened, I didn't believe the run-in with the black truck was anything more than random. Now I was half-whispering into my phone, as if the driver might hear me, through the wall of my house, and the deep throb of the truck's exhaust.

"I figured I'd sort it tomorrow. I just wanted to get home."

I heard an arrested sigh on Michael's end. He reined himself in. "Okay... hold on Tom. I'm on two lines here..."

I was in the darkness of my living room, hunched low on the leather recliner. I'd been afraid to move since I spotted the black truck outside my house. A thin trickle of light bled in from the street, through the slit dividing the picture window drapes.

I heard Michael say, "Okay, roger that, and thanks... Sorry, Tom, I'm back with you."

The black pickup's low rumble rattled the picture window.

"What should I do?"

"Keep away from the windows." Michael said. "Don't turn on any lights."

"Someday soon you'll have to tell me how a guy who runs a sandwich shop can call in the troops so quickly."

I didn't think the Naloxone kit in Michael's car was a

retirement gift.

Michael ignored the probe.

"Keep low, partner. You should head down to Gwen's suite. Use your phone to light the way. Aim it at the floor."

"I'd rather not wake her, but that might be a good idea," I said, as I slid out of the recliner, hunkering down into a squat. Pain lit up both knees. I gripped the recliner armrests with both hands, and my phone thunked hard on the wood floor.

That might wake Gwen anyway, I thought.

Crouched on the floor, groping for the phone, I had a perfect eye-line with the bottom edge of the front room's picture window, the part not quite covered by the drapes.

I crammed the phone in my pocket, and crab-crawled closer, staying low as Michael suggested. I peeked out but couldn't see who was driving the truck.

I heard a strange, uneven, and menacing beat. The mystery driver trampled down on the truck's accelerator like a pedal on a bass drum. The ponderous, rumbling rhythm roused a memory that still made my stomach tight.

"Listen to that," My father had demanded from under the hood of his Crown Victoria. He'd prod at something, and the massive motor would roar. Exhaust clouded us with hydrocarbons no child or beast should breathe.

JP lounged inside on the big comfy couch, watching Magic School Bus with Mom, while I endured that hot summer Saturday morning with our father in his garage. I handed him tools or ran for fresh cans of beer while he tinkered. He replaced grease-blackened bits of metal with shiny new ones he'd smuggled home from the plant.

"The cylinders need to fire in order," he yelled. "You probably think an engine burns gas, but you're wrong. It's more like one controlled explosion after another. Feel that raw power!"

My father shifted his gaze from the engine to me. He ran greasy fingers through his thick black hair, while he searched my face for a spark of enthusiasm that would never ignite.

Three more beers with lunch doused the strange fire in his eyes. When I was sure my father was totally out, I said, "He was like a playground bully going vroom, vroom, with some other kid's Hot Wheels."

My mother flashed a sad smile and said we could take our bikes to the park.

The menacing rumble grew louder as the black pickup backed into my driveway, halting just inches from my already embattled car. Grey salt spittle stained the truck's fenders. Brake-lights glowed red like demon eyes through the fog of exhaust. High-mounted headlamps lit up the street.

The raucous engine lulled then roared loud. With a disturbing crunch the rusty bumper rammed the rear of the Suzuki. Carrie's car.

The sour contents of my stomach gushed upwards like I'd been gut-punched. I swallowed down the fear and the harsh taste. Something else arose in me.

Ignoring my throbbing knees and Michael's advice to lay low, I stood to step towards the door. As I unclenched a fist to work the doorknob, the hallway light came on. I felt a cool hand on my shoulder.

"Tom," Gwen said from behind me, "where are you going?"

My knees sparked with pain as I pivoted to face her. I'm a foot taller than Gwen, but the look in her eyes made up the difference.

She asked, "What's your plan?"

I backed closer to the door. Even with the powder blue fleece bathrobe tied tight around her, and the flowered yellow night bonnet she wore to hold up her braids, Gwen was an imposing presence.

"I'm well... I need... I'm going out there to stop the guy in the truck from pushing my Suzuki into the back of your Cadillac."

Reaching behind me, I turned the knob and pulled hard

at the door.

"Barefoot, and in your pyjamas? In the snow? Are you serious?"

"That's your company car…"

"So it's insured."

Cold air whirled in at us as I swung the door inward.

"I can't let him… sometimes you have to stand up to bullies."

"What are you going to do? Limp at him? Look at you! Your knee is bleeding again. It's soaked through the dressing and your…"

A huge engine roar cut her off. I pulled the door open. Gwen and I watched the truck power out of the driveway. Knobby tires threw back dirty chunks of snow and ice. The chill wind wafted thick black fumes our way.

I pushed the door shut. I was shivering. It was suddenly quiet.

"You're right. I just…"

"What's going on, Tom?"

"That's a good question, Gwen." Michael's muffled voice came from the phone in my pocket. "You okay there, partner?"

I retrieved the cellphone and flicked on the overhead light. Pointing to the living room couch, and my recliner, I said to Gwen, "Let's sit," and holding up the phone, I said, "Michael, I think it's the same truck. I think maybe it's Virgil that sideswiped me.."

Gwen's eyes were wide. "He what?"

Michael said, "You didn't make it to the basement. Maybe you both should get down there. I just got off the line with Halton Police. They're rolling units to close off your street."

"He's long gone Michael and honestly, I've had enough of basements for today…"

A police cruiser shot past the house, siren wailing, red and blue lights flashing bright.

"Okay. Sounds like they've got you covered Tom. I'll

check in with you in the morning. Keep the lights down. Listen to Gwen. Stay inside. Try to get some sleep."

"I don't think I'll be able to," I said.

"G'night partner." Michael clicked off.

Gwen said, "I'll fix us some tea."

"That'd be great," I said. "But shouldn't you be going back to bed?"

"I think I'm up now, for the day, even though it's stupid o'clock. And you, Thomas M. Book, are going to tell me what's going on, yeah?"

18

"What would your Carrie think of you hobbling barefoot through snow and ice to throw yourself at a truck?" Gwen asked, as she out brought out a tray of tea things from the kitchen.

"Um…" I said, as I struggled to climb out of the recliner. "Let me help with…"

"Sit, you," she said. "When I picked you up from the hospital you were more than done for. I thought you were a fool to go out again."

"You made that pretty clear. But sometimes in this job…"

Gwen deposited the tray on the coffee table, and passed over my favourite mug, from the Piano Box in New Orleans.

"The job! You let those church ladies run you. What would your Carrie say about that?"

While she'd been at work in the kitchen, I'd cleaned up my bleeding knee, and changed into jeans and a flannel shirt.

We'd turned on the lights. Whoever'd been out there already saw me in the doorway. Not my smartest move, but I wasn't ready to admit that to Gwen.

"She'd have wanted me to stay home, and she might have been right, except…"

"Except what?"

I swallowed tea, and said, "If I hadn't gone to Attie's, I wouldn't have heard Kat's story."

"What's going on for that one, besides having the grumpy duchess for a great aunt, and a crazy boy for a brother?"

We've held each other's confidences for years. I gave Gwen the gist of what Kat told me in the kitchen.

"So Ed's been doing Kat, and maybe that Virgil as well? What a shit."

"I don't know if it's sexual with Virgil. But they're both lost souls, and vulnerable…"

"And your Ed Wilder should know better."

"Yeah, he should."

"You know I've never liked him. And you and Michael, who I do like, almost got killed today trying to track him down."

"Betty wanted to make sure he wasn't sick or lying dead on the floor."

"And we're back to that, Ms. Betty cracks her whip, and you're like her little trained bear-cub, up on your hind legs."

"Betty isn't the whip-cracking type."

"She knows how to play you."

I thought about telling Gwen how I'd deviated from Betty's script that night, and how it may have led to Kat confiding in me, but I was curious about the DVD.

"Speaking of playing…" I said, pointing to a padded envelope next to the tea tray. "Betty handed me that when she left Attie's. It's from Eric."

Gwen picked it up. "In tiny perfect letters it says Ed clears the temple."

"Eric was in banking long before computers. He's very precise."

"He wants you to watch this? Why?"

"He found it when we set up for the board meeting. It's from when Ed had Kat video his sermons."

"So she's been working under him for how long?"

"Yeah, I wonder. She was a college student then. So an adult, technically… but still, he's her pastor."

"I'm liking this guy less and less."

"Can you drop the disc in?" I grabbed the remote.

19

The video opened with a wide shot of the Saint Mungo's sanctuary from the balcony. A graphic scrolled over, declaring this an Odious Kat Production. The same simple drawing of a feline face I'd seen on Kat's black sweatshirt.

The camera tightened focus on Ed Wilder, behind the communion table. His hair was longer than I'd ever seen it, and a little unkempt. Was that the shadow of a beard?

Ed's white robe and clerical stole- and the presence of bread and grape juice- told me it was Communion Sunday.

Gwen asked, "What's he doing?"

Ed took two steps back and raised one bent knee high, as if aiming a karate kick.

"Acting," I said.

If he'd actually knocked over the communion table, I'd have heard about it.

It appeared that in those days Ed wore jeans and runners under his robe. By the time I came on staff he'd upgraded to Harry Rosen suits.

"What would happen if I toppled this table, sent the trays of bread cubes flying, and splattered grape juice everywhere? I'm sure Doug, our loyal sexton, would be less than thrilled."

Kat shifted the camera to the back of her great uncle's head. Doug sat in his usual spot on the right side, on the aisle. His silver-grey hair was trimmed neat above his collar.

The shot widened to show the centre aisle and the pews on either side.

"Good crowd," Gwen noted.

The camera went back to Ed behind the communion

table. He lowered his foot from the Bruce Lee pose and said, "Many of you would ask why the minister was acting so disrespectful. Attie and the rest of the church council might decide I'd lost it and talk about my future here, or the lack of one."

There was scattered, nervous laughter.

Kat focused on her great aunt, blue-robed, in the choir loft behind Ed. Attie's lips were pursed in her default mode, visible disgust. I imagined her priming her verbal cannon to fire the phrase "made a spectacle of himself."

"There's your Betty, thick as thieves with Attie," Gwen said.

"I don't think so. Betty looks worried. Attie just looks smug. Like Ed's proving her point, that ministers should be on a short leash."

"And who pulls your leash Reverend Book?"

"Let's just watch."

In a tone dripping with sincerity, Ed said, "We've been taught, most of us, to see this table, and the bread and cup we share as sacred and essential to our lives of faith. It would be disturbing to see them poorly treated."

I wondered how far Ed would push.

Ed lifted the white cloths that covered the plates of communion bread. He folded each with exaggerated care and set them aside.

"Ivy just read us the story of Jesus storming the temple. He confronted the sellers of livestock and the moneychangers who converted Roman coins to Jewish shekels, which were then used to buy animals to be sacrificed. These traders and their tables were as much fixtures of life in the Jerusalem temple, as this communion table and our brass collection plates are to us."

Gwen said, "I wonder what the folks in the pews were thinking."

"Yeah, I wish Kat had a camera up front. We only see the backs of their heads."

Ed continued, "The temple leaders would be at least

as horrified, confused, and angry about Jesus' actions, as you would be if I ran amok here at Saint Mungo's."

Gwen asked, "Is that man actually comparing himself to Jesus?"

"Shh," I said.

Ed asked, "So what was he on about? The story says Jesus yelled at those who sold the doves for sacrifice, 'Get these out of here! Stop turning my father's house into a market!'"

I've used this story in the run-up to Good Friday, to describe Jesus' collision course with the temple authorities. Where was Ed headed?

"Some ancient religions taught it was a faithful act to kill a living creature and burn the carcass as a sacrifice. You sent the fragrant smoke up to gain the favour of your chosen deity. You'd need to do this if you'd been stained with some social stigma and were considered impure. You had to buy an animal, have it sacrificed, and then present yourself to the priests to be declared clean."

Ed looked out at the congregation for a beat before adding, "How terrible it would be, to be considered unclean, not worthy of joining in the prayers, or being in the company of the 'good people.' How much worse might you feel if you couldn't afford the price of the sacrificial animal?"

There was silence in the sanctuary and in my living room. Gwen stared at the flat screen.

"The inner circle had side deals with livestock suppliers and the moneychangers, who flipped a percentage from every transaction back to the temple treasury. It was a great fundraiser."

Nervous laughter came through the TV speakers.

"Jesus despised this pay-to-pray business model. He hung out with ordinary messy people on the streets, at the beach, on hillsides. Most didn't have two shekels to rub together, or buy bread for the day, never mind paying the temple's purity tax. And Jesus loved them all."

Ed raised his hands over the bread and the communion

chalice.

"We pray over these things. We bless and share them and proclaim they represent divine love. We say we want everyone to feel welcome. But what if we've put up barriers that make it near impossible for some to feel welcome?"

Ed paused for a longer beat. He certainly knew how to play for the camera. Didn't Eric say he'd been in broadcasting?

Gwen said, "See them squirming in their seats?"

"Before you tell yourself the preacher's exaggerating and good Christians like us would never push people away, take a breath. It wasn't that long ago this church, like most others, taught that people who identified as anything except white bread heterosexual needed to get themselves right, get pure, make some huge sacrifices, before they'd truly be welcome."

Ed took up one of the white cloths he'd folded, snapped it open, and dropped it over a plate of bread.

"To be honest, we're still not doing great. And before we got as far as we have, there were a lot of folks who got the message from us, that they'd better hide their true selves. I've heard it said, not far from where I'm standing right now, 'Of course they can be with whoever they want, but do they have to flaunt it? Do I have to see them holding hands?'"

Ed snapped a second white cloth, and let it drop over the communion chalice.

Kat chose that moment to focus her lens on Ivy in the soprano section, who seemed to be glowing. Her smile radiated joy. She held her palms pressed together at chest level. Was she praying, or waiting to applaud?

The camera scanned back to Ed's face, which in stark contrast to Ivy's was devoid of emotion.

Ed said, "Our shameful history, and our history of shaming others, should never be forgotten. We owe so many apologies, to so many people wounded by the church. Beyond that important work, we need to be vigilant and honest about our remaining biases. We need to think about who else we actively leave out, and who we've already driven away. Amen."

A swell of organ music was the choir's cue to rise as one to sing their anthem.

Kat's camera panned across the choir loft. She zoomed in to fill the screen with an image of her great aunt Attie's face, her eyes bright with fury.

So were Gwen's.

"I suppose I'm meant to like that sermon… but, the man has a lot of nerve, talking about people wounded by the church. Kat made this video for him. Was he already grooming her? Or were they already…"

"Yeah, that's a good question," I said. "One I'd very much like to take up with Reverend Wilder."

20

"Hope called. She'll fly into Detroit and take VIA Rail from Windsor to Oakville. Her train will be in a little before ten tomorrow night."

Gwen and I were perched on stools at the end of the kitchen island closest to the coffee machine. I'd ground the last of my Blue Mountain beans when I saw her car was still in the driveway.

"That why you're up so early, and already doing chores? I hear the washer going and it actually smells… clean in here."

"I'm bleaching the sink, the way Carrie used to."

"Where'd you get all this energy? After yesterday and especially last night I thought you'd sleep in."

"Yeah, me too. But once I got to sleep, in my real bed, I slept the best I have in months. But… what about you? It's almost 8 o'clock, and you're still in jeans."

"I took a personal day."

"You what?"

"I've got lots banked. I wasn't sure we'd be able to move your car and I didn't want you to worry yourself. Pat's up on all the current arrangements, says he'll call if he needs a word."

"The car is okay, mostly. It started and I ran it backwards and forwards in the driveway. But what are you going to do with a day off?"

"Help you clean this house for one. This man-cave vibe you've had going is…"

"I'm on top of it. I've been picking up, even got an online grocery order in."

Gwen topped up our coffee and asked, "What else you have going on?"

"Michael texted, wants to meet at the church."

"Maybe he'll know what to with your Ed Wilder."

"It's not that simple. Ed may not have done anything illegal. But if he doesn't turn up soon, the police may need to know about his run-in with Virgil."

"I'd like to run in to your Pastor Wilder. Or run over him. Preying on those young ones."

Gwen has a way of saying it out loud.

"Kat asked me to be there for her video shoot tomorrow afternoon. I want to help her. There's the added bonus that it'll annoy Attie and remind Betty I can't be run."

"You're full of piss and vinegar today."

I stood to stretch my legs.

"I had a moment last night…"

Gwen said, "I'll bet."

I took a few steps towards the living room, to get my knees working.

"It sunk in I could have died."

Through the picture window I saw a plow-truck scraping our street.

"That's what I said when I picked you up at the Emergency."

"Yes, Gwen, you were right." I kept a straight face for that. Almost.

"Uh hunh."

The plow's flashing blue light was brighter than the sun this morning, which was still shrouded in grey clouds.

"I could have died, but I wasn't dead yet. It kind of jolted me. I've been stuck for a while."

"Sometimes stuck is where people need to be."

"Until it's not," I said.

"Until it's not." Gwen said.

We raised our mugs, tapping them in agreement.

"I'm going out to Annika's tonight."

"Your dog lady?"

"She called wondering if I was part of tomorrow's

shoot. We seemed to connect… She asked me out to her farm for supper. That way she doesn't have to leave Zeke on his own."

"See, I knew it. Your dog lady."

Gwen's smile glowed, then faded. "But seriously… this is… You haven't really…"

"I haven't even thought about… any of that, since Carrie died. It was as if that part of my life… that part of me was buried with her."

"You had plenty to deal with. Single parent to a grieving daughter. And things with your Mom…"

"She started downhill after Carrie's death."

"So your heart and mind have been occupied. But now…"

"Now there's this… something, with Annika and I am almost certain Ella Sayers flirted with me yesterday when we met over coffee."

"Sorry. I wouldn't have passed on her message if I thought…"

"No, I know you wouldn't, not with a client. But don't think I missed what you tried with Mary Ann at the Port Credit chapel."

"That was all her, Tom."

"Every time I go there to meet with a family she comes into the clergy office early, with a plate of warm cookies, and that big smile."

"She likes you. The cookies are part of her job. Hospitality."

"Last time, after the family left, she showed me pictures on her phone from paddle-boarding at Brandy Lake. Spoke about getting back to nature, with her warm hand on my arm."

"Hah! I bet she looked good in her wetsuit. Like Batwoman with her long red hair."

"She scares the crap out of me. That's why I stopped booking family meetings there."

"But… you like your dog lady, Annika?"

"It's comfortable. Doesn't feel like we have to try too hard."

"So yeah, go see Michael. Then your dog lady. I'll take care of your laundry, and deal with the groceries when the truck comes. I might call Jill, see what shift she's on."

"Yeah, give her a call."

I moved to the sink and pried up the plug. Bleach water gargled down the drain, leaving the stainless-steel basin smelling clean and shining bright as a new day.

21

"I remember your big party, when they presented that badge you told Attie about, that's stamped retired. I helped you sketch the floor plan for Amazing Sandwich Powers. Is that all a sham? Are you undercover like at the real estate firm?"

We were in the church's parlour, which I'd begun thinking of as a crime scene.

"Not exactly."

Michael reached inside his jacket. He was in another dark suit, one that didn't smell like a house fire. He flipped open his wallet like a tv cop and thumbed back a leather flap.

"I did retire from the Halton Regional Police Service."

"So what's with the new badge? I guess I should ask about the warrant card."

"You're catching on."

He held it closer. Michael's name, a service number, and a 'head shot' were printed over a gold foil hologram of an official looking crest. I saw my friend's signature and that of the Commissioner of the Ontario Provincial Police.

The laminated card declared Michael Ian Powers to be a duly sworn officer holding the rank of inspector.

"You know I'd thought about the restaurant for a long time. It's what I wanted. Still do."

"And?"

"There's an inter-agency task group called Criminal Intelligence Service Ontario."

"Sounds like a TV show."

Michael pocketed his wallet.

"Believe me, partner, it's not that exciting. They mostly analyze data from local police services. They take a wider view, look for patterns. They work strategically with the Crown Attorney's Office."

I leaned back in my chair, to take the wider view. "And you?"

"A few months after I opened the restaurant, I was called in for a meeting on the top floor at the Lincoln Alexander Building, OPP headquarters in Orillia. There's a situation I know something about, and they asked me to keep my eyes open."

"You needed a shiny new badge for that?"

"Things evolved. I was sworn in all over again, issued credentials and they gave me a number to call if I need help."

"Okay… that explains a lot," I said.

I looked directly into Michael's eyes, and said, "Can I ask something else?"

Michael met my gaze. "I'll answer if I can."

"This situation you're keeping an eye on… is it something I need to know about?"

I was thinking of the pills and money, and the files we found at the manse.

"I have things to tell you," Michael said. "but we don't have the whole story yet. Do you want to hear what I've got, or can you tell me what's going on with you first?"

I paused to breathe. The parlour smelled like stale cake, as if decades of crumbs had been ground into the carpet and pushed out of sight under the cushions of the antique chairs.

My gaze rested on a framed print on the wall above the big horse-hair sofa. It was identical to the print that hung in Doug's workroom. A pristine image of how Saint Mungo's was meant to look from the outside.

"There's something eating at you. Just tell me Tom."

Did Ed's forehead leave a mark when it smacked the gleaming wood of the coffee table? Maybe Michael's friends in forensics could check for traces of blood. Was that real, or just another television thing?

"When I called last night about the black pickup," I began, "I didn't say why I thought it was Virgil. I needed time to sort something out."

I shifted in the stylishly uncomfortable wing-back chair, which reminded me of the one I'd sat on in Attie's front room. According to the plaque on the door she'd footed the bill for this room.

The furnishings had such an antique air of respectability. Did Ed meet Kat here because the contrived civility enhanced the thrill of breaking the rules?

"Let me get you started." Michael prompted. "Someone confided in you, and you aren't sure what you can tell me."

There was no way to arrange myself in the chair that didn't stretch the skin around my open wounds. The memory of Kat's story felt as raw as the cuts on my knee.

"I was tired," I admitted, "and not exactly firing on all cylinders."

"It was a hell of a day."

"Kat said she was here in the parlour with Ed and then also Virgil. On Friday night as the blizzard kicked in."

Michael was good at his job. He sat quiet and listened without interruption to my summary of Kat's story.

A few breaths in silence, then he said, "Can I ask some questions?"

"Yes." I nodded.

"Do you believe her?"

I nodded again.

Michael gestured at the low coffee table.

"Someone's cleaned and polished this, but the crime scene techs may be able to get some blood trace from the seams in the wood."

"I never liked this furniture," I said. "This table looks like a Victorian coffin."

"Yeah, it kind of does," Michael agreed, and then asked, "What do you make of Virgil calling him Eddie?"

"A minister getting involved with one member of the congregation is bad enough. The idea Ed crossed the line with them both... I'm angry. Angry at Ed, and..."

"You think you should have seen signs, done something before it got that far."

"That's part of it. If I'd been a better colleague to Ed…"

"He'd have to be open to it. And you've had your own challenges. We all have. How are things with Hope these days?"

"She's on her way home for Easter. She wants to be here, which is a good sign, I think."

"She's a great kid, and she loves her dad."

"We had a… it was a tough time after Carrie died. Hope was very angry. At me, at life, at God, and at Carrie, although she couldn't say it. It's part of why she went to school in the States."

"I remember. She was rough on you."

"She'd just lost her mother. She's entitled to grieve, and anger is definitely part of the package, for all of us."

"I remember that too. You helped me a lot when my mum died."

"You've been there for me, too."

Michael looked at his watch, and then checked his phone. He cleared his throat.

"I'm sorry to cut this short Tom, but I've got a thing… and will have to leave soon."

"It's okay." I nodded. It was still hard for Michael to talk about his mother.

"I said I'd bring you up to speed."

"You did. What can you tell me, Inspector Powers?"

He sat up a little, and said, "First off, I don't think I need to ask you not to talk about my new assignment."

"I won't say a word. It's your news to share."

Michael reached inside his jacket and brought out a small black notebook.

"Had to say it, sorry. Second, the Halton guys did not get the driver of the black truck last night. Virgil, if it was him driving, got out ahead of a sand and salt truck that came by just as the cruisers got there to seal off your block. They lost him."

"That why there was a police car idling in front of my house all night? I hope this can be over before Hope gets home."

"Me too, partner. Me too. We'll find him." Michael flipped pages of his notebook. "Next thing is about what we found at the manse. The pills tested positive for opioids. Fentanyl, with wide variance in dosage from sample to sample."

"Which means what?"

"Non-standard dosage confirms they're not from a legitimate source. Our lab also looked at the compounds in the filler. You would not believe what they use to cut this stuff. The pills we found were dyed to make them look like oxycontin. They're called meany greenies."

"You've seen them before."

"They've been showing up in Bronte, Burlington and Milton. It's evil stuff. Customer might get their expected buzz or they might get enough to stop breathing."

"So how does this connect to Ed?"

"Too soon for conclusions. After what you just said, I like the guy less and less, but we don't know enough."

"What about the money?"

"That gets interesting. It's all large bills. Fifties and hundreds. Surface swabs picked up normal levels of trace but not enough to connect it to the pills. They'll take a closer look at the bills. Any idea why he'd have thousands of dollars stashed?"

"Not a clue. What are normal levels of trace?"

"Sorry. Too much jargon. Let's just say you never know where your money has been. Especially now since most of our bills are plastic. They float around out there a long time and pick up something from every hand that touches them."

"Gives a whole different meaning to dirty money."

"Partner, you have no idea."

Michael flipped his notebook shut.

We stood and headed towards the parlour door.

"Michael I know you'll have to fill this Detective Kitchen in on what I told you about Kat and Ed."

"He'll need to know and may want to talk to you. Especially if Ed doesn't turn up soon."

22

"Reverend Book, might I offer coffee?"

Brad Kazinski asked this with a smile involving more teeth than warmth.

His desktop was a panel of smoked glass, thick as a prayer book and roughly the dimensions of an open grave. There wasn't a sheet of paper or speck of dust on the massive work surface, which despite its sheen seemed to absorb rather than reflect light.

I shook my head. I had no desire to prolong this meeting.

"I can ask Ms. Sayers to bring some for us."

"Nothing for me but thank you."

Ella Sayers had described The Cash Box as a bank vault. It felt more like a crypt. The air was very still and just a little cooler than comfortable even though I'd kept on my topcoat.

When Kazinski ushered me in the side door of his building, I thought of the live mouse trap my mother set out in our basement apartment. My brother always wanted to pop the lid and look inside. Not me.

"I'm forgetting you and Ella are acquainted. You had a… visit with her just the other day at that quaint little sandwich shop. A follow-up to officiating at her mother's funeral?"

"I don't talk about my pastoral work, Mr. Kazinski."

My cell number is not exactly a state secret, but I did wonder how Kazinski got it. His "I'd like you to stop in at my office" had sounded a lot like Ed.

There was also a physical resemblance. Hair dark as crude oil. The grey of his finely tailored pinstripe suit matched his eyes. I suspected he spent more than Ed on clothes, which is saying something.

"I appreciate your discretion, and your compassionate care of one of our own. We're like a family here. I see why Reverend Wilder speaks so highly of you."

I doubted Ed spoke of me at all but kept that to myself.

"I didn't realize you knew each other that well."

"Ed and I share... concern and enthusiasm for the neighbourhood. Bronte's potential mustn't be squandered."

"I know you're... involved with the Bell Tower proposal," I said. "But Ed doesn't keep me in the loop on that."

"Ed mentioned you have a division of duties. Would it be fair to say he handles the worldly concerns and you focus on the spiritual?"

"I think it's all spiritual work, whether I'm leading a book study, or Ed attends a planning commission meeting. I respect his gifts and I'm grateful for what he does."

Kazinski nodded.

"Well said. You'd do well at town hall if Ed had to miss a meeting. Which reminds me... can you tell me how I might reach your colleague? He and I had an appointment for Sunday evening. It seemed strange he did not call. I've heard there were emergency vehicles outside his home and now there are windows boarded up. I hope there's no cause for concern."

When he called I'd been walking past The Cash Box on the way to get things I'd left out of my grocery order. Ingredients for Hope's favourite dessert.

A chill ran through me that had nothing to do with the wintry air, when I saw two black pickups parked in front of the payday loan store. One was showroom clean while the other was streaked with salt and filmed with road grime.

"Reverend Book, is there?" The deep voice reclaimed my attention. He had both hands flat on the desktop and was leaning in to hear my response.

"Sorry?"

"Would you tell me if there was cause to be concerned

about Reverend Wilder?"

"I can let him know you asked after him."

Kazinski settled back in his chair.

"Of course. I won't keep you any longer. You are likely occupied with preparations for your daughter's arrival. I... pray Hope has a safe trip home. I'm sure she's precious to you."

I could not have spoken, even if I'd found words.

Kazinski rose to offer his hand. His grip was cool and smooth and just a little too firm.

"Thank you for this. It was good to meet you, Reverend Book. Please give my best to Reverend Wilder. Let him know we still have a lot to talk about."

23

"So I talked to Slick Willy," Gwen said. "He said yes to the funeral for Stephen Peretz."

"Slick Willy?"

"Sorry, William Morrison, my managing director," Gwen said.

"You call one of the Morrison brothers Slick Willy?"

"Willy's actually a grandson," Gwen said. "You remember him. He's the one who wished I could be a little less black, back in the day. We worked that out years ago, yeah."

"You called him after taking a last-minute personal day and asked for a favour?"

I'm not surprised Gwen's company agreed to cover the funeral when Stephen's remains are released. For years they've had an unpublicized policy of refusing payment when the deceased is an infant, or a victim of violence. It's a big part of why I try to say yes when Gwen, or anyone at Morrison's calls me for a funeral, whether the family can afford to pay me or not.

Gwen said, "I wasn't asking a favour, but even if I was, he probably owes me."

"You really call him Slick Willy?"

"Only when he calls me Ms. Gwendolyn, or at the Christmas party, when he's had a few, or I have. How'd you make out tracking down the family?"

I said, "Not as well as you. I climbed up and down the phone tree at the church's head office for at least an hour."

"And?"

"Let's just say those who would take my calls expressed minor sympathy along with major concerns about confidentiality."

Gwen said, "It might get easier when the coroner signs a death certificate."

"Thanks for doing the groundwork about the burial," I said.

"Was that pun on purpose?" Gwen asked.

"That depends on whether you think it's funny."

24

I wondered if Doug had more to say about the man who gave him the journal. I flipped pages until Stephen's name leapt out, then worked back to the start of an entry.

I've switched out the first toilet in the Sunday School bathroom. The child-size toilets will make it useable only by children, (which may not 'sit well' with some) but we have so many little ones down there on Sunday, and for the mid-week tots group, it makes sense. I did not run this by the property committee. If they object, I'll remind them the fixtures were free.

A co-op preschool near Lila's home in East Oakville was redecorating, and someone on the committee decided plain white porcelain did not "fit their vision." Attie heard about it from one of the parents at Colborne. I picked up two small size toilets and 3 junior sinks for the price of driving over and asking. They were happy to have it all hauled away. I've stored the pieces in the old boiler room for the time being.

I wish it was as easy to sort things out for people. Somehow switch out the bits that don't fit with their "vision" of themselves.

I was locking up the church tonight after choir practice, and saw Wendy Peretz, Pastor Stephen's wife with the "movement and art" teacher, Ivy, who's just started at the church.

Ivy is in her mid-20's, so she's almost a decade older than our niece, Dido. I make that comparison because she behaves more like Dido's 15 years than her own age. She wears bright-coloured exercise tights, with woolen leg warmers pulled up from her ankles, and long sleeve t-shirts layered one over another, and pulled down so it appears she is trying to cover herself, but not really. The effect is more revealing, at least to my eyes, than if she bounced around in a leotard like Dido did when she was our blonde haired happy little dancer. (I miss those days!)

Ivy's t-shirts all seem to have their neck rings torn out and have been cut down in front to show more of her than I want to see, especially during choir practice.

I see young women dressed like that at the school, crossing through the tech wing on their way to acting and music classes. I will admit here I am a little more tolerant when adolescents are trying on their dramatic personae than when it's someone Ivy's age.

Curmudgeonly old coot I am, it's a good thing I am closing in on retirement. At least from teaching. I plan to carry on as the church sexton as long they'll have me. Attie says they'll probably have to carry my body out of Saint Mungo's twice. Once when they find me collapsed over my work. The second time will be after my funeral.

Some might call Ivy a free spirit, but I see a lost soul. She's taking big bites out of life to see what might taste right for her, but even so, she always looks hungry.

There has been something fermenting and bubbling up between her and Wendy since Ivy appeared in the choir. They stand together as sopranos, between Attie and Betty. Their covert gazes and suppressed giggles started the first week. Betty, who's not much older than the pair, gives them her 'now girls' look. My wife's looks are decidedly more condemning.

The two act like some students I see at school, who seem to find the intoxication of young love that much sweeter when they can challenge social conventions with their public displays in the parking lot, in a hallway, in a stairwell.

Tonight, I was pushing the broom down the upstairs hall on my last walk-through of the church before locking up. Choir members often forget the lights in the choir room after they've returned their music folios to their numbered slot.

I used my broom to push open the choir room door and caught a flashing glimpse of Ivy and Wendy in a close embrace. They were not looking my way, but I am certain they heard the door open, because they quickly fell away from each other. I might have thought less of it, had they not moved with such speed to separate. By the time it registered with me I was intruding on something I did not care to see, the door was a third of the way open. I pulled it shut and pushed my broom further down the hall.

Wendy and Stephen have been with us for just over three years. I don't know her all that well, just what I see. She's looked lonely. Oakville is not an easy place to break in. They don't have children, so she doesn't have child and school things to connect her to community outside the congregation.

It has not been easy for Wendy. The Saint Mungo's folk, especially the women, have no template for relating to a clergy wife who doesn't live to pour tea at their luncheons, and chair the rummage sale. Attie refers to Wendy as "a loose cannon. If people get wind of what she is up to, it will be a disaster for this church."

Attie's worried that if word got out about Wendy and Ivy, certain people, even more curmudgeonly than this writer, would rouse themselves for a repeat of the uproar that came last year. The national church voted to extend full rights of membership, including being ordained as ministers, to gay and lesbian people. You would have thought, by the reaction of some people at Saint Mungo's, that the world was coming to an end. To this date, as far as I observe, it has not.

When asked for my opinion, which is happily a rare event, I say that during my brief military service, at the tail end of the Second World War, I saw much that worried me far more about human nature, and human behaviour, than to whom a person is drawn romantically and physically. I served with some fine young men, honorable and courageous fellows, who did not deserve the war waged against their persons, over who they were allowed to be.

Wendy hasn't found a job. She takes classes at the Bronte Wellness Centre. It's the kind of place that offers yoga sessions and pottery classes and how to bake without actual food ingredients. Gluten free, free range, fair trade, organic, low sodium, no preservative, lactose free. That's where she met Ivy.

Stephen's busier than he should be. He spends far too much time putting out fires, dealing with folks who can still get themselves worked up over any number of nonsensical issues, since the one they are actually fuming over about seems to be a fait d'accompli.

Tomorrow after work I'm going to start in on the second toilet, and maybe one of the little sinks. It would be good to have the repurposed bathroom in working order for Sunday morning. If only some other problems were so easy to flush away.

25

"Everybody suffers, Reverend Tom. I know you get that," Ivy said. "especially at this time of year."

This was her day off from the rec centre. Ivy's red Canada Goose parka was unzipped, so I could see she'd traded out the usual Town of Oakville polo for a lavender T-shirt. It was printed with a self-portrait by the Mexican painter Frida Kahlo. I only know that because I asked about it, to divert her from talking about the anniversary of my wife's death.

"This hasn't been an easy time for any of us," I said. But we've made some small progress. The police were able to release the old boiler room but I'm afraid the deep cleaning won't be done in time for Good Friday. The main building still smells pretty ripe, but there's hope we'll have the all-clear for Easter."

Our words echoed in the gymnasium of Brown Hall, the Christian Education wing in which we'd held the emergency meeting on Monday.

"I'm sure this will be fine," Ivy said. "We can keep the lights down low. That will be easier than taking down all the daycare's posters."

Earlier in the afternoon, Eric had helped me pull stacks of chairs from storage to set out in rows resembling sanctuary seating. My knees weren't happy with the exertion, but I'd pushed myself hard to keep up with the 85-year-old retired banker.

We'd also tucked most of the day-care's play equipment into the side class rooms to clear the sight lines for the Good Friday service.

I said to Ivy, "I realized after council met that we hadn't made a plan. We've kept the doors from the main building closed, and the heat down, so we should be okay."

We could not quite see our breath, but the air in the gym was cool.

I pointed to the array of round banquet tables I'd set up on my own, after I sent Eric home.

I said, "We'll have the service at the far end of the gym and your installation right here."

"The smell isn't that bad in here," Ivy said. "And Betty picked up scented candles for the tables."

Each winter Ivy throws and fires dozens of small clay vessels, more like 'v' shaped drinking bowls than goblets. Her design was inspired by first century Middle Eastern pottery and a story from the New Testament.

Before getting arrested at the Mount of Olives and being put to death, Jesus spent a long dark night in prayer. Luke's Gospel records him asking God, "if you are willing, take this cup from me..."

"I can help with this," I said.

Ivy pointed to seven white cardboard file boxes.

"There's a box for each of the tables. We just need to unpack them."

Ivy invites worshippers to visit her installation after the Good Friday service. It's called Take this Cup. She says choosing a cup to bring home is a way to acknowledge that none of us can escape suffering, and that we're meant to help each other in this life.

The pile of crumpled newsprint grew as we unwrapped the cups and arranged them on the rough burlap draped over each of the tables.

The cup I held felt crafted to warm and comfort the palm of my hand.

I said, "Ivy, they're all a little different, but they also belong together, like one big set."

Ivy smiled.

"Thank you, Reverend Tom. It looks like you may have found yours. Take it home if you like."

After we'd emptied the final box I said, "Can we sit? My knees are about done, and I need to talk to you about Wendy Peretz."

Ivy ran a hand through her short black hair, revealing emerging hints of silver grey.

"I haven't heard anyone say her name in a long time."

We took seats in the back row at the 'sanctuary' end of the gym.

"It hasn't been officially released, but the remains we found in the basement were identified as…"

"Reverend Stephen," Ivy said.

"Yes, that's right."

Ivy looked away from me.

"I didn't know him well. I was new, and kind of in and out of church back then."

"That's just before I came here as a student," I said. "I heard about them, but not much."

I wasn't ready to admit I'd read about their relationship in Doug's journal.

I asked, "What made you think it might be Reverend Peretz?"

"It just fit. He disappeared without a trace. Then an unexplained corpse turns up years later in the church where he spent all his time."

Ivy shivered.

"You didn't know Reverend Stephen well. What about Wendy?"

"We were… close, for a time."

Ivy zipped up her red Canada Goose parka, hiding Frida Kahlo.

"I'm trying to arrange for his remains to receive a proper funeral. I haven't been able to track down any family."

"That could be difficult."

"What do you mean?"

"Like I said, Reverend Tom, I didn't really know him. I just heard things back then… Wendy wasn't happy. Neither of them were. Not just when Stephen disappeared, but before.”

“Do you know how I could find Wendy? Have you stayed in touch?”

“She flew back to Vancouver. She told me… she said there was nothing here for her.”

“That must have been…”

“It was all too much. I wasn’t able to help her.”

“What happened,” I asked.

“Three weeks after Stephen just vanished, Wendy died. She… well these days they’d say she completed suicide.”

26

"For a moment in the sanctuary you froze," she said. "I wondered if you'd seen a ghost."

There was humour in Annika's amber eyes, but she was also waiting for something.

I said, "Um…"

We sat across from each other at a round maple table in Annika's farmhouse kitchen. She'd lowered the shades of a large picture window, and the smaller one over the sink. The overheard fixture was dimmed, in favour of the inviting light of a pillar candle on the table.

Zeke lay on his sleeping pad, close to the side door where I'd entered. He'd roused for a moment when Annika let me in, but after her reassuring pat he'd laid his big head back down on a fuzzy pink mass that might have been a stuffed toy rabbit.

Annika said, "My father would've said someone must've walked over your grave."

"I haven't heard that one."

"It's a saying the Dutch have for when you get goose-bumps, or shiver with a chill, for no apparent reason."

"I definitely wasn't chilled," I said. "You could have roasted this chicken under those big movie lights. It all looks great by the way."

The table between us bore a platter of chicken, a flat serving dish of grilled vegetables, a bowl of creamy mashed potatoes, and a tossed salad. Rich aromas of chicken, herbs, garlic and butter floated in the air.

Annika persisted. "But did you?"

Would it have ended the evening early if I'd told her I saw the ghost of my old friend the church caretaker?

"It was more like I was stewing in my own juices. My fault for wearing a wool suit."

"No, I mean, were you spooked by something?"

I'd been anxious as I drove out to Annika's for supper. I'd avoided thinking too hard about it most of the day, until I was almost out my front door, and Gwen handed me a gift-bagged bottle of wine.

"It's a Malivoire Chardonnay," Gwen said. "Should go with almost anything your dog lady might serve. Unless you already went…"

"Hadn't even thought about it. Thanks, Gwen."

Memories of my father's thunderous excesses always shadowed me when I walked the aisles of a liquor store.

Gwen smiled.

"At least you put on a nice shirt for your first date."

"Until just now, I'd managed not to think of it as a date."

"Dear, dear Tom…"

Gwen laughed as she sent me out the door.

I worried I might sweat through this new shirt.

Annika seemed calm and cool, even though she'd been over the hot stove. She was dressed for comfort in loose-fitting jeans and a collared white blouse. Her long blonde hair was pulled back and loosely tied behind, out of the way for cooking. She bore a cool floral scent I recognized from standing near her during the video shoot.

I pulled the wine out of its bag.

"The vineyard's not far from here," I said. "Do you know it?"

Annika nodded at the bottle, and said, "That's a good choice for tonight."

Her movement repositioned a fine gold chain around her neck. Candlelight glinted from the plain gold band suspended on the necklace.

Fresh anxiety sparked in me. We knew so little about each other.

"My housemate made sure I didn't arrive empty-handed."

I asked about opening the wine, and Annika provided glasses. I managed the screw-top without incident.

Annika gave me her look. Her question still floated amid the inviting food smells.

"I had a lot on my mind," I said. "I think you could tell I didn't want to be there...oh. I just realized how bad that sounds...I mean I'm glad I was there, because we met, but..."

The room was a little brighter when she smiled.

"You were meant to be on vacation and got called in once again to cover for Reverend Wilder. Do you have any idea yet of why he didn't turn up?"

My mind went to an image of Virgil standing over Ed Wilder while he tried to pull up his pants. That was not a story to share with Annika.

"I was annoyed he'd missed Sunday," I said. "When it happened again, and for his pet project... I began to worry. For him but also about the rest of my week. Selfish."

"Is that selfish? You mentioned you took the time off to be with your daughter."

"So, yeah, I was thinking about that, and trying not to take out my frustration on Kat, who has her family's knack of getting under my skin."

Annika said, "I don't blame you. I was in her van when Kat called you. I heard her tell, not ask you to rush down to the church. Reverend Wilder's absence really got to her. I don't think she'd have been able to hear you say no."

I shook my head.

"That's not something her family does well."

"If I'd known how... directive she'd be as a director, I might have declined myself," Annika said, with a laugh.

"I am glad you didn't but meeting you and discovering you knew Carrie... It was a lot."

Again, I worried how that sounded.

I picked up my wine glass, then set it down again,

realizing she hadn't touched hers.

"Not… a lot in a bad way. I'm kind of stumbling here," I said.

Her smile rescued the moment, again.

"We should probably eat while it's still hot," Annika said. "Would you like to…"

I said, "Say grace? I can…"

"Is it a thing you do? Pray before meals, I mean."

"When they ask me at a church thing, I pray out loud," I explained. "But with family or friends it's usually just a quiet moment of thanks."

"That sounds good," Annika said.

I closed my eyes and without thinking, extended my hand across the table. She took it in hers. The room was still for a few heart beats, except for Zeke's huffing breaths in his sleep, and quiet jazz coming from another room.

The warmth of Annika's hand registered on my palm, and the tips of my fingers. Sensations traveled to places I'd somehow forgotten. I opened my eyes. Annika's were already wide, and she was looking at me. I slid my hand out of her gentle grasp, to gesture at the food.

"This is… wonderful," I said. "Thank you for this."

We passed serving dishes and spooned food on our plates.

I sampled the mashed potatoes. A tangy hint of sour cream.

"These are great," I said.

Annika nodded thanks, and said, "I remember when Carrie met you."

"Really?"

"We used to grab coffee between classes. She was a good listener. I loved her dark brown eyes. We fell out of touch when she moved to Oakville…"

I listened to Annika and wondered, not for the first time, about how it is that people find each other.

"I heard she'd met this local guy who was a student

minister," Annika said with a wide grin. "That sounded... unlikely to thrive, but she must have seen something in you."

The crinkled lines around her eyes helped me see the humour.

I smiled and said, "I always told her she could have done better. I didn't meet many of her school friends. We were both pretty busy, and the socials were on Saturday nights."

"And you had to work on Sunday morning."

"That's why you thought I'd be a bad match?"

"I used to go with my dad to the Dutch Reform church. There was always a new student pastor someone wanted me to meet. Young men who were desperately sure of themselves and clutched their opinions as tight as they did their big black Bibles."

I said, "The older I get the less cut and dried things seem."

I swallowed some wine. It hinted of apples and melons and was a good match for the salt of the chicken. Gwen had chosen well.

"The answers they were so fervent to sell... didn't fit any of my questions, as a young nurse learning to care for the sick and dying."

I saw why Carrie spent time with this woman.

"Selling is an interesting verb," I said, "You seem to choose your words with care."

Annika said, "I've thought about some of this for a while."

"And yet you took a chance on a guy with a bible."

"You don't seem inclined to use it as a shield, or as weapon..." she said, "and I liked the way you stood firm with Kat, when we found the remains, without being hard on her."

"Thanks. I find her difficult, but I don't think she's had an easy life."

Annika said, "More chicken?"

When she leaned forward with the platter, the candlelight made highlights in her hair.

"Please, it's excellent."

She saw me eyeing the gold band that hung on the thin chain around her neck. She set down the platter, then held up the ring between her thumb and finger.

"It was my dad's. He always wore it, even for outside work. I like to keep it close to me."

My wedding band was in my pocket. I'd tugged it off at a stop light on the way to Annika's farm.

I swallowed, and said, "Have you been married?"

"A long time ago. Andre is from South Africa. Turns out he was even more traditional than the guys at my dad's church. It took a while for him to accept I wasn't like his mother."

"I'm sorry. That must have been… challenging."

"We met when he'd just come over from Pretoria. I thought he was open-hearted and adventurous. I think he thought so for a while too."

"Did you…I mean, are there children?"

"No, and that was part of it. My dad raised me by himself. I never saw myself as a mom. I loved nursing, and Andre tried for a time to be okay with that… He's happier now. He married someone Carrie and I were at school with. They take their kids to South Africa every Christmas."

I held up the bottle.

"Can I offer you more? I'll stop with the one glass, because I'm driving, but…"

Annika said, "No, I'm good."

I hadn't dated much before Carrie, and that was long ago. Gwen said just keep asking questions. Under my anxiety about doing this right, I was also interested in the answers.

"So how did you and Zeke get involved with The Ghost Toucher?"

"When Jerry from the unit called, I wanted to say 'over my dead body' but we use that joke too often. I said only if it didn't keep us from something real."

"How did you get into search and rescue?"

"It starts with how I found Zeke in the first place. My

friend at the Flamborough animal shelter called to say there'd been a raid on a puppy mill, and they were full to overflowing."

"Were you planning to bring one home?"

"I only agreed to go and help for a few hours."

"And then..."

"I saw this guy."

Annika pointed to Zeke, still sprawled on his dog bed.

"He was skinny, and jittery... could barely stand." Anger flared fierce in her eyes. "They'd beat, and near starved him."

I said, "He's thriving now."

"I nursed Zeke back to health at the same time I was caring for my dad..." Annika said.

I cut into a tender sprig of asparagus, and lifted it, and a bit of chicken to my mouth.

"He was timid, and very anxious when he came here. My friend suggested obedience classes. She said larger breeds, especially the smart ones, thrive with clear tasks and rewards. Zeke loved it, and literally came alive. I jumped when they offered us more training."

"And the cadaver part?"

"He stood out when they tested all the dogs for good nose."

"Had you already named him Zeke?"

"He took to Dad from the first day I brought him home," Annika said. "He'd lay at the foot of his recliner chair all day. Dad would finish a coughing fit, and say 'Hey Ezekiel, what do you think? Any life left in these old bones?'"

The big tan and black German shepherd shifted on his padded mat but didn't wake.

Annika pointed to a framed photo on the wall above Zeke's bed.

"That's my father there. Maarten Vanderlugt."

I saw a grey-haired man in blue jeans and a bright orange polo shirt. He was perched in the crown of a barren fruit tree, legs wide, work boots planted on thick limbs. A battered

John Deere cap at a rakish angle, and a cigarette stub hanging out of his smile.

"What was he doing up there?"

He was poised to cut through a thin branch that shot straight up from a thicker limb, using the long-handled lopper he held with both hands.

"Pruning. Cutting back the new growth just before the leaves come out."

"He looks happy. Great, mischievous smile."

"My dad loved getting up in the trees," Annika said. "Even after he leased out the orchard, he helped every spring until he couldn't climb the ladder anymore."

"What happened to him?"

"COPD. I moved back when he got really bad. Took care of him here, until…"

Annika waved at the shaded picture window which faced the orchard behind the house.

"Everything he loved is right here," she said. "Sometimes it feels like he never left."

Her eyes glistened and glowed in the candle's golden light.

"You said he raised you on his own."

"My mom died when I was a toddler."

"I'm sorry," I said. "Do you have other family?"

"Uncles and aunts and assorted cousins, mostly on the Niagara Escarpment. Close to where that wine came from."

Annika raised her glass, and we both drank.

She asked, "What about your family?"

"I mentioned my daughter, Hope. She's on her way home for spring break, from Emory in Atlanta. My brother JP is out west. My mom's at Millstream in Oakville. On the memory care floor. They are still assessing, but it seems her dementia is progressing."

"I'm sorry. Are you close?"

"I go in to see her every week. She doesn't do so well on the phone anymore."

"And your father?"

"Retired from the Ford assembly plant and bought a year-round cottage up near Parry Sound. He was, and likely still is, a mean drunk. He was rough on my brother and me, and worse with my mom."

I felt heat in my face, and it wasn't the wine.

"This meal is great," I said. "And the supper smells are a definite improvement from the odour the last time we were together."

"We call it decomp. It's worse in a closed-in space," Annika said. "Do they know yet whose remains they are?"

"A former Saint Mungo's minister named Steven Peretz. He disappeared overnight, more than twenty years ago."

"And his family had no idea what happened to him?"

"It seems not."

I told her about Doug's journal and summed up what I'd read about Stephen and Wendy Peretz.

"I learned today that Wendy died just a few weeks after Stephen's disappearance."

Annika said, "They sound like sad and lonely people."

"As my friend Michael says, there's a lot of that going around."

"Michael?"

"Michael Powers. Big guy. He used to be a detective with the Halton Police. He said he knows you, and that you were 'good people,' which I think is high praise, from him."

"I remember him from a search up near Milton. I didn't know he'd retired."

"He opened a sandwich shop close by the church."

"This is a change of topic, but you mentioned your daughter is at Emory in Atlanta."

"She's in her second year at Oxford College," I said, "it's a smaller undergrad college just outside of the city."

Annika stood to clear our plates.

"Georgia..." she said. "That seems pretty far away."

I pushed back my chair and rose to help. I picked up the

platter of chicken and the potato bowl.

Annika pointed to the counter.

"Right there's fine for those, on top of the dishwasher."

I nodded. "After Carrie died, Hope… we both had a hard time. In different ways. It's been good for her to have some distance."

"How did she choose Emory? She know someone there?"

I stretched plastic wrap over the remaining mashed potatoes. I did the same with the grilled vegetables.

Annika stood before the open refrigerator finding places for the food.

"Hope was actually born down there. Carrie and I lived in Georgia for a while before I was ordained. An old friend teaches at Emory. Kate and her wife are Hope's godparents."

Annika leaned in to pull out the freezer drawer. She held up a carton of ice cream and pointed to a Dutch apple pie on the counter.

"It's good to have friends."

She closed the freezer drawer, and the refrigerator door, and set the ice cream on the counter, near the deep-dish pie.

"It is," I said. "It's also good to have pie."

The phone buzzed in my pocket.

I said, "This is terrible, but I just got a text, and want to check it."

"You should," Annika said. "It could be Hope."

"Thanks."

I peered at the screen.

"Everything okay?"

"It's from Michael Powers," I said.

"Do you need to call him?"

"I don't think so. He's just letting me know the police ran the registration on the truck that sped off from the manse fire but haven't found it. He also said to watch myself, but I'm already kind of doing that. Looking in the rearview mirror a little more often."

"But you came out tonight."

"It, you... felt like something I didn't want to say no to. My life has been... I have been in a still place for a while."

27

"Jesus Rev, what the hell happened?" was Little Ray's greeting as I limped through the door of Vince's Barber Shop. Vince and the other haircutter, Vanessa, looked up at Ray's question but like always, they let Ray do the talking.

Maybe because of the reopened wounds on my knees, a wrist that felt sprained, and my bruised elbows, the big man's gruff welcome almost brought me to tears. His concern was as honest and embracing as the smells of the shop. Eucalyptus and menthol shaving cream, burnt coffee and Vince's sandalwood cologne.

Little Ray is almost seven feet tall and well over 300 pounds. He's square-shouldered and built solid as a wrought iron fence. As Vince's gatekeeper he knows the regulars by name and tracks who's next up for one of the red leather and chrome barber chairs. You sit in the waiting area until he gives you the nod.

Vanessa looked almost done with a young blond guy almost as muscled as Ray. She had the talcum brush out, to powder the back of his neck.

Vince, the boss, was reclined in his barber chair watching soccer highlights on the flat screen mounted on the shop's back wall.

"Need a water, coffee, maybe a little shot? Some of Vince's grappa, it'll take the chill off," Little Ray said, combing fingers through his well-oiled thick black hair.

I was sure Ray noticed the scuffs on my pant legs and the spackling of dirt on my face.

Ray's the kind who makes anything he wears look good. Today it's a turquoise sport shirt untucked over glossy black dress pants and polished pointy-toed black boots.

"A water would be great. Thanks Ray."

Little Ray can cut hair but mostly he sweeps up, works the cash and runs the espresso machine. He serves stronger stuff on the sly when Vince gives the nod.

"Say the word, I'll pour you a little something. What'd you do Rev, go tobogganing, without your toboggan?"

"Just about Ray."

As I hung my coat, I saw grimy scrapes on the elbows from when I'd hit the ice.

When I bent to peel off my overshoes, I felt nauseous and the room spun.

Little Ray moves quick for a big guy. He slipped behind me, a steadying hand under each of my arms, just as I keeled over. He took my weight and guided me to a chair.

The waiting area was empty except for a nearly bald older man who studied the pages of his Football Italia and ignored my distress.

Ray turned to the old guy and said, "Tony! Don't worry my friend. Vanessa's got you next."

"Rev, catch your breath. I'll get your water. Vince says I should take care of you."

All the times I've come in I've never heard Vince speak. He's a wiry little guy with a halo of white hair that always makes me think of an old monk.

He dug the foundation for this place by hand. At least that's what Little Ray says.

Vince's shop is a concrete block storefront on Kerr Street that juts out the front of a wartime two-storey house. There's space for four barber chairs, with room in the back corner for Ray's little coffee bar, the cash register and a dusty display of hair products no one buys.

For at least fifty years Vince's shop has been a constant in a neighbourhood where cheap rent draws an ever-changing roster of start-ups that graduate to a tonier part of town if they make it. There are places to pawn your stereo, learn pole-dancing, buy a hash pipe, get a guitar restrung or wire money to the Philippines.

"You gonna make it Rev?" Ray asked. "Your tires kinda went flat there."

"Just had the wind knocked out of me. I'm already better. Thanks for the water."

"You feel ready to get up in the chair? I can take care of you. Vince says on the house, as long as you tell us what happened."

I looked past Ray to Vince, who seemed occupied with last week's match between Roma and Napoli. Beyond Vince I saw Kerr Street through the storefront window. Did that black pickup slow down as it rolled by? Ray followed my gaze without comment.

"That's generous Ray," I said, as I dropped into his chair. "It's not much of a story."

I thought about where to start as Ray draped the wine-red barber cape over my shoulders and clipped it under my chin.

"So what we doing here today?" Ray asked, as he tucked in the paper towel collar to keep clipped hairs off my neck.

I saw myself in the big mirror. I still had splashes of road dirt on my face.

"Just clean me up for Easter. Can I get a tissue?"

"Vince says we can do better than that."

Ray pressed a hot towel from the steamer against my cheeks. The moist warmth was like a blessing. Once again, I was close to tears.

"That feels... thank you Ray."

"No problem, Rev," Ray said, as he dropped the towel in the hamper. "Now, let's see…we'll trim up around the ears, clean it up some on top. But what's this here? Looks like you lost a fight with a stapler."

"The nurse had to shave around where I banged myself the other day."

"We'll fix you up. Seems like your week needs a do-over. You know your clipper number? Never mind, Vince says you're a two and you like it tapered at the back."

I felt Ray push his comb one way then another as he figured how to handle the bald spot.

"So Rev, what's the story?"

"Good question, Ray."

I'd slowed my car before the lights at the corner of Kerr and Stewart and looked down the driveway beside Vince's. Normally I'd park in behind the shop, but they hadn't cleared the heavy dump of blizzard snow.

I was startled by a long, loud honk. A jolt of fear charged up my spine. It morphed into peevishness when I checked the mirror. No scary black truck, just a guy in a navy-blue Jaguar letting me know his light was green.

Two blocks down Kerr I fed coins in a meter and turned into the wind to hike back up to Vince's. The brisk air whisked away my annoyance at the Oakville driver and I enjoyed the walk. Even with the skin on my knees pulling against the bandages with each stride.

The town had scraped away most of the snow in front of the cafés and shops and sanded the sidewalk.

Pastel cardboard bunnies and chicks brightened the thrift store window. I thought of how Hope and I'd skipped the chocolate eggs last Easter, when we were just one year out from Carrie's death. Was it too soon to try to reinstill some of the fun?

I offered a respectful nod to Master Choi, out scattering sidewalk salt at the entrance to his studio. My brother and I took Taekwondo when Mom moved us to this neighbourhood.

I paused at the metal light post set in the sidewalk near the entrance to the Lucky Seven corner store. Waiting for the light to change, I remembered how I'd run to the store for bread and milk from our apartment in the basement of Mrs. Varghese's green bungalow.

Cooking smells wafted over from the Thai place on the opposite corner. Mom loved their yellow curry chicken. I wondered if I could sneak some past the nurse's station at Mill Stream when I went in to see her.

I stepped out to cross Stewart Street. The image of smuggled noodles was blasted out of mind by the loud roar of an engine. I looked right and saw a black pickup barreling through the intersection on the wrong side-- my side of the street.

I froze for a breath, then pivoted to get back to the corner sidewalk. I slipped on the ice and fell forward. I threw my hands out like I was swimming through the cold air.

My knees. My poor knees hit the edge of the curb and my elbows hit the sidewalk. I scrambled forward in a desperate crawl until the soles of my overshoes caught traction on the gritty sanded ice of the sidewalk. I grabbed at the metal light standard to pull myself up. I ducked behind the pole.

The black truck's front tire was up over the curb, powering through where I'd just been crawling. The rear wheel followed, and the tail end of the truck swerved toward the light pole as the driver steered hard to avoid a transformer box barely visible under the snow. Spinning rear tires churned the boulevard and tossed up chunks of dirty snow as the truck sped away.

Ray said, "Holy shit, Rev! Pardon my French, but that doesn't sound like an accident."

"It's okay, Ray." I didn't think so either.

"You need me to call the cops? Probably won't help, but..."

I said, "When I caught my breath and could hear over my heart pounding, I called it in on my cell."

"That's good," Ray nodded. "You say a black pickup? You catch the make?"

Michael asked the same thing when I called him from the corner. He said Vince's was closer than my car, so head there, and get off the street. He'd send a cruiser by for a look.

"I have no idea what kind of truck. I was focused on getting out of its way."

"It's just that a black truck has rolled past the shop a few times since you been in. Two guys in it, we know them. They... run some errands in the neighbourhood. Hey Rev, tuck your head so I can finish in back."

It was soon my time for the talcum brush, then Ray held the hand mirror behind me so I could check the back of my head in the big wall mirror.

"It looks a lot better, Ray. Thanks."

"No problem Rev. You want a little product in your hair this time? It'll help the hair sit down where I've combed it over that spot."

"Yeah, that's a good idea. I'm headed to visit my mom and don't want her to notice."

"Moms worry. Hell, Rev! Vince and I are worried about you too. Those guys in the truck, I hope it's not them. They don't work for good people; you know what I mean?"

28

"And the poor man's corpse just flopped out into the puddle on the floor?"

The gleam in Mom's clear blue eyes told me she was more intrigued than shocked by the image of Stephen Peretz's body secreted behind a wall in Saint Mungo's basement. On her better days she still loves a story.

She'd had help dressing for my visit. They had her well turned out in a grey jacket and skirt and a vintage cameo brooch. Remnants from her Colborne days. Her collared white blouse hung a little loose and her hair matched the silvery grey of her wool suit, but I could still picture her holding forth at the front of a class.

She was sharp today. I was glad I'd slipped home to change my clothes before I came.

Mom asked, "Who'd profit by killing a pastor and hiding the fact of his death?"

It's good I'd closed Mom's door. It wouldn't do for the staff to hear us flout the third rule for visitors: "avoid topics that may cause distress".

I said, "You mean, what's the story under the story?"

As I stepped out of the elevator, I'd considered how much to tell Mom.

I'd paused to smile at Jenny, who looked up from singing her sweet lullaby to the baby doll in her lap. Her wheelchair was parked in her regular spot near the nurse's station.

On the wall behind Jenny hung the framed poster of the "Guidelines for your visit to the Memory Care Floor".

On good days I chat with Mom the way we always did.

"It must have been… distressing," Mom said.

"It was a shock. But later, when Michael asked if I'd heard of anything like that at a church, it tickled the back of my brain. I had a vague memory of one of your stories."

When Hope and I brought her for the first look at "Oakville's premier senior's residence" Mom had eyed the lobby, which was posh as an old railway hotel and said, "Let's go, Tom."

For more than 30 years Mom taught the offspring of the wealthiest families in Canada, and we couldn't afford vacations or a new car until they made her a department head.

Waving towards the gleaming polished wood, over-stuffed couches, and gilt-framed pictures she'd declared, "I can't manage this. Not on my pension."

"I can help, Mom."

Mom said, "I can't expect you to do that. My name is on the region's assisted living list. They said a placement could be just a matter of months."

Hope wasn't speaking to me that week, but she'd nodded her head to a short truce for the sake of her Grandma Jean and came along to check out Mill Stream. A condition of our ceasefire was my silence about the ragged sweat pant, torn tee-shirt and jean jacket ensemble she sported. The jacket had been Carrie's, and Hope had worn it every day since the funeral.

My kind-spirited daughter was still in there, underneath all the angst and grunge. She slipped a denim-clad arm under Mom's and guided her into the lobby.

Hope said, "Gran they won't charge us to look around. I think that lady's coming over to give us the tour. Her name tag says she's Nira the sales director."

Nira was a petite woman in her twenties, in a tailored blue linen blazer and skirt. She shook Mom's hand and passed me a folder of brochures, including the "handy budget guide."

Moments later we were on the Memory Care Floor. A period street sign indicated the hall was named Chisholm Avenue after the founder of Oakville. Brass wall sconces on the wainscoted walls sustained the hotel-like atmosphere, despite the antiseptic sheen of the vinyl flooring, which was like every nursing home I'd ever visited.

Nira said, "Mrs. Book, I hear you taught history."

Mom blinked as if caught dozing. She looked at her feet. Her shoulders clenched and I moved to put my arm around her until it passed.

Hope broke the silence.

"Gran was head of history at Colborne. She's still the only woman to hold that post."

"You might appreciate what we've done here," Nira said, waving an arm.

Above the wainscoting, the blonde wood grain panels between the doors to resident's rooms were hung with framed photos from Oakville's past. Sepia toned images of bearded white men in high collars and stiff suits who managed to appear quite pleased with themselves without cracking a smile.

While watching for Mom to settle back into herself, I'd inwardly celebrated that Mill Stream's disinfectants smelled less acrid than the hospital. I'd picked up only a light hint of urine. Compared to the air in some facilities where I've visited church members, this might be worth the high-end prices I saw in the sales brochure.

Mom met Nira's eyes, then stepped out from under my arm and aimed a finger at one of the bearded gents on the wall.

"You have all the usual suspects. That fellow there and his cronies amassed fortunes in ways their heirs don't like us to mention."

Smiling, Nira said, "Every Mill Stream residence is firmly rooted in the history and tradition of the community. We feel that..."

"Young lady!" Mom's moments of "lowered inhibition" had become more frequent.

Nira's eyes widened.

"I'm sorry, Mrs. Book, is something wrong?"

Mom's voice grew louder.

"If you wrote that in an essay for my class, I'd fail you

for plagiarism. You're mouthing some corporate party line and what's worse, I can hear your heart isn't in it."

"I… yes… it's in the talking points. I thought…"

"Gran." Hope stepped between Mom and the sales director. "Nira's just doing her job. This is a nice place, isn't it?"

Mom's stern gaze shifted from Nira to Hope and her face softened. After a long moment said, "It's lovely." Turning back to Nira, she said, "Please forgive my rudeness. My granddaughter's correct. It's your job, and I've no right."

"Actually Mrs. Book," Nira began, "I agree with you. Notice the absence of people who look like me?"

Mom nodded and smiled. "That's what I meant by the usual suspects."

Nira gestured towards the framed photos, "By this period, Oakville was home to hundreds of black people, both freed and escaped from slavery."

Mom nodded and said, "Let's not forget the indigenous people pushed off the best land to accommodate British settlers. Choices are made about whose pictures we see and which history is celebrated."

Nira still drops by to visit Mom, even though she's transferred to another location. Her family's been rooted in Oakville since before Confederation and none of their ancestors' faces are on the walls at Mill Stream.

Mom asked, "So you expect a doddering old woman to jog your memory?"

"You are hardly doddering, Mom," I said, "Does a body in the wall ring any bells?"

She flashed a rare full smile and quipped, "Do you mean church bells, Tom?"

"I mean I think you told me a story a long time ago."

Mom pulled a thin volume from the low wooden bookcase next to her reading chair. It's where she kept copies of the texts she'd loved to teach from as well as a few she helped edit.

Her small collection of books, a family photo album

and two Norval Morrisseau prints were the only artifacts of her former life. The flat-screen television, the dresser and matching headboard and side table belong to Mill Stream, as do the neutral toned window coverings.

Outside of each private room Mill Stream provides a wall-mounted display case. Most contain a few photos: the resident, their family, Sparky the Golden Retriever.

Mom's displays a map of the traditional territories of those who lived and travelled along the northern shore of Lake Ontario.

Nira could have given a heads up to the floor manager who'd said, "Residents typically choose mementos of a more… personal nature."

"I drew that map for my students," Mom explained, "to show them this land had a rich history before the white men on your walls arrived. I take that very personally."

Mom likes her maps. She pointed to the historical atlas she'd balanced on her lap and said, "Not far from here, on Lake Erie. The Methodists in Port Rowan dug up the remains of their founding pastor and his wife, to re-inter in the wall of their new church. But that's hardly the same as hiding a body."

"No… but almost as gruesome."

"Another story came to mind, when you said your Reverend Wilder has been missing since the big storm. Have I told you about the perilous quest of Canon Worrell?"

"Sounds like Arthur Conan Doyle."

"More like G.K. Chesterton. The Anglicans built a lovely big rectory on the edge of Old Oakville, on prime land over-looking the lake. For decades each of their priests resided there. One Sunday evening after vespers their beloved Canon Worrell became disoriented and lost trudging home in a snow squall. He very nearly died…"

"That's a terrible story, Mom, "I said, wondering if Ed had gone astray in the blizzard.

"It gets better. The brave and true family dog found him and guided him home to warmth and safety."

"If it was me, I'd have been too embarrassed to tell anyone. How did the story survive?"

"Excellent question. It was recorded in the vestry minutes, when they voted to move the rectory downtown and place it on a new foundation just up the street from St. Jude's church."

Ed had taken a wrong turn with Kat. I didn't mention his misadventures to Mom.

"They may have done it so they could keep an eye on Canon Worrell."

"Canon Worrell was well thought of by most everyone, unlike your Reverend Wilder. Would it be such a bad thing if he slunk away under the cover of night?"

"Mom, I know you don't like him."

"I worried when you took the job at Saint Mungo's."

"It was a way to be here. For you, and for Carrie's treatments. We wanted Hope to have you in her life, especially when we knew…"

"And I am so grateful you came back to Oakville. I just wish you didn't have to go back there, and not just because of Ed Wilder. That Attie Beacham. I kept my distance from her when you were at her church as a student, but I still heard a lot."

Attie was secretary to the Colborne principal and she'd run the school like another tight ship in her personal fleet.

"Attie is Attie. The rest have been kind. They remembered Carrie and I from the old days and they love Hope."

"But that Wilder. Don't trust that bastard. When I finally saw through your father I swore I'd protect you and your brother from…"

"Mom, I…"

"…people who pretend to care about you, but really…"

"Mom…" I reached for her hand, which was trembling.

"only care about whatever sick thrill they get from controlling or hurting…"

The rest of her words were lost in a struggle to catch her breath.

"It's okay, Mom. We're okay…"

She'd never been this forthright about Ed, and it was rare for her to speak against my father. She looked about to cry.

"Mom, I don't have any problems with Ed. Since he realized I don't want his job he just lets me do my thing."

Mom let loose a long sigh, and her gaze shifted from me to her window. The curtains were pulled in the hope of sun but grey clouds had won the day. After a few breaths, she spoke.

"Carrie couldn't come? Is she working today? Please tell her I'd love to see her."

"Mom…"

"Tom, what is it?"

The words catch in my throat every time we repeat this loop.

"Mom, Carrie died."

"Oh Tom. I am so sorry. What's happened?"

"Carrie was very sick, Mom. There was a tumour on her brain."

"That's so… terrible."

One morning as I was packing Hope's lunch and snacks for preschool she was "helping like a big girl." A coffee mug she'd just lifted from the dishwasher slipped through her small hands and crashed to the floor.

When Mom recognizes she's stumbled in a conversation, she looks as bereft as Hope did when the mug shattered.

"How are you, Tom? How is our little girl?"

"We're… we're okay, Mom. Hope's doing well. She's flying home from university for Easter and wants to come see you."

"And what about Carrie? She couldn't come today? Is she at work?"

Tears turned to happy squeals when I swung Hope in the air for the short flight to her booster seat. She picked up Cheerios one at a time and popped them in her mouth but kept her eyes on me as I swept up the scattered ceramic shards.

"I'm sorry, Daddy."

"It's okay, sweetie. Accidents happen. We have a cupboard full of mugs."

29

"It feels like we're flying."

The small display offered a virtual bird's eye view of Saint Mungo's bell tower. When I looked up from the controller in Hassan's gloved hands, I could just make out the black X of the quadcopter drone hovering high above the church.

"It's amazing," I said. "Like a superhero movie."

Hassan thumbed the joysticks to dip the drone closer to the tower.

"It's more intense when you wear FPV goggles," he said. "First person view."

Hassan had been the camera operator when we found the body in the wall. He was well dressed for the chilly afternoon. Kodiak boots, heavy parka, and a black wool cap bearing the neon logo of Odious Kat Productions.

The bright lines of the crudely drawn feline had caught my attention as I stepped out the rear door of Saint Mungo's to the snowy back parking lot.

I'd been looking for Kat when I'd found Hassan standing between the open loading doors at the back end of a white rental van. Black instrument cases lay open on the van floor.

I hoped Attie would be relieved the video crew had parked their vehicles behind the main wing of the red brick church, away from the eyes of interested onlookers. Unless of course they were peering down from the windows of the senior's condo next door, or the tall apartment towers behind the church.

Two paces in front of Hassan a sleek black drone hovered in place at shoulder height above the icy pavement.

Rotor blade wash kicked up a dusting of new snow.

"Hi, Hassan. How are you?"

"Pretty cool, hunh?" Hassan said. "The stabilizing software uses an onboard compass and GPS."

The remote control looked like a child's toy in the big cameraman's hands. I resisted asking for a turn to play. Hassan must have seen the little boy gleam in my eye.

"Hey Reverend Tom," he'd said with a grin. "Want to see how it works?"

"That would be very cool." Cool? I'd felt ancient as I said it.

I watched with keen interest as Hassan worked the controller.

Dark slate tiles of the belfry roof loomed large on the screen as the drone dropped closer to the top of the bell tower. I saw what looked like a large, ragged nest sheltered in an inside corner of the parapet wall. What odd creature would make a home up there? I lost sight of the straggly mass when the drone swung up over the belfry access hatch and away from the tower.

"Home inspectors use them to check out roofs." Hassan said. "Pest control companies are also getting into it."

Hassan piloted the drone in a wide orbit around the bell tower.

"The camera is on gimbals that let me pan right and left or tilt up and down even when the drone is stationary. I can aim the lens in practically any direction."

I dropped my eyes back to the screen for a rapid and dizzying 360-degree tour. The camera captured the outward view as the drone orbited the tower. I saw the brassy mirrored windows of the seniors' condo to the east whiz by. Then the balconies of the apartment towers behind the church property. The fir trees on the hillock to the west and the high rigging of vessels in dry dock at the yacht club across the road. Beyond the shrink-wrapped boats loomed the dark water of Lake Ontario and the grey sky.

I looked up again at the X shape of the black drone, just

as Hassan slowed then halted its orbit and set it to hover above the belfry.

"Anything you want to see, before I hit 'return home' to call it back? I want to switch out the battery pack before Kat starts her shoot."

"Can you show me the tower roof again?"

"Reverend Tom," Kat said, "I need you to join Annika and Zeke at the main entrance."

Kat is back to being about what she needs from us. Maybe her way of holding it together. Here we were again, searching for the spirit of her great-uncle while her twin brother was in hiding, and her pastor, who'd also been her lover was injured and missing.

Hassan shrugged. "Maybe I can show you later." He held the remote out towards me. "Might even let you try the controls."

"Thanks Hassan," I nodded. "Good to see you again."

Kat had made less accommodation for the harsh weather than Hassan. Her tightly-fitted black leather coat was more about fashion than warmth and she'd skipped the Odious Kat wool cap in favour of a white mohair headband that allowed the frigid air to frost her blonde hair. I hoped this meant she'd want to work fast and be out of the cold sooner.

The lofty heels on Kat's glossy black boots looked less than optimal for the icy parking lot. Even so I was pressed to keep pace with her as she strode away from the equipment van.

"Kat, how are you today?" Despite twinges of protest from my knees I caught up and matched her stride as we rounded the corner from the side driveway and approached the wide front stairs.

"Good... no, not really. I'm surviving. Hey Candace!" Kat nodded toward a short round woman with a camera rig on her shoulder. "Can you set up at the base of the stairs? Reverend Tom and I are going up to connect with the woman from Search and Rescue."

Candace wore a bright blue parka and white knee

length snow boots. Lavender hair with black tips hung loose from under a woolen Hudson Bay toque, white with the classic trading blanket stripes, bands of green, red, yellow, and black. She nodded all those colours in agreement.

I turned to look at Kat.

"How are you, honestly?"

"Reverend Tom I just have to push through, get the shots I need, and hope no one else... that nothing horrible happens."

"I get that."

We reached the base of the steps up to Saint Mungo's main doors. They'd not been cleared since last night's snow fall.

The church was built against the grade of a small hill. You had to climb a steep cement staircase to reach the big double doors to the main foyer, which was also the base of the three-storey red brick bell tower. This impressive design was from an era when no consideration went to the requirements of the disabled, the aged, or clergy with carved up knees. I tried to ignore the sharp stabs that came with each step.

I rested at the top. I looked beyond the yacht club's hibernating boatyard and made out the candlestick of the automated lighthouse at the end of Bronte Pier. It was a flare of white and red in contrast with the dark waters of Lake Ontario.

Saint Mungo's was founded back when Bronte Harbour was a busy fishing and trading village and Lakeshore Road was part of the 'Number 2' highway. The route from Old Fort York to Burlington Harbor had obliterated the ancient waterfront trails of the Anishinaabe, Huron-Wendat, Haudenosaunee and Ojibway peoples. I'd fallen in love with the rhythm of those names when Mom recited them.

Kat waited beside me.

"Reverend Tom, are you ready to start?"

"Sure Kat, just catching my breath. What do you need me to do today?"

"I'll explain when we find Annika and Zeke."

Kat halted at the ornately carved oak doors of the main

entrance to the sanctuary, and said, "Let's kick the snow off our boots. No need to make a wet mess for Virg…"

I read her face. Virgil wasn't here.

Opening the heavy door meant pulling through several inches of snow. My wrist was still sore from my tumble on Kerr Street. The pain must have shown on my face when Kat and I stepped into the foyer, where we met Annika and her search dog.

Annika said, "Tom, are you all right?"

Zeke was sitting back on his haunches. A battlefield soldier takes their rest when they can. The bright orange tactical harness was his uniform.

"Just a little winded from climbing the stairs," I said. "Can I rub his ears?"

"Sure. He's not working yet."

Zeke leaned into my hand.

"Good dog, Zeke," I said. "You're a good dog."

Kat said, "I just need to check something. I'll be right back."

Kat's heels clicked and clacked as she walked away, and she left a melting trail, despite her efforts to knock the snow from her boots.

The foyer fell quiet, except for Zeke's breathing.

"He's comfortable with you," Annika said.

"It's good to see you… both."

I really was terrible at this.

Annika smiled. "Is Hope on her way home?"

"Yes, it's all good. She flew to Detroit this morning and took a cab downtown, then the tunnel bus to Windsor."

"That's great."

"She said it was a quick walk to the train station. and she'll be on the train from Windsor coming in around ten tonight."

Annika said, "When I was her age I'd never been out of the GTA, except a bus trip in grade eight to Quebec City."

"Ours was to New York," I said. "The UN building, Carnegie Hall and a Broadway show."

"Must be where you got the bug for show business," Annika said.

Kat's clacking and clicking seemed deliberately louder on her return to the foyer.

"So I need the three of you for two scenes."

It wasn't until then I realized Kat no longer wielded her clipboard.

"Okay," said Annika. "Will you want Zeke to work, or does he just walk with us?"

Kat seemed to ignore Annika's question.

"For the first part I want the three of you here at the top of the steps. Hassan will shoot from his UAV camera... Annika, do you know what that is?"

"A drone." Annika gave me a look. "We've used them on searches."

"Good," Kat continued. "Hassan will do a few orbits of the tower, shooting you from above. It will look like someone, or something, watches from on high. Something mysterious that soars around the belfry."

Kat led us out the double doors.

"Kat's short on people skills," I whispered to Annika. "But she does seem to have a vision for this."

"You seem to have a little more... grace for her today," Annika replied.

Hassan's drone was in a stationary hover above us. The colorfully accessorized woman in the blue parka waited at the bottom of the steps, camera rig on her shoulder.

"Candace, are we good? I'll get out of the shot."

As Kat stepped behind Candace and her camera, at the base of the stairs, she keyed the mike on a small yellow radio. "Hasson, you see us? Good to go?"

Two short bursts of static seemed to be Hassan's response.

"Reverend Tom," Kat called up to us, "I need you to point up at the belfry and tell Annika something. Anything."

Kat keyed the mike again. "Hassan, after we get the

overhead from the tower orbit I want you to follow them."

Two more static bursts.

"If it looks like Zeke has picked up a scent, stay on him. If he finds something, you need to come down close and capture the image."

I raised an arm, and said, "This is the part where I say things that don't matter, and you still have to look interested."

Annika grinned. "This all seems vaguely familiar…"

Kat called up to us. "It wouldn't hurt if we could see a little chemistry between the two of you. Reverend Tom, maybe take Annika's hand as you lead her down the stairs."

Annika held out a gloved hand. I obliged.

"This may be the only church I've ever seen," Annika said, "this bright a red. It's almost like a fire truck."

"The story is that sometime in the 1870's the elders collected subscriptions to replace the original wood frame church," I said. "A brickyard owner offered to donate the materials if he could pick the colour. The shopowners, lawyers and up-and-comers who ran the church swallowed hard and accepted his offer."

"Do you believe that?"

"I got this from my mom. She pointed out that back then, banks, schools and churches were usually clad in far more sombre tones. There had to be a reason for this brilliant exception. As my mom said, the bright-red brick stood out like sunburn on a fisherman's neck."

We paused to look with feigned interest at the dates carved on the cornerstone, then walked along the west side of the building toward the back parking lot. The snow had been plowed back, but the driveway was slick with ice. If Virgil had been around, it would have been his job to throw down more road salt.

"Mom also believes Saint Mungo's was built on the site of an ancient burial ground. Before European settlement First Nations people had a seasonal camp where Bronte Creek spills into Lake Ontario. Makes this a special place."

"Your mom sounds like a good teacher," Annika said.

Zeke kept station beside us until we rounded the northwest corner of the building.

When we reached the church's rear exit, Zeke halted, and lowered his dark snout to sniff at the snow-crusted pavement near the door. He looked up at Annika and let loose with one of his short sharp barks.

I saw Candace jump a little, which couldn't be good for her camera work.

"Tom," Annika said. "You remember what that means?"

"You think he's picked up a scent?"

Annika knelt next to her search dog. "Kat, what do you want us to do?"

Kat called to us. "Reverend Tom? What do we do? I…"

Kat's mask of control had cracked.

"Kat," I said. "I think we let him do his job."

"Okay. Annika, can you…"

"Yes," Annika said. "But can you have Candace keep back with that camera?"

Kat nodded.

Annika unclipped the leash.

"Zeke," she said. "Bones. Find the bones."

30

I wondered how we all looked from the "God's eye" shot. The black X of Hassan's quad-copter camera was all but invisible against the wintry grey sky.

There were times it would be so much easier to soar above it all and never come down to earth. I thought about how Kat's first video shoot had ended with Reverend Stephen Peretz's corpse landing with a murky splash on the floor of the old boiler room.

The up-close and personal view had little to recommend it.

Annika had issued her quiet command, "Bones."

Zeke raised his head from the trodden snow near the church's back door to sniff at the cold air.

I said, "Do you think he has something?"

Kat murmured into her handset and gestured in the search dog's direction.

Candace, the camera operator, fell in behind Zeke. She followed at a respectful distance as the cadaver dog weaved his zigzag pattern across the parking lot.

Zeke's breathing sent up little puffs of steam as he worked.

"There are only a few scents he responds to that way." Annika said. "Human decomp, which you remember…"

I shook my head. "I won't forget it for a long time."

"He's also sensitized to human tissue and blood, for tracking. If someone was wounded and bled here Zeke can pick up on it."

I read the fear on Kat's face as she asked, "Could it be a false positive? Do search dogs have those?"

Candace halted about 10 paces behind Zeke. His mahogany and black coat, and the bright orange of his tactical harness stood out against the white hills of snow plowed to the outside edges of the parking area.

The search dog zeroed in on a particular snow mound at the north end of the lot. From a distance, I saw nothing special about it.

Annika said, "He seems interested in something."

Zeke halted at the mound's edge and issued a loud bark. He assumed the pointing arrow stance I'd first seen in the boiler room. Zeke would hold that position until Annika released him.

Hassan brought the camera drone down from the heights, to hover twenty feet above Zeke and the snow mound.

Annika led me closer to her search dog, who issued two more quick, sharp barks.

"That's a definite tell," Annika said. "He's serious."

Behind us, Kat spoke into her handset, "Hassan, can you come in a little lower?

Static bursts answered.

The quadcopter dropped another ten feet, then pulled back up. The wash from the drone's rotor blades stirred up a cloud of powdery snow.

I said, "Is there something there?"

I saw dark patches. Fall leaves rotting under the snow?

Annika knelt near Zeke.

"Good dog. Stand down, Zeke."

Zeke relaxed and fell back on his haunches.

Annika said to me, "I'll call 911," then to Zeke, "You're such a good dog."

Zeke looked up at Annika to receive the praise and the treat on her palm.

I was thankful I didn't have to kneel. My battered knees couldn't take it.

I stepped a little closer.

What I'd thought were decayed leaves were shoes. They were men's shoes. I knew those shoes. Where were his overshoes?

I was certain the wing-tip oxfords that protruded from the mound of parking lot snow belonged to my colleague, the Reverend Ed Wilder. The shoes, about which Ed was always meticulous had weathered the snow, road salt and frigid temperatures far better than their owner.

My mind flashed to the first moments after Carrie's final breath, when it had seemed so very important to find and clean her eyeglasses.

The wash from Hassan's drone blew out loose snow, revealing more than Ed's oxfords.

Who else might recognize the ice-stiff trouser cuffs, crusted with snow?

I heard myself say, "We need to keep Kat away from here."

There was the wail of approaching sirens.

"We'll keep everyone away until the police arrive." Annika said.

"Sounds like it won't be long."

31

The homicide detective looked a few years younger than me. No silver in his close-cropped dark brown hair. He was clean-shaven, and thin in the face. His hazel eyes were alert.

I didn't ask why we met in the church parlour, but assumed the investigators were taking a close look at the church offices. Ed's, and mine. I'd read enough mysteries to realize they probably viewed me as a suspect.

"I'd like to lay things out for you as I see them," said Lawrence Kitchen.

The detective sat on the edge of one wingback chair, and I the other. Attie must have had a hand in choosing this furniture. It's all for show rather than comfort. At least that what's my knees were telling me.

"Okay…" He must hear the doubt in my voice.

"Perhaps you can fill in any gaps as we go along," the detective sergeant said.

"That sounds…" I hesitated.

Kitchen seemed at ease; hands relaxed in his lap. He wore tan cords and a navy sweater over a collared white dress shirt.

He said, "You're worried I'm trying to pull something on you. Trick you into revealing more than you want."

"Well… yes," I said.

Lawrence Kitchen came across more like an English teacher than a homicide detective. But what did I know? Michael was the only cop I knew as a person. My brother JP's encounters with law enforcement had never been this informal. This felt almost collegial.

The detective sergeant gazed up to the parlour ceiling,

and to the right. The look of someone accessing their memory.

"A wise detective once said nothing clears up a case so much as stating it to another person."

I said, "It sounds like you want my help."

I chose not to admit I knew the quote.

"Yes, that's my hope. You're not a suspect as far as I'm concerned."

I felt the tension release from the space between my shoulders.

"It's only two hours since we found Ed," I said. "How did you decide that so quickly?"

"We've been on this since the first remains were discovered. I've had time to collect… impressions."

"I thought you'd be all about evidence. Facts, clues, that sort of thing." I risked a smile, and said, "Maybe I've read too many mystery novels."

Kitchen's black notebook looked like the one Michael uses. Were they standard issue? The detective flipped through pages.

He said, "Evidence… the facts, as you call them… are like puzzle pieces. They often get fitted together to support a narrative… but…"

I leaned forward with interest.

"There is always a story under the story," Kitchen said. He smiled for the first time in the interview.

I had the impression he'd been itching to use that line.

I said, "You were at Colborne?" It wasn't really a question.

"Oakville really is a small town," Kitchen said, "especially for people like us who grew up here."

I looked close at him while I worked it out. I thought again about his likely age.

"You could have had my mom for Canadian History, or the History of Revolutions. She was a department head by then but held on to teaching those. You would have had to dig a little, to make the connection. She always went by her maiden name at the school."

The detective smiled again. There was more warmth in his eyes now.

"We called her Mrs. P.," he said. "Jean Paterson; sorry Jean Paterson Book changed my life. I took every class I could with her."

"Did you ever tell her that?"

"Never had the nerve. I would love to when this is all over."

"It may be too late. Her dementia is progressing. I've had to move her in to Mill Stream."

"I'm so sorry to hear that."

"They have her in memory care, on the secure floor. She loses the plot sometimes."

"I didn't know that." Kitchen leafed through his notebook. "She's only about seventy."

I looked down at the floor. The Persian carpet was worn from years of vigorous vacuuming, sucking away all the cake crumbs.

"The doctors theorize she suffered repeated concussions when she was younger."

"Your father?"

I winced at the thought.

"You did do some digging."

"There were reports, calls from neighbours but never any charges."

"For years, my mother worried about word getting back to the school. The appearance of propriety was everything."

"You weren't at Colborne. I would've heard of you."

"My father wouldn't allow it. Looking back, it may be the only thing he was right about."

I rose to stand, and my knees sharply protested the movement. I stepped towards the door.

"Look, Detective Kitchen. How is the fact you were in my mother's class pertinent?"

"Reverend Book she wasn't just one of my teachers."

Kitchen met my eyes.

He said, "She taught me how to think. I remember learning about residential schools in Canada. She took us to the Art Gallery of Ontario, to study Norval Morrisseau. Not just to look at his paintings but learn about the formative conditions. The what and the why of his work."

I felt the muscles in my face relax.

"She had his prints in our home when I was growing up," I said.

I returned to the wingback chair closest to the detective.

"You don't have to call me Reverend Book. It's Tom."

"Okay, Tom. Then I'm Lawrence."

I said, "Lawrence. What do you want to talk about?"

Kitchen flipped a page of his notebook.

"This will be more a summary of findings, and less about my impressions. I'll try to stick to what we can support with evidence, or research."

"Sounds fair."

Lawrence gestured in the direction of the church parking lot.

"I should also say our team is still at work, gathering physical evidence, and conducting interviews. Part of why I asked to meet in here, is there are scene of crime technicians in the administration area, working through Reverend Wilder's office."

"Do they need to go through mine as well?"

"Thank you," he said, "but not at this point."

"Before you get to stating the case, and before I forget to tell you," I began, "I'd suggest you have your team look in the belfry and if they can, use the access hatch and take a look on the belfry roof."

"Okay. We can do that. Can you tell me why?"

"Before the shoot began today, Hassan, the camera operator showed me his drone. He's like a big kid with a great toy."

"You must have made a good connection with him," the detective said.

"When he flew it over the tower, I saw something tucked behind the parapet, in the northwest corner. It looked too big to be a bird's nest. It's been bothering me."

He thumbed a message into his phone.

"I've just asked the tech team to go up and look. Will they need anything more than the master keys they picked up from the church administrator?"

"I don't know for sure," I admitted. "I've never been up there."

There was a faint buzz from the detective's phone. He nodded, tapped an answer, and pocketed the device.

"Can I tell you what we have so far?"

"Please."

"The remains discovered in the church basement are most likely those of the late Reverend Stephen Peretz. He was 40 years old and in good health when reported missing 28 years ago. It appears his remains and, interestingly, his wallet and keys were deposited in a disused exterior coal chute before it was capped and paved over in the fall of 1989. This fits with the date he was reported missing, having last been seen in this building. His car was left in the church parking lot."

"When was he reported missing?"

Flipping the pages of the little black notebook, he said, "Tuesday, September 26, 1989. The statement bore the name and signature of Ms. Ivy Torrance, who indicated she was a friend of the family."

"Ivy."

I stared at the print hung above the sofa, of the Saint Mungo's building. Was I acting like Attie, trying to protect the image of the church?

"Your eyes went wide when I said her name," Kitchen prompted. "Want to say more?"

"Ivy is very involved in the congregation. She comes to some of the classes I offer. She's quiet. Expresses herself with her hands, through her art. I have trouble imagining her filing a police report."

Could he read on my face that I wasn't saying everything I knew?

"Okay, we'll leave that for now. The age and condition of the remains make it difficult for our pathologist to be definitive about cause of death. There is cranial damage and a cervical fracture. The strongest indicator of foul play is that the body was so deliberately and successfully hidden. I want to know who wished harm to this man and why."

"This was all well before my time." I heard myself hedging.

"And as I said, Oakville is a small town. Bronte is like a village within Oakville. Your congregation is an even smaller subset. Someone knows something about what led to this man's disappearance and death. This was a major event. A big stone that made ripples in a small pond. And as your mom might have said there's a story under it all."

"It's hard to argue, especially when you invoke the wisdom of my sainted mother."

"Moving on," Kitchen said, "we have a cluster of events involving your late colleague."

"So you've spoken with Michael Powers." How much did Michael tell him? Would he have mentioned Doug's journal?

"Inspector Powers brought me up to speed earlier. We had a previously scheduled conference on another matter."

Detective Sergeant Kitchen was not telling me everything. That helped me rationalize my own vagueness.

"The remains of the Reverend Edward Patrick Wilder, who was last seen alive on Saturday night, were discovered three hours ago by a cadaver dog on loan from Halton Search and Rescue. His handler, Ms. Annika Vanderlugt, and yourself acted quickly to secure the scene, and call law enforcement."

"Annika kept her head," I said. "I was frozen in my tracks and not because of the cold."

"You were in shock," the detective offered. "Surprised

by the sight of the corpse of someone you know in that awful state. That can… stir things up."

"You already know, then…" I cleared my throat. "My wife died two years ago this Easter."

It was no easier to say it today.

"I was saddened to learn that," he said. "My condolences."

Kitchen even sounds like an English teacher.

"Thank you."

The detective stood and paced the parlour.

"I want to know more about what happened in here. Our techs took a quick look but will work this room tomorrow. Judging by the shine on that coffee table and the state of the Persian rug the parlour has been sanitized but they'll look anyway. We'd expect to find a few of Ms. Daniel's long blonde hairs on this couch."

"I don't know any more than what I told Michael," I said. "Kat…"

Lawrence checked his watch.

"One of my team is with Ms. Daniels as we speak. We hope she won't need much prompting to tell her story. My colleague is very good at her job and will avoid giving the impression you violated her confidence. We know she is under duress and may need your care."

I took that in with gratitude. This detective seemed to have genuine concern for Kat.

"We also want to talk to her brother Virgil about Saturday evening, and about the events of Monday afternoon and late Monday night. I especially want to know about his relationship with Reverend Wilder."

"Any idea where he is?"

I suddenly felt cold.

Lawrence stopped pacing and dropped into the wing-back chair across from me.

"There is no comfortable way to sit in these chairs. They're the antique versions of those plastic booths at

McDonald's," Kitchen said, with forced hilarity.

He asked, "Tom, are you okay?"

I took a moment before I spoke. I realized I'd been trembling.

"In my world, I deal with death, other people's grief, all the time. But not raw violence. The fire… the explosion… being sideswiped. I was almost run over today. The sight of Ed's body carelessly discarded in the snow. I don't know how you face this day after day."

Kitchen leaned forward to set his notebook on the table. Then he sat back and returned his hands to his lap.

This detective knew about listening a person into speech. I chose my words with care.

I said, "Virgil is a strange… lonely young man. He's always been protective of his sister. They haven't had it easy. I don't know what he might do if he felt she'd been wronged."

I paused. The wound in my scalp was pulsing.

"In my estimation," I said, "Kat has absolutely been wronged." I heard my voice grow strident. "Ed crossed a line with her. I don't know how it went with Virgil."

The detective lifted the notepad from the coffee table.

"We are looking for him. Inspector Powers identified a black 2012 Ford F-150 as it fled Reverend Wilder's home. The plate number matched that of the vehicle observed leaving your home late Monday night. It's registered to Virgil Daniels, at the address of his great-aunt, Athaliah Beacham."

"Is Virgil connected to the… to the things we found at the manse? Ed's home is owned by Saint Mungo's. We call it a manse."

"Tom, I know the term. And I've seen the title document for the property. At this point we don't know what to think about the money or the illicit pharmaceuticals. Those are definitely on my long list of questions."

"Speaking of questions, can I ask about some things?"

"You can ask," he said, "I'll answer as I am able."

"Where does Brad Kazinski fit in to all of this? When I

talked with Michael this morning, he didn't mention the folder marked 'Bell Tower'. You left that out as well."

"This may sound like I'm ducking your question," the detective said. "I don't mean to. But what do you know about Mr. Kazinski?"

I thought a moment before offering edited versions of my conversation with Ella Sayers, office manager at The Cash Box, and my own unsettling encounter with her boss.

The detective listened with care and jotted in his black notebook. He closed the book when I stopped talking.

"I'll come back to Mr. Kazinski's disturbing comment about your daughter, but first can I say something else? Something that goes beyond the scope of my earlier summary?"

I nodded. "You mean something you think is important but can't prove?"

"Yes. Exactly," he said. "This absolutely falls into the area of impressions."

"Okay, but I do want to come back to the other thing."

"I mentioned that when the first body... I'm sorry, that sounds cold. When the remains of Reverend Peretz were discovered, we began gathering background on persons connected to Saint Mungo's."

"Including me," I said.

I reminded myself I could be a suspect. I also wondered if he'd dug up my brother JP's record.

The detective nodded.

I rose from the wingback chair. One leg had gone to sleep. "I need to stand. My knees get stiff since the... excitement at the manse."

"I found Reverend Wilder to be a disturbing figure," Kitchen said. "He seems, or seemed, to be one of those people with numerous acquaintances, a wide network, but no actual friends. My impression is he made adept use of relationships, without being emotionally invested in them. He appears to have been very successful at getting his way."

It felt good to stand. I put a hand on the wingback chair

for balance. I lifted my foot and shook out the pins and needles, enjoying the warmth of returned circulation.

"That sounds like Ed," I said.

I felt something loosen in my chest.

"Since he went missing, I've been feeling I should have tried harder to connect. But I just couldn't get any traction with him."

The detective scratched his head and formed a question.

"Did you find he deflected personal inquiries and preferred speaking about tasks?"

"I think I see where you are going with this..."

"We've discovered he spent a lot of time with Mr. Kazinski."

"They were working together on the Bell Tower deal."

"I spoke with Mr. Kazinski," the detective said. "He is, as police say in mystery novels, well-known to us. He was forthcoming about the development project. He seems keen to accomplish at least two things, which I think have become... enmeshed in his thinking."

"You sound like a therapist," I said, pointing to the horsehair sofa, "You want this couch for your office? I'd be glad to see it go to a good home."

"I'd want something a little more comfortable," Kitchen answered with a smile. "Mr. Kazinski has made it his mission to clean up Bronte. He also wants to rehabilitate his family name. The Bell Tower project seems central to his efforts. He viewed Reverend Wilder as an asset."

"It surprised me to hear how well he knew Ed."

"Did you get the sense he cares about Reverend Wilder?"

I shook my head. "More like he needed something from him."

"That does seem more likely."

"I still wonder," I mused, "how the two of them are connected."

"We have significant resources devoted to that line of inquiry. Sorry if I'm sounding like a cop from a mystery novel again. It's how they talk at some of the meetings I attend."

"So what is it that you think, but can't prove?"

"Your description of Mr. Kazinski is consistent with my own experience, and with our gathered intelligence. He is intellectually bright, emotionally detached, highly motivated and very effective in his work. He is manipulative. He does not appear to have close friends. He is not close to his ex-wife or their children. Who does that sound like to you?"

I was caught for a moment in my memory of my time in that crypt of an office.

"Kazinski seemed cold and ruthless. He scared me without making a direct threat."

"I suspect he used the information he'd collected about you and your daughter to make it appear that he knew a lot more. He's a skilled manipulator."

"He knew how to play me," I admitted.

"He has adapted quite successfully to the world he lives in, and which he dominates."

The detective pointed to the print of Saint Mungo's hanging above the sofa.

"If he found himself in a different environment he might adapt, wear a different mask, but underneath, he might be..."

"A lot like Ed Wilder."

Kitchen nodded. "It's my unqualified opinion that both men have displayed characteristics consistent with what forensic psychologists call ASPD. Antisocial personality disorder."

I let that sink in. It shed light on Kat's story and helped me understand why my efforts to connect with Ed always failed.

I don't have a degree in psychology, but I did clinical training at a hospital with a psych ward. I learned my way around the diagnostic manual and worked with patients who had that particular notation on their charts.

"You're saying Ed Wilder was a sociopath. And Brad Kazinski, a powerful and dangerous man who knows far too much about me and my daughter, may also be one."

32

"That trauma scene guy'd make a good action hero," Deborah said with a smile. *She looks better when she smiles and is a little scary when she doesn't.*

"Um…"

When Detective Kitchen mentioned getting keys from the office, it reminded me to check in with Deborah Judge, the Saint Mungo's church administrator.

"I told Rod he could call himself the Wiper," Deborah continued. "He swoops in when tragedy strikes. Helps clean up so life can go on."

"Sorry I didn't get to meet him," I said. "Didn't even know he was here."

Deborah might be close to my mother's age. I'd never ask. She has black shoulder length hair without a hint of grey, and bright blue eyes that often flash with humour and occasionally what she calls tetchiness. She claims to be related to a midfielder for Colchester United, and she's a big supporter. Her passions are football and her Irish wolfhound Brigid.

"They got here before Kat's video crew. Unloaded then parked their van over at the yacht club so it wouldn't show in any of her shots."

"Was that Kat's idea?"

Deborah's office overlooks the back parking area. I sat in one of her visitor's chairs, with my back to the big window. She was behind her desk, in the chair Michael used when we first opened Doug's journal. Brigid was under the desk, a mound of grey hair snoring at her feet.

"No. Rod said he knows to keep a low profile. Some clients don't want it known they need trauma cleaning."

Like Attie dangling the big cheque. Make it like nothing happened.

"It does smell better in here," I said.

"Which is good for tomorrow. For the Good Friday service," Deborah said. She has that way of reminding me of things.

"I just finished with Detective Kitchen," I said. "Never thought to ask if we were cleared to use the sanctuary."

When Deborah started at Saint Mungo's the job was church secretary. Paul Bennett proposed a new job description.

She'd said, "It doesn't matter what you call me. Take me off the hourly rate and give me a salary."

The church gave her the title and a raise, and she's been in charge ever since. Not even Attie dares take her on.

Deborah said, "You had other things to talk about. But it's okay. I checked with someone from the detective's team. She said they were done with the basement, and once they were out of the offices, which they are, the building was all ours. I've already called Betty to bring her up to speed."

"What about…"

Deborah said, "I watched the whole thing, while you were in with the detective. They traced the path that lovely dog followed…"

"Zeke," I said. I resisted the urge to turn and look out the window to the parking lot.

"…the path that Zeke followed, and took photos and scooped up snow," she said. "You and the other bystanders had already been shifted out of the way. The officer with the camera took a lot of snaps before and after they lifted out…"

"Ed's body," I said.

"Ed's body," she agreed. "They lifted it into a big white duffle, zipped it up, and slid it in the back of a van."

I looked at Deborah.

"You seem to be handling this a lot better than me," I said.

Deborah met my eyes with kindness in her own.

"You have a big heart, Tom. I can see how this would get to you. Especially after the other fellow, in the basement."

"You've known Ed longer than me."

"You were still trying to figure him out. I already saw Edward Wilder for what he was."

"And what was that?"

"My gran would've called him a toe rag. A shrewd-eyed snake who used people for his own ends."

I saw gemstone hardness in her sapphire eyes. No wonder Attie never messed with her. I wondered who'd hurt Deborah, and what their fate would have been.

"I'm sorry, Tom, does that shock you?"

"It might have even a week ago. To be honest, it lines up with what I've been hearing. I'm not bothered you'd say it. I question myself because I wasn't seeing it."

Deborah said, "It's the kind of thing you can only see if you can see it…"

"When I first came back to Saint Mungo's I tried to connect with Ed, get to know him. After… I just didn't have it in me."

"I know, Tom," she said. "But don't trouble yourself. He really wasn't worth it."

"I, um…"

"I saw what he was up to with Kat, who may come on all claws sometimes, but who's really a scared little kitten. He had way too much money for someone on a pastor's salary, even though he got about twice what they pay you. Sorry if you didn't already know that. He spent a lot of time with Virgil, and you just know that wasn't right. Then there was the business with Kazinski…"

"If you knew all of that," I asked, "why did you put up with him?

"What makes you think I did?" Deborah half-smiled and held out a plate. "Have a muffin. I made them fresh this morning."

33

"I didn't know if I should help Ed or strangle him," I said. "Now he's laid out at the morgue, and I still can't decide."

I set two large brown paper sacks on my kitchen island. The bags were stapled at the top, to keep in the heat, and blotted with the greasy promise of takeout goodness. A small ziploc bag held accessories from Thai-m 4 Thai.

Last vestiges of evening light shone in my kitchen window. It had been a grey day.

Gwen said, "Like we tell the families, shock can dull your feelings. As if you've been hit by a truck. You'd never survive if you felt all the pain, all at once."

"Weird you'd say that," I said. "I was hit by a truck this morning."

I was letting her know it needed to be that kind of conversation.

She grinned, "How's the truck?"

"Well..." I said, "I was almost hit."

"What happened?"

We tore open the brown paper bags, releasing steamy air redolent with aromas that spoke to me. Cardamom and lemon grass. Coriander and curry.

As we shared out coconut soups, mango salads and skewers of chicken satay I described my close call on Stewart Street. How I was sure I'd be run down before I got my hair cut.

"No worries, Tom. We'd clean you up good in the prep room. Even cover up your new bald spot. We have a special spray for that."

"Yeah, thanks," I said, holding out a white clamshell container. "Here's your spicy glass noodles."

"Smells great," Gwen said. "Did you get the license plate or at least the kind of truck?"

"All I managed to do was not get hit."

She gave me her 'oh really' eyes.

"What?" I asked.

Gwen was already out of her work suit, and into sweatpants and a Morrison Brothers zippered fleece hoody. She'd come upstairs to set out plates after I called from the church, to tell her about Ed.

We'd both wanted Thai food since she mentioned it Monday.

"Tom, your knees are still pretty torn up. You're not exactly setting land speed records.

"Yeah…so?"

"So, if someone wants to hit you, you're a barely moving target. They were just trying to scare you."

"It worked. But it's not just that."

I told her Little Ray's opinion of the guys in the black truck, and about seeing the trucks parked at The Cash Box.

"Kazinski sounds like Darth Vader. Why'd you go?"

"After what Ella Sayers told me, and what we found in the manse… I was curious."

"And what do you think? Could he have hurt Ed?"

"Seeing two dead bodies in a week and now talking with this homicide cop has rubbed off on me. I'm starting to think like an amateur detective. "

Gwen forked some noodles and smiled.

"Okay Father Brown. What's your theory?"

"When he told me about Stephen, Kitchen said hiding the body points to foul play. So maybe that's true for Ed."

Gwen said, "Did your Detective Kitchen really say foul play like he was on Law and Order?"

"He really did," I said.

"So you think Brad Kazinski could have been the foul player, yeah?"

"I don't think that's what they call them. But this is the

part where I start looking under rocks and find more rocks."

"What?"

"On Tuesday, Ella Sayers told me Kazinski and Ed argued and she saw them both storm away angry. But Kazinski asked me how to reach Ed and said he'd missed their meeting on Sunday night. If he was looking for him, that means he didn't know he was dead."

"Did you believe him?"

"What do you mean?"

"It sounds like he scared you, when he talked about Hope."

"Yeah. I didn't like him knowing about her."

"And he's got trucks at his store like the ones that have been messing with you."

"Trucks, or maybe just one truck. I don't know."

I realized I hadn't told Kitchen any of this. I told myself it was because I was caught up in what he said about Kazinki and Ed. The truth is the soft-spoken detective had an unnerving way of getting past my defenses.

"You know he was willing to scare you with words. Maybe he'd use other tools to get what he wants."

"You're saying he could be playing me, pretending to worry about Ed."

"You think he worries about anyone besides his own slick self?"

"Why would he bother with me?"

"That's a good question, Father. Why mess with the humble parish priest?"

Which is the real reason I hadn't told Kitchen about the truck attacks Monday night and Thursday morning. It made no sense that Kazinski, or anyone else would make me their target.

"Bless you my child," I said, waving double crosses in the air with my open chop sticks.

"Bless this," Gwen said, and tossed a packet of hot sauce my way.

I said, "It's got something to do with Ed, and whatever

he was into."

"Yes, it has to be about Ed," Gwen said. "But I'm worried about you."

I shifted on my stool.

"I'm worried too," I said. "The detective said something about Ed and Kazinski that bothers me. Especially when I connect it with Kazinski dropping Hope's name like a grenade."

"What did he say?"

"They both fit the profile of a sociopath. Smart, emotionally distant, hard to get to know, but they know how to use people, and get their way."

"That does sound like your Ed Wilder."

"Yeah," I said. "But are we seeing him that way just because of what this detective said?"

I told Gwen what Deborah had just told me about Ed Wilder.

Gwen said, "So what does your gut tell you? You believe Kat. You believe Deborah. Do you trust the detective?"

"It's hard to be objective. The detective, he said to call him Lawrence, talked about having my mom for a teacher and how much she helped him."

"Who's more likely to be playing you," Gwen asked. "Lawrence, the homicide cop who likes your mom, or Kazinski, the scary guy with mob connections?"

"You are pretty good at this," I said. "You could be the amateur detective."

I searched my memory for a literary reference but could not think of any mysteries featuring Jamaican-Canadian funeral directors. Too bad. I'd absolutely read them.

"I'm a woman of colour in an industry run by scheming old white guys. I know to read between the lines. So how's your dog lady?"

Dessert time. Gwen turned to the fridge for butterscotch ripple ice cream, our usual after thai food. I grabbed the bowls and spoons.

"We're shifting from murder to questions about my

love life?"

"Is that what we're calling it? Okay, Tom, so how's your love life?"

"Annika is... good. I called her while I waited for the takeout. They interviewed us separately, which makes sense. She knew the officer from Search and Rescue work, and it seemed to go well. Then she took Zeke home."

"I haven't talked to you since the big date. How'd that go?"

"It was good. Comfortable. But it's happening at such a strange time. This Stephen Peretz, and now Ed. Trying to get Hope home, and seeing how that goes. Things with my mom."

Gwen said, "After such a long time of nothing happening."

"There is always life and death happening, things changing. But now it feels, I feel, more…"

"Part of it?"

"Yeah," I said. "I feel like I'm in the story, not just watching it from a distance."

34

My niece Dido loiters around Pastor Stephen in a way that worries me. I've seen it before, at the school. A teacher, more often than not a middle-aged man, has by some stormy happenstance been cut loose from their moorings, and mislaid their inner compass. A man who does not know how to be alone with himself, seeks what might generously be termed an affirmation of their manhood. (Not that I am disposed to such generosity of spirit when I hear one of these sordid tales.)

The misguided teacher offers a calculated excess, just a little too much of the wrong kind of attention to a student, and she responds. It will have been a cunning predation, that could easily be denied if observed and questioned.

Do women teachers prey on students this way? I am not sure I wish to know. I have only noticed it work this way, with male colleagues flirting with certain of their female students.

Dido, I fear is a candidate for such attention. She has the physical type of one of those girls who would present as attractive, if she were generally friendly, and if she had an inner glow by which people would warm, and then see her reflected in that positive light.

I have often heard Lila implore her to take more care with her appearance, to do something with her hair, which is of a light brown colour that can, I admit, easily look 'mousy'.

She has expressive, clear blue eyes. In rare moments I have seen them shine with joy. Most of the time, I sorrow to say, her eyes seem vacant, and her entire presentation of self is dimmed, drained of any possible vitality.

Friday, September 15, 1989

Dido may be predisposed to respond to Stephen's predatory attentions. Ralph, her father, is so beaten down by Lila, her mother, that he is almost a ghost in his own life and in his daughter's life. She has watched her mother run and run down her father. She has been robbed of a strong and benevolent male presence in her life.

I worry Dido is seeking to fill the gap with the wrong kind of attention, from the wrong kind of male authority figure.

My brother-in-law Ralph Daniels is a dismal drunk, who has spent the entirety of Dido's life in an alcoholic stupor. Despite his persistent self-immolation he has somehow managed to be successful in his actuarial practice. They are well off and contribute a great deal of money to Saint Mungo's, at least this is what Attie tells me. Neither their wealth nor their largesse mitigates their essential misery, as far as I can tell.

Dido has grown up with the understanding, reinforced daily by her mother, and by my wife, that her father is a carefully managed disaster who is barely tolerated, mainly for his cheque book.

I remember when that role for Ralph was irrevocably written into the family narrative. There was an incident from which he could not recover, even if he dared, or cared to try.

Dido was a round little toddler at the time. Lila was still in some degree of denial about Ralph's drinking and had left Dido in his care while she and Attie attended a lady's function at the church.

When Attie pulled into the driveway to drop her sister at home, Dido was sitting alone, bawling her eyes out, on the front lawn of their huge East Oakville home.

As Attie and Lila both said, many times in the years to come "It just isn't done, allowing your child to upset the whole neighbourhood."

I continue to hope their dismay at disturbing the neighbours, none of whom Lila cared for, was peripheral, and their real concern was for that poor little girl.

The way Attie tells it, Lila barely waited for the car to stop before she threw open her door and ran to her child. She scooped Dido into her arms and made for the front door of their home, to find it locked.

Attie brought her sister's purse from the car and dug out the house key. She shared Lila's desire to get the wailing child into the house and out of earshot and sight of the neighbours.

Once inside, the sisters were able to comfort and calm Dido. Lila held her "precious Dido" close to her bosom, as she later said, 'caring little about the effects of her dripping nose and drooling mouth' on the bodice of her dress, even though it was a 'Hugh Garber, all the way from Montreal.'

It was Attie who found my brother-in-law Ralph passed out in the easy chair in his study. In her words, "He reeked of liquor, and his snoring was so loud it is no bloody wonder he couldn't hear his daughter's pitiful cries."

I only heard about Ralph's drunken neglect weeks after it had happened. The story was justification for their ill-conceived plot to either "teach him the error of his ways," or to "cure him once and for all". The object changed depending on the season, and which sister was recounting the tale. It might have been amusing if they hadn't almost killed the man.

They conspired to acquire a quantity of a drug called disulfiram, also known as Antabuse. It apparently has use in legitimate alcohol treatment programs. Their application was certainly not legitimate. They dosed every bottle in the liquor cabinet in Ralph's study, which was where he would retreat every day after work.

Ralph, who because of his lifestyle and habits was already a prime candidate for a cardiac event, managed to call 911 before he passed out. He later told me, "I had trouble catching my breath, and my heart was pounding. I felt like my chest was going to explode.'

The fact that he remembers that much tells me the drug kicked in before he was fully inebriated.

As Lila tells it, "He was laid out unconscious in that study of his, again, when the sirens and flashing lights set all the dogs barking and tongues wagging up and down our street. I didn't even know he'd called for an ambulance. What an affront to answer my own door and be firmly directed to step out of the way!"

Ralph survived, of course. I don't know what Lila said to

him, that convinced him to tell the people at the hospital he'd self-medicated. But I can guess.

(Saturday, September 16, 1989)

I have not personally witnessed anything untoward going on between Stephen and Dido, but I worry. She is in his office, with the door closed, too often. Stephen has taken to picking her up after school and driving her home after their visits.

It was emptying the garbage cans in the church that clinched it for me. We don't have a good place to put out trash in front of the church, and I don't like the look of that anyway, so I usually bag the office garbage two or three nights a week, and the kitchen and classroom garbage on Sundays after church and take it home with me. Later I throw it in the dumpster at the school.

I don't work at seeing what's in the garbage, except to pull out things that might go to recycling, I generally prefer to let it all drop in the big green bag and move on to the next trash can.

I have been picking out a lot of glass to recycle from Stephen's garbage. Smirnoff Vodka bottles have been appearing for months. Why doesn't he dispose of them somewhere else? If I were a closeted drinker, I expect I would be more devious.

He's been drinking behind his office door more and more, especially on those nights when it seems there is no earthly, or heavenly, reason to stay here. He just doesn't seem to want to go home. That much I can understand.

I haven't known what, if anything, to say, or do about the bottles. People at Saint Mungo's like him, despite the sharp and speculative whispers about his failing marriage, and Wendy's "close friendship" with Ivy. His services are full of life-- he puts so much of himself into them. He speaks well. I hear him differently now.

I can see why Doug kept his journal in a box on the top shelf in his workroom. I wonder if Attie knows what her husband wrote.

I'm disturbed by the picture that's emerging of Attie and her sister Lila, and of Stephen Peretz.

I remember helping Mom clean up after my father's

binges. In the months before we got out, he left a long trail of broken glass, bruises and hard feelings.

Sunday, September 17, 1989

When Pastor Stephen asks us to trust that God's love is constant, and always with us, and without condition, even when life feels otherwise, I think now he is speaking loudest to himself.

When he talks about there being no road we can walk, or place we can go, that God is not already there, walking with us, or waiting for us, it now makes me wonder if he is actually looking for a way out, or a place to which he can run away. I heard that undercurrent in the psalm he quoted this morning,

"Where can I go from your Spirit?
Where can I flee from your presence?
If I go up to the heavens, you are there;
   if I make my bed in the depths, you are there."

I have been thinking of all those bottles in the trash- as Stephen's pathetic and failing effort to get away, without actually leaving.

I have tried to reserve judgment on his drinking. That's a challenge, as I have seen too much of it with Ralph, and with some of my co-workers. Intelligent, if not wise, essentially good people, who step off the normal path of walking through life, and divert themselves, in a way they tell themselves they can manage. Then they find themselves tumbling down into a very dark place.

What are they running from, or to? What hungry or thirsty aspect of them is so demanding, and so insatiable? I can't judge these people, because I also have hungry places in me. How different am I from this man who hides in his office and doesn't care to be home with his wife? Stephen's Wendy may be looking to Ivy for what she no longer wants from him. Or maybe she is finding herself. How did their lives get this way? I have no way of knowing, and maybe the why doesn't matter, because it just seems to be. What profit would there be in my judging this man, his marriage? My own marriage does not bear any more than superficial scrutiny.

Stephen hides in his office, and I closet myself in my sexton's room, scratching away in this dim light, in a notebook he gave me, because he thought it would do me good to keep a journal.

It does help pass the time.

I am here most nights and as much of the weekend as I can claim. Attie and I maintain the fiction she would rather I was at home, and she therefore must challenge and seek justification for my not being with her-- what important task keeps me away from her yet again?

I, to a lesser degree, for my role is secondary in the drama, play the part of the husband who would rather be at home, were it not for the demands of caring for this holy temple. The Lord of the Universe, Maker of Mountains and Keeper of the Celestial Clock needs me, for a few more hours, to strip the floors in the upstairs hallway, and to unclog a toilet.

Speaking of clogged toilets, and my other more or less mundane acts of hands-on devotion, I am happy to report the project to salvage the old boiler has gone well. The students from my school's industrial arts program have gained great experience with the cutting torches. The scrap metal hauler has been happy to take away the cast iron and steel. The students have been able to cut pieces small enough the metal can be carried by hand-- well, in gloved hands, up the back stairs and out to the parking lot, and Sid's waiting one-ton truck. If what Sid pays us for the weight of the scrap comes close to covering the cost of refilling the oxy-acetylene tanks, I will be happy. The space will be cleared out, the coal chute will be walled over, and the room will have a new life.

The project has afforded me a great boon. The tech students needed supervision for all those after school and evening work periods. I kept the cold drinks and salty snacks coming for the young men, and women, as they took their breaks. It was sweaty work in that small room.

I set up an old table and chairs in the Sunday School office, ones that would not be harmed by a little grease and soot and had a capital time chatting with these kids. There is something good about seeing them outside the formal context of the school.

I learned about The Dead Poets Society, a motion picture that could actually tempt me away from my nightly duties here at the church.

I heard about a television program called Seinfeld, which apparently is a show about nothing. That does not interest me at all.

I also heard enough about a popular singer called Madonna to know I would likely not care for her music.

I talked with Attie one evening about how much I appreciate the hard work of these students, and the pleasure it is to get to know them in a different way. It is so unlikely that I would hear about the things that interest them in the exchanges that happen at the school.

"Why would you wish to know them? They are students. Students push their way in to our front office at Colborne every day. Most often they are complaining about something or scheming to find a way around an academic requirement or get out of a compulsory duty. I have little time for their wheedling noise, and the last thing I want is for them to waste the time of the head of school. We have important matters with which to concern ourselves."

In my lesser moments, I think she would have made a great commandant for a Hitler Youth summer camp. I imagine her marshalling straight lines of students all bright and blond and shining with achievement, to outward appearances, but secretly filled with fear and despair.

I laughed out loud, then chided myself for being amused that Doug would compare his wife to a Nazi youth group leader. What kind of life did they have together? I needed to keep all of this in my own little tin box, and not let Doug's story change the way I treated Attie, if she came to the Good Friday service.

I still had work to do on that service. After seeing Ed's body frozen in the snow, it felt even more important to resist the insidious notion that violence and death are legitimate solutions to our problems. I needed to tell myself that, even as I was reminded of the pain we humans are capable of inflicting on each other.

Tuesday, September 19, 1989

Attie seems happy with the progress we have made in the church basement. The idea of this old hulk of a church building running a little more efficiently, cutting costs, appeals to her. Her administrator's temperament was soothed at the thought of all the free labour I brought in.

The upgrades to heating the building have been done with a minimum of change to the appearance of the building, which also pleases my wife. She's always been one to care more about the look of the gift box, and less about what's inside.

Her one passion, outside of her administrative duties at Colborne College, consists of shaping and carving at the outside edges of this congregation, with the keen edge of her mind, her ruthless heart, and her knife-like words. She does not hesitate to cut deep, if it's in defense of something precious to her. I take comfort in the knowledge she would never hurt anyone to protect me.

I have settled for finding my own way to be in the church, to escape her by serving this place, in a manner that does what good I can manage. So I fix broken chairs, and paint everything on a rotating schedule, and make sure things work. Very seldom does my mending or tinkering involve people and their hurt and tarnished hearts. I don't know how to make them shine, as I do the candlesticks and the cross, and the oak table in the chancel.

I have grown to love this place, and to see fleeting glimpses of why it matters to people. They may not be able to articulate it, but they need to come here. They gather, and sing, and whisper faintly along with the prayers. They dare to hope their prayers will find their way to a God that loves us, as Pastor Stephen asserts, with reckless and creative abandon.

Wednesday, September 20, 1989

Tonight, in addition to the vodka bottles, I salvaged some empty "cooler" bottles for recycling. The teachers at school who run the dances talk about wine coolers as "Koolaid for big kids"-- the beverage of choice for students who are trying to drink themselves into some kind of loosening from all their various bindings.

I find the very existence of these products deplorable.

I am old-fashioned enough to believe intoxicating drinks, that fuel and give licence to wildness, should at least taste a bit threatening. They should not so closely resemble, in name and packaging, scent and flavour, strawberry shortcake and pink lemonade. There is an evil in the way their power is wrapped in such saccharine disguise. Like a poisoned Halloween apple.

The appearance of drained cooler bottles, and their sickly sweet rotting fruit smell in his office garbage feeds my dread, my gnawing suspicion that Stephen is now proffering these treacly, potent drinks to Dido. Did this begin in response to his thirst, or hers?

Does Stephen know the spectacularly awful history Dido's family has with alcohol? If he does, and still uses it to ply her, I find that even more reprehensible.

Is he so far fallen into that dark crevasse that his lower, predatory instincts and strategies have overtaken Christian charity, and his fundamental humanity? By humanity I mean the shared, if largely unspoken, agreement that the fully grown among our species should know not to deliberately harm or confuse the young. On some level, I want to believe he knows better.

This man who preaches so movingly on Sunday morning of love and the necessity of social involvement to relieve suffering knows, in some way, that we are meant to do good rather than harm to children. Even children who wear the masks of adulthood.

I hate that this is happening and I cannot help but despair over what flows from this cynical conviviality. What will become of my niece? What is actually left of this man who has been my pastor?

The previous day, Gwen and I had both spent time trying to arrange a decent burial for the remains of Stephen Peretz. Would I have bothered if I'd read this about him earlier? If Doug is a reliable narrator, there is a part of me that understands why Stephen wound up where he did.

At the same time, I was touched by Doug's loneliness, and Stephen's, and I wonder where I would be without Hope, and Mom, and Gwen.

Thursday, September 21, 1989

I came back here to the church right after supper with the desire to write out this conversation as close to verbatim as I can remember.

"Attie, I need to talk to you about Dido."

Attie looked up from her plate and across our table at El Spero's. We meet here occasionally for supper, when her duties at the school run late. Attie likes it because most of the parents of her day-schoolers would never consider eating here. "After all," she once said, "the restaurant is in a shopping mall that has a bowling alley in the basement."

Attie put down her fork but kept hold of her knife.

"What about Dido?'

"She is spending a lot of time with Stephen, and I am not sure that's a good thing for either of them."

"Pastor Stephen? Maybe he is offering her religious counsel. She could use some direction. Lila has her hands full with her, and of course, Ralph has never been of any help."

"It doesn't look like pastoral counselling to me."

"What are you suggesting? Look, I have real things to worry about. I have a trustees meeting this weekend for which I need to prepare, and our math and science head teacher strolled in the office this morning and announced he is leaving us for Upper Canada College. I will have to initiate a search for his replacement, and also be seen to have made progress on it, all by the end of the week."

"Stephen is going through a pretty rough patch lately."

"You're talking about that wife of his and her special friend in the choir. We knew nothing good would come of that. Lila and I told you after last year's disastrous Good Friday service. How does a person commit to sing a duet, attend practice for weeks ahead, and just not 'be up to it' on the day? It was such an embarrassment."

"Stephen is pretty broken up about Wendy leaving."

"He should be. I don't think he's grasped how this will make our church look. Just because some of those Toronto churches have divorced men in the pulpit doesn't mean we care to follow their sad example."

"Stephen and Wendy are not divorced."

"Lila's housekeeper saw Wendy at the legal clinic at that 'women's well-being' centre. She takes her daughter there for self-defence classes. She told Lila that Wendy and Ivy were sitting in the waiting area, holding hands and whispering together. A week later we hear she's flown off to Vancouver, to be with family we've never before heard about. What else are we to make of that?"

"Attie, I don't know what to say about Wendy and Ivy. I want to talk to you about Dido. I think she and Stephen are closer than they should be."

"Why would you say that?"

"She's a lonely young woman, who is in the pastor's office almost every day after school. He picks her up after class, and she's with him…"

"What are you saying?"

"I am trying to tell you. I think they are drinking together."

"Dido knows better. She knows what it's done to her father. She would never. And it would shatter Lila. She would never… No, it's not a possibility."

"There are vodka bottles in Stephen's trash. And those wine coolers."

"You're telling me you search the minister's garbage? Does anyone see you do this?"

"I don't have to search. I empty the office trash cans, and they are there in the open. I sort for recycling. I bring the trash to the school and put the recyclables out in our blue box."

"So you put empty vodka bottles out in front of our house? What are you thinking? We have to live in that neighbourhood. What would happen if your blue box was overturned?"

"Attie, I think you are missing what I am trying to tell you."

"The image of broken vodka bottles on my driveway will haunt me for days. Tell me you will stop bringing those things home. You'll make us look as bad as Ralph."

"You are worried about a few bottles in our blue box? Attie think for a moment. You don't want Saint Mungo's to suffer the scandal of having a divorced minister. If Stephen and Dido are

*involved in some unseemly way, and it became public knowledge,
what would people say then?"*

35

"There are things I failed to mention," I said.

After a pause, Detective Kitchen said, "You weren't being formally questioned."

My cellphone had rung just as I parked in the spacious lot shared by Via Rail, the GO regional commuter trains, and Oakville Transit. The long-haul passenger service uses the same tracks as the commuter and freight trains that run between downtown Toronto and the suburbs.

The screen indicated the call was from Lawrence Kitchen. His personal phone, not the Halton Regional Police.

I said, "Even so, Detective Kitchen. I could have been more… forthcoming is a word you used earlier."

"In my somewhat ironic description of Mr. Kazinski. And it's still Lawrence. What do you want to add?"

I told him about being sideswiped on the way home from Attie's and described the black truck rumbling up my driveway to ram my car. I left out the part about Gwen staring me down and stopping me from sliding and stumbling across my skating rink driveway to confront the driver.

When I got to my story of the close call on the way to Vince's barber shop, I caught myself scanning the brightly lit parking lot. Without realizing it, I'd been watching for salt-stained black pickups, like the one that almost hit me, and the one I'd spotted at The Cash Box.

I was at the station an hour before Hope's train was due. It was better to be early, and I could use the time to push through Doug's journal.

There were perhaps a dozen commuter cars with frosted windows scattered in the parking lot, which was built to accommodate hundreds. A few vehicles queued up in front of the train station, sending up thin tendrils of exhaust as they idled. The lot was very well lit, and there were no black pickups that I could see.

I'd turned off my engine and was beginning to feel the chill.

Kitchen said, "My team noticed recent damage to your car. There's no incident number linked to your name, so you haven't yet reported those… altercations."

"I called Michael Powers, but I'm guessing that doesn't count."

"Inspector Powers did fill me in. I was also made aware of the officer assigned to watch your home Monday night."

"Yeah. Michael said whoever it was got away."

Huge mountains of snow had been pushed to the western end of the lot, furthest from the station buildings and the bus loop. No trucks at that end either.

Shivering, I started the Suzuki's engine.

"As you say, whoever it was. We will look into what Little Ray told you about the Kerr Street neighbourhood, as well as the vehicles parked at Mr. Kazinski's office."

"Thanks for that," I said.

"We have a little more information about one particular black truck. As you know, the vehicle that fled the scene of the manse explosion is registered to Virgil Daniels. It seems when he last renewed his plates, he used the street address for Saint Mungo's Church. That may have been prescient on his part."

"What do you mean?"

"My team, acting on your information, searched the bell tower. The strange shape you picked out from the drone's view was a backpack cocooned in layers of black garbage bags."

"Why hide it up there?"

"The stash included many packages of fentanyl pills similar to those recovered from Reverend Wilder's residence and a large quantity of cash."

Despite the warmer air now issuing from the Suzuki's vents, I shuddered as I thought of the proximity of those dangerous pills to the nursery school that rents space at Saint Mungo's. Cubs, brownies, scout and girl guide groups also call the building home.

"I have trouble seeing Virgil as a drug dealer. Are you sure it was his backpack?"

Kitchen said, "On their way up to the roof my team found signs of someone squatting in the belfry. A portable heater, sleeping bag, several changes of clothes, and takeout containers. Whoever it was prefers Tim Horton's hot chocolate with double cream."

Probably reminds him of his mother, I thought, remembering the care Kat took with our hot drinks.

"That could be Virgil, but was there anything to confirm? Where's his truck?"

"That was our question. Taking a cue from Hassan's drone footage, we visited the apartments behind the church, and the condo tower next door."

I said, "All just steps away from Saint Mungo's."

"We looked at the security logs and videos. It didn't take long to discover Virgil's used the underground parking in the condo next door every night since Saturday."

"How'd he get in?"

"Using a key card issued to Lila Brown. Recognize the name?"

The big portrait over Attie's fireplace. The grim faces of Cyril and Mabel Brown.

"That could be Virgil and Kat's grandmother, if she's reverted to her family name."

"We agree," said Kitchen. "She owns a condo in the building and leases a spot in the garage. The property manager said she winters in Florida. Sarasota Police are looking for her."

I heard the muffled voice of an announcement over outdoor speakers, and the warning bells of an approaching train. A blue Toyota started up a few parking spots over, and the driver maneuvered toward the passenger pick up lanes.

"Any idea where Virgil is now? He'll need a new place to sleep."

Kitchen chuckled. "We'd put him up for a few nights. We'd like to talk with him."

Doug's journal mentioned Lila Brown's condo, looking down on Saint Mungo's. That's where she'd taken refuge when she signed over the big house and her grandchildren to Attie.

It struck me it could have saved the police some steps, and they might have already picked Virgil up if I'd come clean earlier and told them about the journal.

"Detective Kitchen…" I began.

"Lawrence."

"Lawrence," I said, "I have more to tell you."

"I heard a train in the background Tom, do you have time?"

"That was a GO train. My daughter is on VIA."

A trio of buses rolled towards the Oakville bus terminal. Their arrival was well-timed to meet the de-training commuters. The dash clock read 8:55 p.m. Half an hour before Hope's train.

"I'm good. I need to start with Wendy Peretz. Do you know that name?"

"Yes. She was married to Stephen Peretz. We have a report of her death at a hospital in Burnaby, British Columbia, within weeks of her husband's disappearance. The coroner determined it was suicide by means of an overdose of prescribed sedatives."

"I've been working on arrangements for a proper burial for Stephen's remains and trying to track down his family."

"That's very kind. We may be able to help."

"Thank you for that," I said. "Yesterday I talked with Ivy Torrance-Martens. She was romantically involved with Wendy Peretz."

Kitchen said, "I mentioned Bronte is a small pond."

"You did. The thing is…she told me about Wendy's

suicide."

"You held this back earlier," the detective said.

I said, "Yes, I... wasn't sure..."

"Is it another situation involving the need for confidentiality?"

"That's... part of it. But there's another wrinkle."

I told him about Doug's journal and summarized what I'd read to that point. I didn't mention a ghost sent me looking for the book, but I did admit asking Michael not to tell the police of its existence.

There was another pause, longer than earlier, before Kitchen said, "Tom, I think I'd like to read that."

"I can bring it to you tomorrow," I said. "By then I'll have read what I'm meant to read."

"Interesting..." Kitchen said. "Why tell me now?"

"Because it was wrong to hold the journal back this long. And because of these men and their stories. I think Doug was a lonely guy. I don't know enough about Stephen or how Ed ended up as he did, but I don't think keeping secrets was good for any of them. And I've decided to trust you."

Detective Kitchen's third long pause of the evening. I was grateful this was a phone call.

"This is an unusual conversation to happen between an investigator, and a..."

"Suspect?"

"No, not a suspect. A person with insight, information, and a stake in the outcome. At any rate, this is an unusual conversation."

"I'm sorry to put you in a difficult situation."

"I don't believe that was your intention. And we're talking now. If you still have time before your daughter's train arrives, I have more to tell you."

"We're good," I said.

"We have new information about the events of Saturday night, and the death of Reverend Wilder. It is all preliminary, based on video footage we obtained from the buildings nearest Saint Mungo's."

I asked, "What can you tell me?"

"We're looking at the feed from a camera on the west side of the condo building. It's time-stamped, so we see someone who looks like Virgil leave at 6:45 on Saturday evening. Half an hour later we see Kat exit. Soon after that, the blizzard came on strong, which significantly degraded image quality. At 8:00 p.m. we see a figure we believe to be Reverend Wilder exit the rear parking lot door, same as the first two. Shortly after that, it appears the camera was damaged in the storm."

"We all tend to park near that door," I said.

"The figure we believe to be Reverend Wilder slipped and fell on the ice as he went out the door. We think it's the spot the cadaver dog picked up his blood trace."

"It's Virgil job to throw down salt," I said. "Ice builds up outside the doors."

"Both Virgil and Kat trod that same spot and didn't fall."

I said, "Ed's dress shoes were terrible on snow and ice. He didn't have his overshoes when we found him."

"I remember that. Reverend Wilder took quite a tumble. As he struggled back to his feet, the camera captured the image of a dark pickup approaching from the Lakeshore entrance."

"Virgil?"

"The footage is too grainy to tell. The snow was coming down hard, the lighting poor, the camera just too far away. We see the truck roll past the main entrance, travel up the lane beside the building. It accelerated as it came at Reverend Wilder. The impact sent him flying."

"That sounds purposeful," I said. "And horrible."

"Yes," Kitchen said. "The driver stepped out to lower the truck's cargo gate. They wore a winter coat with a hood that cast a shadow over their face. They hefted your colleague over their shoulder, tossed him on the truck's cargo bed, then drove toward the rear of the parking area behind the church."

"Which is where Zeke found him."

"Unfortunately, that end of the lot was out of the camera's range. The suspect's truck must have exited from the other side of the building. Later footage shows a larger truck from your church's maintenance contractor plowing and pushing snow out to the edges of the lot."

"They may have buried Ed alive."

"Our pathologist doesn't think so. She says his death was most likely the result of the massive trauma received when he was hit by the truck."

"That seems a small mercy."

"It's a terrible story. I'm sorry to be telling it."

"But," I said. "This is why you called. To tell me how Ed died. And…"

"I thought you deserved a heads up."

"You wanted to warn me that Virgil, or whoever did that to Ed, was deliberate, and vicious, and might well do it again."

He said, "I fear that's true."

It was my turn for the long pause.

"Lawrence, you know a lot about me. But I haven't asked… do you have kids, a family?"

"My wife and I are no longer together. Hailey, who is 15, is with her mother. I don't see her as often as I'd like, with this job."

"I'm sorry, Lawrence, it's…" I began.

"Tom, take your daughter straight home, and stay safe. My number is now in your phone. You can call any time."

36

"Almost there," Hope's text read. "Train on schedule."

"I'm already here," I texted back.

I clicked on the reading lamp to supplement the ambient glow of the parking lot lights.

I felt an urgency to see where Doug's story would go, even though I feared… dreaded I already knew.

Monday, September 25, 1989

During lunch after church yesterday, Attie announced she'd arranged to use one of her vacation days to take today off. This from a woman who up to now hadn't missed a workday in the current decade, or the previous one.

"Lila and I have conspired to take Dido on a shopping expedition. Her wardrobe is in desperate need of an upgrade. Dido, of course, not Lila. We'll go over the border to the Walden Galleria, on the outskirts of Buffalo. You may recall it being in the same area as the airport."

This turned out to be fortuitous, as it meant Dido would be nowhere near Saint Mungo's tonight. Attie and Lila could not have plotted a better night to keep Dido away from Stephen.

Monday is the traditional day off for Saint Mungo's ministers. There are no regular meetings scheduled. In a normal week, it is when I get the most done around the church.

It did not surprise me to find Stephen holed up in his office. Over the past months he'd had less and less reason to be at home. This was something I could understand.

I'd just done my rounds and had turned the lock on the outside door at the tower entrance. Long gone were the days we could leave the building open. Even a church on Lakeshore Drive, in the increasingly upscale Bronte area, was vulnerable. You never knew who might wander in, and this old building has many places a body could hide.

I could clearly hear Steven's angry voice, even from where I stood in the Bell Tower foyer. I pushed my broom along the corridor, and as I came closer, I made out heavy thumps through the thick wood of his office door. I worried he had someone in there with him and felt immediate relief that at least this time, it wasn't my niece. Before she left in the morning, Attie said they would "take their supper in Cheektowaga" before driving back.

Of late it had been a common occurrence to find Stephen… it was hard in these moments to think of him as Reverend Peretz, drunk to the point of incoherence. He'd never acted out physically. I did not want to believe he'd be a danger to himself or anyone else. I did harbor deep concerns his actions towards Dido were both selfish and destructive.

The office door was locked. Stephen was on the other side of that dark oak. Another loud thump. A crash?

I heard him call out, "What has she done to me? Why would she…"

I used my master key and announced myself as I entered.

"It's Doug, Reverend Stephen. Do you need anything?"

A white marble bookend carved in the shape of praying hands caromed off the door frame just inches from my head and landed with a sharp crack on the hardwood floor. Steven's aim was frighteningly good for a man in his state.

For a moment I stared at the fresh gash in the dark oak and wondered if I could match the stain and varnish for a quick repair, or whether I'd have to replace the trim. This strange reverie was interrupted by the crashing arrival of the second set of praying hands, which gouged an even deeper wound in the wood, just above the earlier laceration.

I looked at Stephen, behind his desk. He turned back to the built-in shelves, grunted, and pawed at their contents. He seemed to be looking for something else to throw. He sent hardbound books flying and tumbling to the floor.

"Reverend Stephen, are you okay?"

It seemed a ridiculous question, even as it came out of my mouth.

"Leave me alone," he screamed. "Everyone should just leave me... like she did! Leave me the hell..."

Stephen pivoted to face me. He was red in the face and sweating profusely. There was a wildness in his eyes. The front of his black clerical shirt was blotchy with perspiration. He was panting to catch his breath.

He looked at me through his tears, and asked, "Why can't you all just leave me alone?"

Before I could think of a reply, he turned back to the built-in shelves. His right arm stretched up towards a high shelf. Just beyond his reach sat his communion chalice. The engraved silver goblet had been an ordination gift from his home church. I doubt he knew how often I had dusted and polished it.

Stephen rolled his desk chair close and raised his leg to step up on it. I could see he meant to gain height enough to grab the cup. I stepped towards him, filled with trepidation.

"Steven! No! Let me help you..."

It happened faster than I can describe here.

The chair rolled out from under him as he tried to plant his foot on the cushioned seat. Before I could get there, Stephen lost his balance, and fell backward.

There was a loud smack, and a snapping sound, as the back of his head caught the corner of his desk. Stephen crumpled to the floor.

I stepped over books and broken glass, and a spilt bottle of Absolut Vodka, to find that Steven's breathing had stopped. My nose told me his bowels had released.

Long dormant army first aid training took over. I leaned in close and pressed my fingers to find his carotid artery. There was no pulse that I could find, and his head lolled over at an unnatural angle.

He was dead.

I'd liked Stephen well enough in the beginning, but his actions towards Dido had cost him my respect. As much as Attie's obsession with appearances baffled me, and grated on me, I could see her point that the breakdown of his marriage to Wendy had taken a certain toll on the congregation.

People were divided in their loyalties. Some seemed to have stopped coming on Sundays, presumably to avoid the tense atmosphere. As Attie says, people are talking and that's never good."

What would happen if he was found this way?

There had been nothing I could do to help the situation while he was alive.

But now that he was dead…

My crew of students had finished clearing out the old boiler room and a wall had been built over the opening for the old coal store.

The contractor was ready to seal over the outside access to the coal chute. They'd fill it in this week, ahead of repaving the lot on that side of the building.

In the old days, when the coal chute doors were opened, the coal truck would dump its load and gravity pulled it down the ramp and into the coal store.

I wrapped the body in three layers of my heaviest plastic drop sheet, sealing each layer with duct tape. I wheeled the result outside on the hand truck I use to move stacks of chairs around the fellowship hall.

There was some delicacy in lifting the wrapped body over the lip of steel frame around the coal chute access. The last thing I wanted was to tear open the makeshift shroud.

Once I got the whole of it over the sharp edge, the plastic cocoon slid with ease down the ramp, and settled at the bottom.

During the liberation of Holland we'd come across mass graves. We were told the Nazis buried people alive and used quicklime to limit the smell of decay. Would crushed limestone have the same effect? I shoveled until my arms and back protested and trusted the contractor would finish the job.

Not a proper burial. A better man than I would have said a few words to send Stephen Peretz on his way. I confess that at the time, my only petition to God was that no one venture into the Saint

Mungo's parking lot before I completed my grisly task.

I do pray, now, that Steven's soul is at peace, even if his remains, and his memory deserved more.

I worked late into the night to restore order to the pastor's office. I spot-cleaned the Persian carpet. I opened the small window on the east wall to air out the room. I poured what remained of the vodka down the drain, and added the bottle, and the silver foil gift box it came in, to my bag of recyclables. I noticed it was not Stephen's usual brand. I am not a drinker, but it looked like one of the high-end spirits Ralph used to keep in the cabinet in his study. While wiping down his desk with bleach, to eliminate any traces of his blood, I came upon his wallet and keys. I wrapped them in plastic and dropped the bag, and a few more shovels of loose gravel into the dark hole.

I heard warning bells. The VIA train had pulled in at the station.

37

"Hope!" I called out, as I picked up my pace to move against the tide of passengers exiting the VIA rail station.

I saw her blonde hair before anything else, flowing out from under a red and white Team Canada toque my mother gave her in August for her move back to Atlanta.

Hope smiled and waved. She was walking with a woman in a bright red knee length parka, accompanied by a service dog.

I broke into a sweat in the heat of the crowded station. It may have been from the effort of walking fast without limping or grimacing at the pinprick twinges of pain in both knees.

Stepping closer I felt warmth on my face and reminded myself not to say Dad things like 'you've grown so much' even though she did now seem almost as tall as me. Maybe it was the winter boots.

Hope was layered for warmth in a grey hoodie with Emory University lettered in blue, a down-filled vest, and the faded and torn jean jacket she'd inherited from Carrie. Mittens matching her Olympic toque hung out of a pocket, waving maple leaf emblems like small flags. The only Canadian in her residence and one of only a handful in her year.

She shrugged off her battered maroon McMaster backpack, also an heirloom from her mother, and stretched her arms wide for a hug.

"Hope…" was all I could manage.

She whispered, "Dad, are you okay?"

"Hope. I'm… it's good to see you."

We broke the embrace and Hope angled towards the person beside her. The woman in the red parka looked to be in her mid-forties. Her long ginger hair was wildly curly. She wore a wide woolen scarf over her shoulders, woven in blue and green with thin bright stripes.

"Dad, this is Susan. We rode together on the train from Windsor. This is her service dog, Norm. But leave him alone, he's working."

Norm looked a lot like Zeke. A large German shepherd, with dark brown and black fur. The fabric panels of his harness were the same tartan as Susan's scarf.

"I… yes, I know about that, Hope. Nice to meet you, Susan."

Susan smiled and held out a hand.

Norm's eyes followed my hand as I reached for Susan's.

"We're good Norm," Susan assured her dog. "He's with Hope."

"Susan, I'm Tom. Hope's dad. We'd offer you a ride, but I don't think Norm would fit in our little car."

"No worries, Tom. My hotel will send a shuttle."

"Can we help you find your driver?"

"Are you kidding? I'm easy to spot in my fire engine coat and with Norm here."

"Good to meet you Susan," I said, as Hope hugged her goodbye.

I felt some regret at parting from my daughter's new friend. Her presence helped break the tension, or at least offered distraction.

"You too, Tom," Susan said.

I led Hope out the station doors and down the ramp to the parking lot. Chemical blue de-icing crystals crunched under our feet.

Hope stepped over to walk beside me.

She said, "Dad, you're limping."

"I'm fine," I said. "Tell me about Susan."

"Dad!" Hope packed a lot in that one strong syllable. Her breath fogged in the cold air. She pulled her mittens on and made boxer's fists.

I pointed towards the car.

"We're over this way."

Hope halted in mid-step and looked me up and down. I saw her questions forming and headed them off with my own.

"What brings Susan to Oakville?"

"She's a consultant in quality assurance, whatever that is," Hope said. "She came over from Detroit like I did. She'll be working at the Ford plant during the holiday slowdown. She's from Halifax, actually Dartmouth."

At the car, I struggled to pop the back hatch.

"Dad, let me try."

Hope made a show of examining the deep dent, and the cracked paint before she worked the latch release. There was a disturbing and loud creak as she raised the hatch door. She dropped her backpack in the trunk beside the broken shell of the driver's side mirror.

She said, "The car's a little…"

I cut her off.

"Sounds like you and Susan had a good chat on the train."

"She has to work the holiday weekend and doesn't know anyone here, so I invited her for Easter dinner at Mama Jessie's," Hope said. "I already texted Gwen. She says it's no problem, there'll be lots of food. They've booked the common room at the complex, and Mama Jessie will save us places at the big table."

Hope raised an eyebrow.

"Gwen says they can also save a seat for your new friend."

I opened the passenger side door, grateful didn't squeal in protest, and made my way to the driver's side. I had to leverage my weight into two hard tugs to get my door open.

The little car rocked and creaked as I sat.

I started the Suzuki's engine to get the heat going and yanked hard on my door handle. There was a disconcerting clunk from inside the door as I yanked it shut.

Hope looked at me with Carrie's deep brown eyes. "Dad?"

I was pleased Hope made it home and proud of the way she'd befriended the traveler. I was also terrified she was in danger. That we both were. Someone used their truck to kill Ed. Lawrence and the Halton Region Police had not found Virgil. The metal of our little car seemed paper thin.

I met my daughter's gaze, and said, "So Susan, and her dog... they both seem nice."

Hope said, "Is this a new thing? I didn't realize you were so into dogs."

"So, Gwen told you about..."

"She said you'd have lots to tell me and wouldn't know where to start."

"She's not wrong," I said. "What do you want to hear about first?"

"The good stuff. The dog lady."

As we passed the Home Depot on Cross Avenue, I stole a glance in the rear-view mirror, hoping Hope wouldn't notice. I saw no vehicles behind us.

"The dog lady. That's what Gwen calls her. Her name is Annika. She studied nursing at Mac with Mom. She volunteers with Halton Search and Rescue, with Zeke. He's her..."

"Her dog. I got that part. Tell me the rest."

Cross Avenue makes a gradual descent as it follows the curve of Sixteen Mile Creek and then climbs steeply uphill alongside Hogs Back Park, which on this wintry night looked like a mound of frosting.

"Your grandmother told me there used to be a tunnel right through this hill. Can you believe that? They re-directed an underground stream to power the grist mill on the other side. Ingenious."

"Dad."

"In the woods behind the hill, there's an old pioneer cemetery where some of Oakville's founders are buried."

"That's... just so interesting, Dad."

"Sorry..." I said. "It's not easy talking about this."

"So you'd rather tell me about tunnels that aren't there anymore, and really old dead people we don't know? Seriously? I'm good with you seeing someone, Dad. Really. It's probably time."

We climbed towards the intersection at the top of the hill. I let the steep grade slow us, even though we had the green. I signaled our right turn and took a careful look. More than once I'd seen a big truck barrel through here.

"We both have new friends with dogs," I said. "Maybe we were wrong in not having pets when you were growing up. Pets other than Bluey, your betta fish. Poor little guy died the first week we had him."

"Dad."

"Mom always said with both of us working and you at daycare and then school that none of us were home enough for a pet."

"Tell me about Annika, Dad."

"She's... I feel comfortable with her."

"So will you bring her to Mama Jessie's for Easter?" Hope asked with a wicked grin. "You know they'll all want to meet her."

I could just see it. The Bailey clan would converge on the common room with their casseroles and knowing looks.

Gwen's mother and all the aunties would welcome Annika with literal open arms and fuss over her. The whole time they'd be checking her out.

I said, "That could be a lot. Especially this soon."

"Gwen says you like her."

Gwen's also been using me as a human shield, to ward off questions about why she left Richard, so there's that.

I pushed down on the gas and wheeled the car right, heading uphill on Speers Road.

I thought about the awkward but warm embrace the other night at Annika's door.

"We're starting to get to know each other."

"Will I like her?"

"I think you will…She's not like your mom. They are very different people."

"I never thought you'd try to replace Mom," Hope said. "That's not you."

"It's come at a weird time. The stuff at the church, and all at this time of year."

I took a peek in the mirror, still worried about being followed.

"I know. Wish I could've been home sooner."

"The weather's on the list…"

"Of things we don't control. I know. But things seem more out of control than normal."

"People, and their choices…"

"Are also on the list. Thanks, Philosophy Dad. I could have used your help last week."

"How do you think you did on the exam?

"If the prof does the marking, I'll be fine. She gets me. If it's the T.A., not so much."

"Hope… What did you do?"

"He kept saying religious faith creates a distracting bias. I pointed out that zealous atheism kind of does the same, and then told him I'd pray for him."

I heard the sharp edge of her sarcasm.

"Did he get you were kidding?"

"Hard to know. It was during an online tutorial."

"You didn't use any of those web things? Happy face emojis?

"Do they have one for you're an intellectual poser, but I have to make nice?"

I said, "Hope Jean, you don't do yourself any favours. You have to think…"

Hope pulled off her mitts.

"You're one to talk. You look like you were in a bar fight after you drove Mom's car in a demolition derby."

"Hope."

"Auntie Gwen said you could've died."

I said, "How much did she tell you?"

"That Michael carried you out as the manse blew up, but not before you both breathed in toxic smoke. And that some crazy ran you off the road the same night."

"Gwen always adds drama. She was pretty upset when I told her."

"At least she got to hear about it. When did you plan to tell me?"

"I didn't want to upset you. Make a bigger deal than it was."

Hope gripped her hands together tight.

"Really, Dad? I saw photos of blown out windows and police tape. The Oakville Beaver website said two people were taken away by ambulance. Was that you and Michael?"

I heard the rumbling exhaust of a jacked-up Honda in the lane next to us.

I hoped she didn't see me shudder or tighten my grip on the steering wheel.

I breathed deep and formed my words with care.

"They checked us out. We were… we are fine. I'm fine."

"I see the way you're walking. You're not fine."

"I scraped my knees."

"And that spot on your head?"

"A few little staples to close a cut. I don't even go back to get them out."

I saw a pickup with a plow blade scraping the parking lot in front of Food Basics. Was it a black truck?

"Why were you and Michael at the manse in the first place?"

"The council wanted us to look around. We were trying to get a line on Ed Wilder."

"You're supposed to be their minister, not some amateur detective."

"Things got a little complicated. But we're okay."

It wasn't easy to tell one dark paint colour from

another in the dim light.

Hope said, "Complicated? Do you hear yourself?"

"Do you hear yourself?" I said, "It's like you want to be the parent now."

"No, Dad, I just want to have a parent. I don't want to lose you, too."

"I know. Which is why I didn't want to worry you. Especially not now, not this week."

As we turned left, I peered at the truck pushing snow in the grocery store lot and decided it was dark blue.

"Auntie Gwen was right. You really could've died. You can't just decide… other people need to have a say."

I said, "Is this still about the manse and the car?"

"Yes… No… Yes… It's all the same. You playing cops and robbers with your friend Michael is just like…"

"Hope?"

"I need you to be careful, Dad."

We were silent as we passed the closed shops on Kerr Street. I turned right on Rebecca.

Hope said, "Can I turn down the heat?"

"Sure," I said. "That'd be good."

If she caught the double meaning, Hope wasn't ready to smile at it. We were past the Oakville YMCA, and Saint Paul's Church before either of us spoke again.

Hope pulled off the Olympic toque and pushed her blonde hair back behind her ears.

"The poor man in the wall… who was he?"

"A former Saint Mungo's minister. Reverend Stephen Peretz. He disappeared without a trace almost 30 years ago."

"That's weird. What do you think happened?"

"It's long and complicated," Tom said, "but I think it was murder."

As I said it, it felt true.

"By anybody we know? Was it the same person who killed Reverend Ed?"

"You know about that?"

"Gwen said you and Annika found him. What's going on? Why is someone killing ministers?"

I braked for a transit bus pulling out from the South Oakville Centre. Quick check of the rear-view mirror. Nothing close, but was that a truck a few blocks back?

"Zeke... her search dog, led us to his body," I said. "The police believe Ed's remains had been there since Saturday night."

We followed the transit bus through the intersection with Third Line. I turned down the Suzuki's heater fan.

"Don't like the diesel fumes," I said.

The truth was I wanted to listen for the rumble of another exhaust.

The bus gained speed, and we were behind it until Saint Dominic's School. I took the left and signaled for the quick right on to our street. Home was a half block away, down this dead-end.

"Dad."

"Hope."

"You could have said no."

"Said no? To checking out the manse? Yes, I could have... I should have."

"No, not that, although yes, you should have," Hope said. "I mean you should have said no to Mom. You should have made her take the treatment the second time."

"That wasn't my call. That's not how we are... we were... with each other."

I pushed in the clutch and geared down. I've always thought standard was better for winter driving. I get a better feel for the road, if not control.

"You should have told her you needed... that I needed her to live."

"She knew we would be okay."

"But we're not okay... I'm not okay! She should have fought harder. You should have..."

This was not the time to share my father's wisdom about "should'ves".

I said, "She did fight. She fought so hard. She took everything the doctors threw at her."

"But then Mom… died."

"Sweetie, Mom did not just die. She lived. She fought and beat the tumor, sent it running."

Snow was piled high in the front yards on both sides of our street. It had been plowed and sanded since I left for the train station.

"And then it came back."

"Yes. It came back."

"And she didn't fight it."

"She'd learned something."

I slowed for the turn.

"Yes, she learned that dying is not the worst thing," Hope said. "She told me that. You told me that. She decided she wasn't going through the surgery again."

"There's more."

The plow had left a substantial windrow. I hoped we could push through the tall skid of snowy chunks across the driveway.

"More what?"

I worked the signal lever and turned left into the driveway. It was then I heard the familiar low growl.

Bright headlights appeared in the rear-view mirror. They filled our frail little car with light as the truck grew closer.

"More what Dad?

I said, "She learned there's more to everything than just life and death. That's what she was showing me, before…

38

I pushed down my panic and pressed down harder on the gas. The car's tiny engine howled. It was no good. The Suzuki's front end had mired in the windrow of ice and frozen snow.

I said, "Hope, I need you to get out."

The black truck stopped just short of the little car. I heard the crunch of gears, then the furious roar of the big engine as the truck backed away.

"Now, Hope. Get out!"

"Daddy, what's happening?"

"I think he's going to ram us. You need to get out, now Hope!"

I pulled up on the handle and tried to shoulder my door open. It did not budge.

The rumble from the black truck grew louder. I heard its transmission grind as the driver threw it in to forward gear.

I said, "Go, now!"

"What about you? I can't leave you!"

"Go, go!" I yelled. "Get to the house and call 911!"

Hope tumbled out, leaving her car door hanging open, and ran towards the house.

I stretched across to the passenger side to pull the lever to flatten the seat back. I did the same with my own. I snaked my body to avoid the shift-stick on the center console.

I was on my side, belly towards the shifter. The seat cushions were cold and hard. I clawed at the passenger seat with the tips of my fingers to pull myself toward the open doorway.

I heard Hope's voice, but the words were overwhelmed by the roar of the truck engine and the rude thrum of its exhaust. I felt and heard a loud slam and saw the driver's side collapse in towards me.

The force threw me upwards, then I felt the shifter jab my stomach as I landed hard on the front seats.

There were bangs like pistol shots as airbags exploded from the steering wheel and passenger side dashboard. A blizzard of fine white powder clouded the cabin.

My chest heaved but I couldn't hear myself cough.

My eyes were smeared with dust and tears.

I inhaled something thick that was not meant for me to breathe. My lungs burned, like I was back in the smoke-filled house.

I felt movement. The black truck nudged the Suzuki sideways across my icy driveway. I was sure it was going to push the crumpled car into the trunk of the big maple on the edge of my neighbour's yard.

Hope's door still hung open. Frigid air whooshed in from her side and blew past me and out the broken glass on my side. Deflating airbags billowed in the chill wind, and sharp cold chunks of snow flew at my face.

I was jolted hard as the edge of the passenger door smacked the trunk of the big maple. The force bent the door backwards towards me, until it snapped off the hinges and disappeared under the car.

The truck roared even louder and pushed my car until the frame crunched against the bark of the tree.

Something heavy clamped down on my left heel, trapping my foot. My ankle twisted in a very wrong way. My leg was wet, and cold. Try as I might, I could not pull my foot free. The pain was dizzying, until my leg went numb. The cabin spun. With both hands, I gripped the cushion of the passenger seat until the sickening whirl stopped. The seat was coated with white dust, like fresh snow.

I lay on my side across the front seats of what was left of Carrie's car, which I guessed was boxed between the truck's front bumper and my neighbour's tree. Through the loose flutter of billowing airbags I saw flashing red and blue light. I prayed that meant Hope had called for help. I prayed she was safe in the house.

I struggled to keep my eyes open, and to hear. My ears were ringing, my head buzzing.

There was the wail of a siren and the screech and slide of a speeding vehicle coming to a sudden stop.

Tired. I tried to speak, to yell.

"Hope!"

The word choked in my throat. Desperate to know she was safe, I tried again.

"Hope!"

She would not hear me. I barely heard myself.

I coughed and choked and struggled to catch my breath. I was so cold.

The rumble of the truck's exhaust halted. A brief strange quiet was pierced by a bullhorn squawk, then an amplified voice that I thought was Michael Powers.

"Virgil Daniels, get your hands on that steering wheel."

"I had to keep him away from my Kat. Auntie Attie warned me you can't trust these ministers!"

"Virgil!" Michael's gruff voice repeated. "Hands now! I need to see them!"

"I'm not the one you need to worry about! It's him!"

"Hope! Michael!"

I tried to call out, before it all went silent and dark.

39

"Woman has a lot of nerve, inviting us to another bridal shower."

"You're not wrong. And does she think a drug rep is a trade up from the last guy?"

The women's voices were loud, even through a door I knew was closed because I saw a thin strip of light at the bottom.

If it wasn't for that faint light, and the small LCD readout on the IV machine, I wouldn't have known where this dark room might be. Where I might be.

"A shower on Easter weekend? Seriously?"

"She's our boss. You going to risk not showing your face..."

They think all the patients are asleep. It must be late. I turned my left wrist, but my watch was gone. That's where they taped the IV tube that snaked up my arm.

The sound of the nurses' voices as they passed in the hallway was a great comfort. The fact they were gossiping told me I wasn't on 4 South, in one of the single rooms they set aside on a quiet hall for the dying.

My fingers brushed against the cable with the call button. I could buzz and ask for something. Water, or a pill to help get me back to sleep. Then I could ask them the time.

There was another way.

I've spent a lot of time visiting people in rooms like this one. As my eyes adjusted, I strained my head to look around.

I caught a glimpse of the service panel on the headboard behind me and to the left. Gas nozzles, indicator lights. Outlets to power monitors, and the IV pump.

If I could look close at the screen on the IV machine.

If my vision would clear.

It was better with one eye closed. Maybe I hit my head.

4:43 a.m. Okay. "So day what was it?"

I saw no other beds. Sensed no other bodies. Heard no other breathing. I wondered how I rated a private room, on the church's meagre health plan.

Carrie only got a private room the week before we moved her into hospice.

I opened both my eyes fully. I shifted in the bed. My arms lay loose at my sides, and my elbows rubbed the safety rails. Why were the rails up?

The hall was quiet again. I heard my own breathing, the hushed descent of air from a ceiling vent, and the quiet tick of the IV.

I looked over at the fat bag of saline solution hanging on the stand, and the smaller bag below it. What were they dripping into me?

On my first day as a student minister at Saint Mungo's, Paul Bennett brought me along for a hospital call. Driving over he told me about Donny, the palliative patient he wanted me to meet.

Before the onset of Lou Gehrig's disease, Donny had been a lanky and nimble outfielder on the church softball team.

"He had great hands," Paul said. "Caught anything hit his way and threw to the infield with deadly accuracy. Now he can't lift a finger, but his mind is all there. You'll see that in his eyes."

I could picture Donny laying in that hospital bed. His side rails had been up, and with the white plastic head and footboards, he'd looked boxed in.

Paul said, "He lays there with essentially no muscle control, so now it's part of the regimen to arrange his hands. The way the nurses rests them on his belly, one flat over the other, you'd think Donny was already dead and laid out for viewing."

My younger self had shivered at the image.

"Paul why would you say that?"

"How would it feel, Tom," Paul asked, "to have your unresponsive limbs posed for you?"

"Like I was already dead."

Now I was laid out in a bed like Donny's. Like Carrie's.

After we left Donny's room, we'd passed an empty bed parked in the hallway. Paul traced his finger along the brand name and told me it was a company that also made caskets.

The mattress felt thin and stiff against my aching back and bruised buttocks. Shifting in a fruitless search for comfort, I noticed my left foot and calf were bound up in a heavy cast that came up to my knee.

The quiet dark closed in around me. My mind drifted from beds and caskets to the above ground mausoleums Carrie and I saw on our tour of old cemeteries in New Orleans. The guide from the bus had pointed to a bright white pyramid that claimed the space of two regular crypts.

"That's the one Nicolas Cage had built. He's not in there yet, far as we know. But it's here waiting for him."

Most of the other crypts were the shape and size of backyard garden sheds, except they were made from brick smoothed over with white plaster.

This hospital bed suspended me above the floor at about the same height a casket would rest in one of those Louisiana crypts. They built them up that way to keep the bones of their loved ones safe above the flood waters.

I was high enough above Oakville. Probably a few floors above ground level.

What was in that intravenous drip? Why didn't it help with sleep?

Carrie learned a relaxation technique at a retreat before the tumour came back.

"Breathe in through your nose on a count of four," Carrie said. "Hold it for four, then exhale on the same four count, pause and repeat 17 times."

I said, "Something special about 17?"

"I don't know," she'd smiled. "I always drift off before I

get there."

I was aware of breathing through seven cycles before I slipped into the misty swamp of a dream.

I sat across from Carrie in a booth at the Piano Box, a bistro we'd found off Magazine Street, in the Lower Garden District. They had a concert recording of Go to the Mardi Gras playing in the background. Professor Longhair.

I smelled coffee laced with chicory, and Cajun spices wafting out from the kitchen. They were frying catfish.

I said, "Do you remember Bluey?"

"Hope's betta fish? You were so broken up when it died," Carrie said. "We never even knew if it was a boy or a girl."

I said, "I thought we'd be having the 'everything and everybody dies' conversation, and I didn't think she was ready."

We'd gone to New Orleans for our honeymoon, but in this dream, Carrie sported a sea-blue bandana over her post-chemo peach-fuzz baldness. The bandana was printed with little creatures that made me think of goldfish crackers.

Carrie said, "I don't think her being ready was the problem, sweetie."

I raised a waterglass to my mouth. It was spotted with condensation that left my palm wet and cool.

"It would have been a kind of ending," I said.

"An ending?"

"Do you remember? We talked about this."

Carrie said, "The bubble?"

"Yes," I said. "I think that before Hope knew, she lived in a beautiful bubble. There was just now. It felt like every moment with her was forever. No worries about what came before or what would need to happen next."

Our booth and most of the restaurant's furnishings had been hand-crafted from panels salvaged from old pianos. We loved this repurposing of the richly stained and varnished wood.

Carrie said, "Like she lived outside of time?"

"More like, she was in the only time that mattered."

In the dream, I closed my eyes. When I opened them again, the blue bandana was gone. Carrie's thick brown hair was back, shining and luxuriant as it had been the first time I saw her, singing a solo during an Advent service at Saint Mungo's.

"Tom," she asked, "Do you think that's the way it was for her?"

I said "I don't know. I hope so."

"Your bubble sounds like a dream," Carrie said. "It's a beautiful thought. A timeless, always kind of place."

"Until she learned the truth, that we don't actually live that way."

Carrie said, "No we don't live that way. Time does pass, and people die. But…"

Our server approached, clearing his throat.

"Ya'll had a chance to look at the drinks menu? What's your poison?"

I was in the kitchen in the old house, before Mom got us out.

My father was across the table in his jeans and faded Oakville Rangers T-shirt. His thick black hair was combed flat back, still wet from his after-work shower. This must have been when I was in grade 9. JP was in grade 7, and probably hiding in his room until Mom called him for supper.

"Amateur drunks still think it matters what brand they pour down their throats. They are creatures of habit."

My father's voice was always too loud.

When mom was late getting home from the school, it was my job to sit with him until she got his supper on the table. The kitchen always felt too small when dad was there.

The best thing in that room was a Norval Morrisseau print above the coat hooks at the back door. One of his Woodland paintings. Outlined in black, on a bold crimson background, a mother loon carried her little ones on her back. Mother loon could also have been a fish. She could choose to either fly away or swim. It was the last thing my mother saw before leaving the house each morning.

My father drained his beer can as he crunched it in his hand. He tossed it behind him, casually arcing it towards the kitchen sink.

My mom stood over the stove, giving studied attention to what hissed and sputtered in her frying pan. It smelled like onions and ground beef. She didn't look up. Not even when the crumpled can landed at her feet.

I jumped out of the kitchen chair and went to the refrigerator without being told. I brought him the next beer, then knelt to pick up the crushed empty.

"Good boy. Knew you were good for something."

My mother raised her head at that. "Frank!"

For a few breaths, all I could hear was meat sizzling. Silence was never a good thing in that house.

My father forced a laugh, and said, "Jeanie, I'm kidding. He did good."

He knew my mother hated when he called her that. I needed to get him back on his story. Whatever he was talking about.

I asked, "What were you saying about creatures of habit?"

"Amateurs have a favourite brand. Before they get to the stage they'll drink anything, they tell themselves they drink to relax, savouring the rich flavour."

I knew better than to ask my father what he told himself.

"Never mind that after the first drink you can't taste the difference between top shelf and bargain bin. Serious drinkers don't trouble themselves over the brand. The poison is the poison."

He gripped his beer can in a hand large enough to hide the label. Dark grease lined his knuckles even though he always washed up after work.

"Jeanie, we're wasting away here."

My father's hands never came clean. Even when he moved up to line supervisor at the Ford plant, I could see him wringing his hands under the running stream of water at the kitchen sink, scrubbing them with a soapy sea sponge.

The server at The Piano Box said, "Catfish are bottom feeders, scrounging their food in the murky silt. But they cook up great."

Most of the wood panels in the piano restaurant were polished to a high gloss, like the top of the communion table at Saint Mungo's. Others were scarred with water damage. The booth behind Carrie's head was pockmarked with what I was sure were bullet holes.

Then I was one of Norval Morrisseau's transforming loon fish swimming in dark waters. I watched black ooze drip out of the drill holes in the basement wall at the church. The coal bin was a crypt for Stephen Peretz. He was in that dark box for so many years.

I stopped swimming, and images floated over me, like pages torn from a book, and tossed in a watery ditch.

Doug Beacham leaning over his worktable scratching questions and answers in a book, then hiding all his thoughts in a tin box.

Virgil's loud black truck ramming into Carrie's little car. Boxing me in.

Brad Kazinski's blank white face staring at me from behind the black desk in his armored box of an office, cold as a tomb.

Stephen Peretz raging in his office. Throwing statuary and books at Doug.

Attie Beacham waving her cheque book like a witch's wand. The pastor's office transformed into a parlour but still reeking of swamp water.

Ed Wilder falling. I hear his skull smack the edge of a coffee table shaped like a coffin.

Cold dark water seeping out of the wall.

There's a shiny gift box on the carpeted floor of Stephen's office. I ran my fingers along the embossed typeface. Absolut. Who'd give him a bottle of high-end vodka?

The dirty slurry of water over checkerboard tiles, and the splash as the shrouded body tumbles out of the wall.

The rolled-up blueprint of Kazinski's plan to tear down the church and build a shiny new box behind the façade of the bell tower.

Ed Wilder's catalogue-perfect house filling with thick dark smoke.

A zip-lock bag bursting with ugly pills and a cash-stuffed envelope in the mantle hidey hole.

A spritely little girl dancing around a grave. Her shiny shoes slip on grass green carpet that glints with icy diamonds.

I float above like a low-flying drone and watch myself reach under the plastic tarp for a handful of dark earth.

I close my hand tight like I'm crushing a can, to break up frozen soil.

My hands are not as strong as my father's, but they wash clean.

Paul Bennett taught me to use real the thing if I could, to make the cross on the casket before it was lowered.

"Sometimes you'll get your hands dirty," Paul said.

Since then, I've committed so many to the ground. Earth to earth. Humans formed of clay, returned to its depths.

Ed hadn't stayed buried. Neither had Stephen.

Doug must have been strong in those days, to heft his body, wrapped in its plastic shroud. Human clay in a big zip-lock bag.

I watched my father toss 50-pound bags of cat litter in the trunk of his Ford Taurus like they were couch cushions. The Taurus was a retired cop car bought on the cheap.

My father said, "The bags weigh down the rear end, and if we get stuck, I throw it down between the tires and the ice and snow. Cat litter is absorbent clay."

The last image of my dream was Ed Wilder soiled and wet under parking lot snow.

40

I said, "Do you remember those funky bandanas you bought when Mom was getting out of the hospital?"

The blinds were open, allowing sunlight to brighten the hospital room. The day outside looked cold and clear.

Hope stood near my bed. She read the label on the IV bag.

"What are they giving you Dad?"

"I wondered that too. I dreamed about Mom last night. She was wearing the blue bandana with the little fishes on it. We were getting lunch at this little place in New Orleans."

"Dad, are you okay? Why is there a security guard outside your door?"

"There is? I didn't know. Ask Michael."

Hope wore her navy blue down vest over her Oxford College hoody, and jeans. The same clothes as last night. Her blonde hair was pony-tailed the way she did when she didn't have time to wash it. Did she sleep at all?

She said, "Michael's not here. A tall skinny guy with a badge on his belt is waiting in the hall. Looks like he's been up all night. Said he didn't mind waiting, that I should see you first."

"That sounds like Lawrence… Detective Kitchen. He's a good guy."

"How many cops do you know now?"

Hope dropped into the visitor's chair beside my bed.

"Just him and Michael. But Michael is a friend."

Hope said, "I'm still pissed he took you to play Inspector Gadget at the house that exploded."

"He didn't take me. And don't forget, he helped us last night. At least I think he did. I heard his voice."

"He was there. He got Virgil calmed down and out of his truck, then checked on me in the house. We woke Gwen up. By then there were other cops. And paramedics. And the fire department. They had to crack open the car to get to you out."

"How's the car?"

"Really, Dad? How's the car? You were unconscious when they got you out. Your legs were soaked in blood."

"It was your mom's. She loved that car."

Her deep brown eyes met mine. Like Carrie's. I blinked first.

"Hope. I'm okay. You're okay. We're going to be okay. Take a breath."

"You think I need to calm down? Wait 'til you talk to Auntie Gwen."

"Is she here?"

"She brought me. She stayed upstairs with me all night. There was still a cop car outside the house this morning."

"I'm glad Gwen was there for you."

"She's family. Especially now that Gran is, well, the way she is."

"That detective in the hall... he was one of Gran's students. He thinks a lot of her. Has anyone told her about all of this?"

"No. We talked about it. Gwen said it wasn't a good idea, and she's right."

"Hope, how are you doing? Last night... you must have been terrified."

"I was more scared for you. Michael and Gwen took care of me. She explained about Virgil. He's had a sad life. He and Kat, they lost their mother too."

I looked at my daughter with amazement.

"You're right," I said. "They've had a hard time."

"Can you imagine," Hope asked. "Losing your mom, then being raised by someone like Attie Beacham?"

I had to block out what I'd read in Doug's journal and choose my words carefully.

"She probably did the best she could. She and Doug never had their own kids. Virgil and Kat's mom was her niece. Their real grandmother checked out of their lives after she died."

"Michael told me. I don't get how she could do that. Makes me so grateful for Gran."

"Me too, sweetie."

"There's something Gran told me. I was thinking about it, after watching them cut you out of the car. I need to say it."

I felt my throat tighten.

"Okay."

Hope rose from the visitor's chair and stood close to the bed.

"I was really mad when Mom died. I still am sometimes. Mad at you. Angry at Mom. Just mad."

"I know."

"I told Gran."

"What did she say?"

"She told me how lucky I was. She hugged me tight and said you and Mom raised me to expect good things from life."

"That was your mom… more than me."

"Grandma said that because of Frank… because of your father… the way he was, you grew up always expecting the worst to happen. She said he was kind of an asshole."

I laughed. "She said that?"

"Yeah. It was great. I'd never heard her swear."

"Back then she'd never say anything against him. My dad's an alcoholic. He is… limited."

"Everyone is limited. We're humans. But he hurt Gran. He hurt you, a lot. He hurt Uncle JP."

My daughter made her boxer's fists.

"Something's not right with Frank… my… father. Maybe like things aren't right for Virgil."

"He took it out on the people close to him. Then Gran got you and JP out of there."

"She did."

"But not before you got hurt. She says you grew up

not quite trusting life would be okay, and believing you didn't deserve good things."

I reached for Hope's balled up hand. It unclenched in mine.

"That changed when I met your mom. Then we had you. It was like life was saying 'this can be good, you know.' And it has been. It's not always easy, and it doesn't always go the way we want, but it's good."

I needed my hand back to wipe my eyes. Then I reached out again for Hope. Her hand felt small and warm like her mother's.

"That's what Gran said. She was so happy for you that you could know that."

"That's the way Mom said we needed to raise you. With the idea there is good. That there is love. And that somehow love wins."

"Even when someone you love dies?"

My throat was hoarse.

I said, "The love doesn't die."

"And you believe that, Dad? You believe love is even bigger than pain and death and tragically limited assholes?"

"Yes. I do."

"Then you should live more like you believe it."

"What do you mean?"

Hope tightened her grip, then slipped her hand out from mine. She stepped back from the bed. She clasped her hands then swept both arms open like the host of a game show announcing the big prize.

"For starters you get a new car. It's okay to have new things in your new life."

I smiled. This was about more than a car.

"Maybe you should do the sermon on Easter Sunday."

Hope pointed at the cast on my leg.

"I might have to. You already missed the Good Friday service."

She was right.

"I forgot all about that," I said.

"It's okay, you had a good excuse. Are they letting you out any time soon?"

I said, "I have fractures in my left foot and tibia. They say I'll be in this thing for at least 6 weeks. I probably had a concussion, which is why they kept me overnight. I get out later today."

The lines relaxed around Hope's eyes.

I said, "Why didn't Gwen come in with you?"

"She said we needed time. She's sitting out there with her new friend Annika."

I glanced over at the door.

"Annika's here?"

Hope said, "She's lovely, Dad," and smiled broadly. "I like her."

"I'm glad to hear that," I said. "She's out there with Gwen?"

"Auntie Gwen had some questions for her."

41

"Is the guard out there to keep me in or keep someone out?"

I wondered if Lawrence Kitchen could tell I was only half-joking.

The detective dropped his overcoat on the back of the visitor's chair.

"We don't believe you are in any danger," Lawrence said as he sat down. "We have Virgil Daniels."

The hospital bed's motor hummed when I thumbed a button on the side rail to adjust the mattress angle.

I said, "I heard that from my daughter. So why the security?"

"Inspector Powers pulled strings to get you out of the emergency ward and into your own room. Apparently, you are a valuable witness."

"Witness?"

"Don't question it," Lawrence suggested, with a smile. "You didn't have to sleep in a hallway last night. The guard is hospital protocol."

Lawrence had traded his navy pullover for its wine-coloured twin, but the tan pants and collared dress shirt were the same. He still looked like he should be teaching Macbeth to high school students.

"Where is Michael? I need to thank him for last night."

"He's at an intelligence meeting in Orillia. He said he wishes he'd been 30 seconds faster. He'd been following you. I didn't know that when we spoke last night... before Virgil's attack."

"Following me? I mean... I'm glad he was there, but..."

"He had a gut feeling but didn't want to spook you and Hope if he was wrong."

Lawrence's eyes had dark shadows like he'd been up late marking essays.

"He knew I didn't want a police presence around when Hope came home."

"How is she? Inspector Powers said a friend stayed with her last night."

"She's… good. Actually, very good. My housemate was with her. You probably saw her in the hall."

"She looked formidable. I wouldn't want to cross her."

"No, you wouldn't. Gwen is a force of nature."

"We did keep an eye on your house last night."

"Hope said. I thought you said there's no danger."

Kitchen didn't have to tell me there were other black trucks out there.

He said, "I wanted your daughter to feel safe in her own home. After the tow truck dealt with your car, my team took turns in an unmarked car in your driveway."

"That explains why you look so tired?"

"I was on scene right after Inspector Powers, so I took the first shift. Constable Palmieri, I think your administrator met her at the church, relieved me at 5 a.m. so I could stop at home and clean up."

"Thank her for her kindness. And thank you."

"I'm sorry it came to this."

"What do we do now detective?"

"We? That's an interesting pronoun, Reverend Book."

"I keep thinking you look like an English teacher."

42

"Reverend Tom are you okay? I'm sorry about hurting you, and your car."

"I have fractures in my ankle and foot. I'll mend. My car's another story."

"Are you angry at me?"

Virgil Daniels was 29, but clean shaven, showered and with a fresh hair cut, he looked more like the haunted little kid who used to hover over Kat when I was their student minister.

"I'm not angry, Virgil. But these last few days have been frightening and confusing."

Relief showed in Virgil's face. He looked pale in the bright morning light that shone through the window of my hospital room, which Lawrence Kitchen and I were using for this interview.

I said, "If Hope… if my daughter had been hurt, I'd be angry."

Something like guilt, or remorse, showed in Virgil's deep-set eyes.

I smiled and said, "I'm glad you're here. Would you like to sit?"

Lawrence had asked the security guard to help him shift my bed closer to the window and they'd brought in stacking chairs from the family lounge.

Virgil dropped in the chair closest to me. The grey sweatpants and loose-fitting coral green T-shirt looked like hospital issue. He was thinner than last time I'd seen him.

Earlier, Lawrence had said, "We might get further if we bring him to your room…"

"And he sees me laid out," I said, "with this big cast and

the IV stuck in my arm."

Lawrence now sat in the chair nearest the door. The seat between Lawrence and Virgil was occupied by a woman I'd yet to meet.

Virgil's lawyer had come in with a thin black briefcase under her arm. She wore a grey business suit. Her glasses were over-sized, thick-framed and drew attention to her piercing blue eyes. Her dark brown hair was cut short and carefully styled. She had not spoken.

I said, "Virgil, I'm sorry we haven't talked much since I came back to Saint Mungo's. We don't seem to work the same hours, and there's been a lot going on."

Virgil met my eyes then looked down at his hands. I followed his gaze, and saw he was clasping one hand in the other, in an effort to stop their trembling.

"Your wife died," Virgil said. "I'm sorry your wife died. I remember her from before. She was nice."

"Thank you, Virgil."

Virgil looked up at me, and said, "My mother died. Aunt Attie says things were too much for her. Were things too much for your wife?"

I saw a softening, a hint of kindness in Virgil's face.

"My wife became very ill. She had a brain tumour."

"Aunt Attie says my mother had something wrong in her brain."

"I think that was a different kind of thing. I'm sorry your mother died."

"Me too," Virgil said. "I'm supposed to take care of Kat. That's my job. When we were little, before she… before she died, my mother said I needed to take care of my sister."

"I think you do your best with that."

Lawrence shifted, and his chair scraped the floor.

The detective said, "Virgil, it's important before we go any further, to tell you that Hilda, Mrs. Brecker, is here to serve as your legal counsel. It's her job to make sure you are protected. You have a right to have a lawyer with you when you talk to me."

"You're a police officer," Virgil said. "You were at Reverend Tom's house last night, after I…"

"That's right, Virgil. My name is Lawrence Kitchen. I'm a detective sergeant with the Halton Police."

Hilda scanned the room, icy blues eyes resting first on Lawrence, and then on her client, before she said, "Virgil, you don't have to talk. Anything you say in front of this man could be used against you in court."

Lawrence turned to face the lawyer.

He said, "That's not why we're here. My colleagues and I have been authorized by the Crown to exclude Virgil from prosecution."

"The exclusion was mentioned in the email that came to our office," Hilda said. "I have to note, this is very unusual."

"This is a highly unusual situation. The Office of the Crown Attorney is of the opinion the community would be better served if Virgil were to receive the help he needs, outside of the criminal justice stream."

"And you want something from him," the lawyer said.

I'd been surprised when Lawrence told me Virgil hadn't been arrested.

"We took a different route," the detective had said. "He's actually two floors up, held for psychiatric observation for 72 hours."

I said, "You used a Form 1?"

"You know about those?"

I nodded.

"I did a clinical unit as part of my training, in an ER at a Toronto hospital," I said. "I learned a lot about the Mental Health Act."

Lawrence said, "Michael decided, with the support of my team, to bring him here rather than into police custody. A brief recounting of Virgil's erratic behaviour,and an evaluation of his mental state at admission were enough. The attending physician signed the application for involuntary detention."

"How did Virgil react?"

"I think he actually feels remorse for what he's done," Lawrence said. "He's confused, but I think he appreciates the difference between the psych ward and remand."

"Lawrence, I'm impressed, and grateful. I don't think he'd do well in a jail setting."

"We aren't acting purely out of benevolence, Tom."

Lawrence rose from his chair and stepped towards Virgil and Hilda.

"Virgil," Lawrence said, "I want to be very clear. This woman is here as your lawyer. Your Aunt Attie arranged for her to join us. Ms. Brecker does not work with me. She is here to protect your interests. Listen to her. If she thinks it's better for you to not talk to us, that's okay. Do you understand?"

"I think so." Virgil sniffed and wiped at his nose. "She works for me. She is here to help me."

Lawrence said, "That's right. She is here to help you."

"Okay."

"Virgil," I said, "Lawrence and I wanted to talk with you, because we need to understand some things. Will you help us?"

Virgil looked at Hilda, and asked, "Am I in trouble?"

Hilda came close to smiling.

She said, "Honestly, Virgil, I think you have been in trouble for a while. I will let you know if answering their questions will make things worse."

Lawrence asked, "Are you comfortable with that, Virgil?"

"I think it's okay. What do you want to know?"

"I'll start by asking why you followed Reverend Tom and his daughter Hope last night, and why you rammed their car with your truck."

"I thought he was just like Eddie."

I asked, "Do you mean Reverend Wilder, the other minister at Saint Mungo's?"

"Aunt Attie says you can't trust these ministers with girls. She says bad things happen. They do things to girls."

"But Virgil, "Lawrence said, "Reverend Tom was with his daughter Hope."

"I was driving on Rebecca, on my way to the church, and I saw his car. I could see her blonde hair. I thought it was Kat in his car, and he was taking her to his house."

"But it wasn't your sister, it was my daughter, Hope," I said. "I'd just picked her up at the train station. She was coming home for Easter."

"I didn't know," Virgil said. "Eddie took Kat to his house. She told me it was none of my business. But mom said I had to…"

I said, "You had to take care of your sister."

"I'm sorry I broke your car," Virgil said. "I'm sorry I hurt you. I'm really sorry I scared Hope."

"Thank you, Virgil," I said. "I believe you."

"Virgil," Lawrence said, "Can I ask something else?"

Virgil nodded.

"Why did you think Reverend Tom would be with your sister?"

Virgil said, "The other night when Aunt Attie phoned me. She said she was upstairs, and she could hear Reverend Tom and Kat in the house after everybody else left. She said that's how it starts. She said Reverend Tom needed a warning."

"A warning?"

I asked, "Was it you and your truck that night on Lakeshore Road? That was very frightening."

Virgil said, "I am sorry about that. But I have to keep her safe."

"Safe?"

"I thought you were going to hurt her," Virgil said. "Like the other… like Eddie."

I said, "I'd never do anything to hurt Kat. It's part of my job to care for her and for you, Virgil."

"Aunt Attie says we have to watch ministers. She says we can't really trust them."

I said, "Is that what you think?"

"I thought Eddie was different," Virgil said. "But then I saw them."

I softened my tone.

I said, "What did you see, Virgil? Can you tell us?"

"Eddie turned out to be just like Aunt Attie said. I don't want to talk about that anymore.

"He said he was my friend. He said we were a team. We were going to make things better."

Lawrence said, "What were you going to make better, Virgil?"

"Drugs. Bad drugs. We need to get the bad drugs off the streets, Eddie said."

"I work with people who are trying to do something about that."

"Eddie said that wasn't good enough," Virgil said. "His friend had a way to do it better, faster."

Lawrence said, "What are you talking about, Virgil?"

"Just a minute," Hilda interrupted. "We seem to be moving into new territory. I would need assurance… Mr. Daniels would need assurance, that the arrangement with the Crown applies here."

"That's fair, Ms. Brecker," Lawrence said. "We can leave that line of inquiry for now. I don't want to make you, or Mr. Daniels uncomfortable."

Hilda nodded, and said, "Thank you detective sergeant."

I said, "Can I ask Virgil something?"

"You can ask," the lawyer said. Her eyes were still fierce. "And I will step in if I feel it necessary."

"Virgil," Tom began, "Is that okay with you?"

"Okay."

"I want to ask about the fire at the manse, I mean at Reverend Wilder's house."

Virgil slumped down in the visitor's chair.

I said, "Did you have anything to do with the fire, Virgil? Was that you?"

Hilda snapped opened her briefcase and pulled out a single page. She turned her gaze to Lawrence and spoke with firmness.

"This memo from the Crown Attorney's office indicates you have latitude to exclude my client from criminal charges related to actions allegedly taken against the Reverend Thomas Book. But I'm not sure it's a get out of jail free card."

43

"We brought in a big wheel from the Crown Attorney's Office," Lawrence said. "His coming out to the suburbs on the Easter weekend, and the document he conveyed were enough to reassure Ms. Brecker. She's convinced they're not after Virgil."

I said, "I know nothing about that world but that sounds high level. Is this connected to Michael's new bosses in the Criminal Intelligence Service?"

Lawrence said, "You look a lot better in your own clothes. How are you feeling?"

I smiled.

"Lawrence you could just be honest and tell me you can't talk about it."

"I can't talk about it, Tom. You do look better. How do you feel?"

They'd pulled the IV line and helped me get showered while Lawrence met with Virgil and the lawyers.

An occupational therapist dropped in to give me a lesson on how to use my new cane, which now leaned in the corner near the bathroom.

"It'll be good to get out of here," I said. "I've had a lifetime of beige walls and plastic guard rails, in the last couple of years."

The hospital bed was stripped and recentred in the room. A sports bag Hope and Gwen brought in for me sat atop the bare mattress.

I put a hand on the bedrail for support as I navigated around the two remaining stacked chairs to look out the window.

I said, "My knees were already a mess. The cast will

make walking harder. But I'm grateful. Very aware it could have been much worse."

"Yes," Lawrence agreed, "it could have."

The windowpane was cold to my touch.

I said, "This isn't over."

Lawrence said, "You've been through a lot. I'm grateful for your help with Virgil…"

With a hand on the sill to steady myself, I turned to face Lawrence.

"We're not done," I said. "I'm still in this."

"Tom, these past few days, they'd take a toll on anyone…"

"So should I just lay back down and let your team handle things?"

"What I should say is leave the police work to my team and go home. Be with Hope."

"And…"

Lawrence took a half step back. He raised his open palms like I do when I tell the congregation to stand.

"And what I will say is… it appears to me that despite, or maybe because of these awful events, something is rising in you. Something strong. Something good."

"And?"

"I think you're in this, too."

"You are a very strange police officer."

"And you're like no pastor I've ever met."

"Have you met that many?"

"My ex-wife takes our daughter to the Church of the Sower. It's the one on the edge of Burlington that looks like an outlet mall. They have a large pastoral staff. You seem… cut from a different clerical cloth."

"Is that a good different?"

"The ones I've spoken with seem to have their idea of who I am without actually taking time to know me. I get enough of that when I'm on the job."

I pivoted on my good leg to look out at the snow-covered expanse across the road. There was a frozen marshy pond under that snow. Come spring birds will nest in the wild grasses.

I turned from the window and back to Lawrence.

I said, "What you can you tell me about Virgil?"

"He wasn't dealing," Lawrence said. "He bought the drugs to get them off the street. He stashed the pills at Saint Mungo's until Reverend Wilder could pass them on to Brad Kazinski."

Lawrence flipped a page in his notebook.

"Virgil's actual words were, 'Eddie said we were doing your job for you. Getting that poison off the street.'"

"I need to sit," I said, tugging at the top stacked chair.

Lawrence held the bottom chair. We pulled one from the other and we each took a seat.

I said, "There's a hole in that logic Virgil could drive his big black truck through."

"You sound more and more like a cop, Reverend Book. I doubt Virgil realized what's actually been going on."

"Which is what, exactly?"

"Reverend Wilder passed Virgil the cash, but the project was financed by Brad Kazinski. We've compared currency from the belltower to what you uncovered at the manse. Samples from both carry traces of ink that fluoresces under special light."

I said, "Why would Kazinski mark the bills Virgil used to buy drugs?"

"His payday loan business is used by several criminal organizations to launder their money. A high volume of cash passes through the front door of those places, and the side door as well."

Ella Sayers, Kazinski's office manager had told me as much.

"So..." I said. "Kazinski watches for the marked money."

Lawrence said, "The guys who come in the side door

bring cash from lower on the food chain. Kazinski records where it comes from."

I said, "He can tell who's running the dealers in his neighbourhood by who brings in the marked bills."

Lawrence said, "Our intelligence says Kazinski's family declared the Bronte neighbourhood a no-fly zone. We think the guys selling to Virgil weren't supposed to be there. At least one of them met an untimely end. That car fire at the Lakeshore McDonald's."

I said, "Virgil was a pawn in a plan to draw out the rogue dealers."

"Chess is a good analogy," Lawrence said. "Strategy, tactics, and territory."

"Did Kazinski have direct contact with Virgil?"

Lawrence said. "Limited. Virgil said it all went through Reverend Wilder."

"So, can you use Virgil to connect Kazinski to the drugs?"

Lawrence shook his head.

"That's not going to happen. There's a much bigger picture."

I said, "The thing you can't tell me about."

"There are lots of things I can't talk about," Lawrence said. "We know Kazinski's involved, but we don't have enough. Arresting him would jeopardize the larger operation."

"Do I have anything to worry about? Kazinski seemed to know a lot about Hope."

"Virgil told him you filled in for Ed while you were supposed to be off work, preparing for a holiday with your daughter. I think Kazinski concocted his insinuation from those fragments."

I hobbled toward the cane in the corner.

"Kazinski tossed it at me like a grenade."

"You've heard my assessment of the man."

"He used Ed, and Virgil. Ed used Virgil. That sad young man's been manipulated by almost everybody in his life."

"That's almost saintly sympathy for someone who could have killed you and your daughter."

I tested my weight on the cane. Could I get one with a built-in sword?

I said, "You heard him. Attie aimed him at me like a loaded weapon."

Lawrence nodded.

He said, "I think Virgil had trouble living with all of this, with himself."

"He looks rough even after they cleaned him up," I said. "He's been sampling the goods."

Lawrence said, "His bloodwork isn't back, but we think so. What makes you say that?"

"I worked in an ER, remember? You can almost smell him sweating it out. Did he say how he got caught up in all of this?"

"He says he did it all for Eddie."

I said, "What do you think was going on between them?"

"He's clearly conflicted," Lawrence said. "The closest thing he has to a mother told him not to trust clergy, but then a beguiling male figure befriended him and asked for his help."

I nodded. Lawrence really did look for the story underneath.

"He craved Wilder's approval and took risks to secure it. As you reported, it upset him to discover Ed's relationship with his sister. That's a murky, incestuous mess."

"When you lay it out that way," I said, "do you think he could have killed Ed?"

Lawrence was silent for a moment.

He said, "I told you about the surveillance video we think shows Virgil leaving the church well before your colleague."

"Could he have come back after Kat left and driven the truck that hit Ed?"

"It's possible," Lawrence said. "A prosecutor could sell

that easily."

I said, "But you don't believe that."

Lawrence said, "Virgil told us he was angry at Ed, and he admitted feeling betrayed by them both. But he also said that when he left the church, the only place he could think to go was…"

"The manse," I said. "Which would either have been a very stupid, or incredibly crafty place to hide."

"Virgil does not impress me as crafty. He was there from Saturday night until Tuesday morning, in his words, 'waiting for Eddie.' He slept on the futon in the basement. He feared facing his great-aunt and he was still angry at his sister."

"Kat told me on Monday that Virgil was no longer staying at Attie's."

"My team will check with Reverend Wilder's neighbours, and their security cameras. Virgil had a key to the manse."

Lawrence flipped another page of his notebook.

"Virgil went to the church early Sunday morning, hoping to see Reverend Wilder. While he waited, he cleaned up the mess."

I said, "I've never seen him clean anything."

"Crime scene techs confirm the table was thoroughly sanitized. It bore none of the residual prints and dust they found on other pieces in the parlour. The carpet had been shampooed."

I said, "Who told Virgil to do it?

Lawrence had a question on his face.

Seriously," I said, "he's never been a self-starter. If he was still looking for Ed, and wasn't speaking to Kat, where did he get the idea?"

"Excuse me."

Lawrence pulled out his phone to thumb a text.

"His cell phone," Lawrence said. "If he'd been arrested we'd have gone through it."

"The mention of his phone reminds me of something, but it's just out of reach…"

"You did suffer a concussion," Lawrence said.

I said, "It'll come back. But I have another question. Did Virgil start the manse fire?"

"Yes, he admitted to it. He was driving away from the manse when he saw you pull up. He worried you'd find something connecting him to the drugs."

"Arson seems a pretty reckless strategy," I said.

Lawrence said, "He panicked. He circled back, parked around the corner and hauled a gas can through a neighbour's yard. Risky. He left a trail and might easily have been seen."

"The fire could have spread. He might have endangered more than just me and Michael."

"He said he didn't know Inspector Powers was there."

I said, "But it was okay to blow me up? That… tests my saintly sympathy."

"We know he mistrusted ministers. He was upset by Reverend Wilder's betrayal. That may well have… contributed to his apparent disregard for the value of your life."

"That fits, considering his family history."

Lawrence flipped his notebook closed.

He said, "Oh?"

"Stephen Peretz had an inappropriate relationship with a young woman named Dido Daniels. She was a legal minor, and a member of his congregation."

"Daniels?"

"Dido was Virgil and Kat's mother. They were raised by Attie and Doug, after Dido completed suicide."

Lawrence put it together.

He said, "Peretz's name is not on the birth records. I need to look at that journal."

"It was in my car," I said. "I was reading it at the train station."

"Then it should still be there."

Lawrence thumbed another text. The sight of his phone nudged my battered brain.

"It's come back to me," I said. "Virgil snapped photos of

Ed with his pants down and threatened to call someone."

Lawrence said, "We need his phone. He didn't have it when Inspector Powers brought him to the ER. My team's searching his truck. It's in the same impound lot as your car."

"Can you go through Virgil's phone without his consent, or something from a judge?"

"Constable Palmieri spoke with him a few minutes ago, and he told her the password. That's close enough to consent for me, since we don't plan to charge him."

"But what if he actually did run Ed over?"

"You asked earlier if I believed that. Do you?"

"No… but if he did, couldn't this go very wrong for you? You negotiated his immunity."

Lawrence said, "Tom, I'm tempted to say that sometimes you just have to have faith."

"So I'm thinking more like a cop," I said, "and you're sounding more like a preacher."

Lawrence said, "Does the journal shed light on how Stephen Peretz ended up wrapped in plastic and buried in the coal bin?"

It took some time to lay out all the strands I'd found, and how they wove together in my night of dreams. Once again, I left out the part about Doug's ghost.

"That's quite a story," Lawrence said.

"I think all the threads are there," I said.

Lawrence said, "A good defense attorney could unravel your theory. And the provenance of the journal would be an issue. Even if we could verify Douglas Beacham's handwriting, the journal was in an unlocked room in a building open to the public most days of the week.

I said, "So what do we do?"

Lawrence said, "We, or more properly, the Crown Attorney would need another data stream, to corroborate the narrative as you laid it out for me."

I said, "Doug is dead. Stephen is dead. Dido is dead. There's only one person who can give us that."

"I have an idea," Lawrence said. "It would be overstating to call it a plan."

"I'm in," I said.

Lawrence said, "There are risks."

I said, "The keeping of these secrets has done so much damage. It's time for the story to come out. What do you want to do?"

"Nothing clears up a case so much…" Lawrence began.

I finished for him. "As stating it to another person."

The grim determination on his face did not fit with the schoolteacher persona I'd imagined. Lawrence was a bit of wolf in a lamb's wool sweater.

He said, "We bring the principals together, walk them through what we've got and hopefully it sets something useful in motion."

"I noticed your use of the word we."

"That's deliberate," Lawrence said. "I am going to need you to do some things."

44

The Oakville Beaver, Friday Online Edition

Bronte minister rescued by jaws of life

Emergency vehicles were called to the Applewood Drive home of local minister Thomas Book late last evening. Book's 2004 Suzuki Swift was seriously damaged in what authorities describe as "an incident of aggressive driving" involving a late model Ford F-150 truck.

Detective Constable Barbara Palmieri, spokesperson for Halton Police Services, stated the driver of the F-150 pickup had been observed behaving erratically before ramming the driver's side of Reverend Book's vehicle. The Bronte Rescue Jaws of Life were used to extricate Reverend Book, who was transported to Oakville Trafalgar Hospital with serious but non-life-threatening injuries.

The identity of the truck driver has not been released.

Reverend Book has served as associate minister at Saint Mungo's Church for two years. He is not the first minister from that church to be in the news in recent days.

On Monday afternoon, the decayed remains of the late Reverend Stephen Peretz were discovered during renovations to a basement storage room, directly below the Saint Mungo's sanctuary. Reverend Peretz was reported missing under mysterious circumstances almost 30 years ago.

Thursday afternoon, the frozen body of the Reverend Doctor Edward Wilder, senior pastor of Saint Mungo's, was found buried in a snowbank at the north end of the church parking lot.

The discovery of the remains of each of these former ministers occurred during location shooting for the Natural Wonders Channel television show "The Ghost Toucher." Neither the Natural Wonders Channel, nor the producers of The Ghost Toucher were available for comment.

Detective Constable Palmieri was unable to confirm if foul play is suspected in the deaths of either Reverend Peretz or Reverend Wilder. When asked if there was any connection between these deaths, and the apparent attack on Reverend Book, the detective stated it was against policy to discuss an ongoing investigation.

Ms. Betty Torrance-Martens, chair of the Saint Mungo's Church Council, thanked the local community for their continued support, and asked for prayers for the families and friends of Reverend Peretz, Reverend Wilder, and Reverend Book. She indicated the Easter Sunday service would carry on as scheduled and that all were welcome.

45

"Kat," I said, "can you tell everyone why your video equipment is set up in the parlour?"

Kat looked more like a producer than a lowly location director. She wore a grey pin-striped suit over a smart white shirt. She'd pulled her blonde hair back into a bun and put on black-rimmed reading glasses which I thought added ten years but did not quite hide the nervousness in her eyes. She gripped her aluminum clipboard in both hands.

Kat said, "Thank you, Reverend Tom. The segment I've been filming here at the church is the first project I've been trusted with, and I don't have anything to show for two expensive days of location work. I've got footage of the... bodies being found, but no context, no story to go with them. I was hoping you'd consent to my filming this afternoon."

Eric Halliday was at the north end of the table. He wore a blue flannel shirt that appeared to have been pressed. Retired banker casual dress. He was ready to play his part.

Eric said, "I can't imagine why you'd want my tired old face, but Kat, if it's going to help you, I say go ahead. I've known you your whole life, and I trust you."

I thought Eric sold it well.

Betty Torrance-Martens, the council chair said, "Would we need to pass a motion or something?"

Michael and Lawrence had earlier pushed the horsehair sofa up against the built-in bookshelves and slid the casket-like coffee table out into the hall. They'd also rolled up the Persian carpet, and stood it on its end, beside the sofa. This cleared the space for the 8-foot plywood table now in the center of the room, around which they'd placed wooden stacking chairs.

I said, "If you're agreeable, Kat needs us all to sign a waiver like I did for the other shoots. There are forms and pens on the table."

Kat had hung tiny grey boxes on each oak-paneled wall. The size and shape of matchboxes, they were loaded with memory cards that could record for hours. Looking at one, I couldn't even guess where the lens might be.

During set up, Lawrence had said, "They're bigger than we use for surveillance, but not much. This is high end equipment."

Kat said, "We bring them in when seeing a camera crew would put people off. They don't need extra lights, and they each have an onboard mike. After a few minutes, people forget they're even there."

I looked around the table. Eric had signed his form. Michael Powers made a show of reading the document, but he had his pen in hand. I signed mine and made a stack with the ones signed by Betty, and her partner Ivy, the council secretary.

Beside me, I heard Kat say to Attie Beacham, "Just sign it, Aunt Attie, or leave."

Attie signed and added her form to my stack. She also stole a glance at the battered tin box I'd placed at the center of the table.

I said, "Have you all met Detective Sergeant Kitchen? I asked him here to shed some light on things."

Lawrence wore tan cords, and a navy cardigan over a collared white shirt. On the table in front of him, next to Kat's form, was a small black duty book.

Lawrence said, "I've signed my form, Ms. Daniels. Are you recording now?"

Kat tapped her phone, and said, "We are now, Detective Sergeant."

He said, "I added a note to the bottom of your form, that I should repeat out loud. The proceedings being recorded are not a formal interview, but I am here in my role as a homicide investigator with the Halton Regional Police. I've also noted that my team may request access to the footage."

Michael Powers, from his seat next to Eric said, "Which means you're on the job."

He'd dressed down to look more like the property guy on the church council than a reinstated police inspector. He's a big man, built for football, and he'd sweat through his Amazing Powers T-shirt from the effort of setting the room the way I wanted it.

Lawrence said, "Yes, I am."

Michael and Lawrence had worked together on the phrasing.

Kat said, "My company has already shared the earlier footage with the police and just want to help. I feel the same way."

I said, "I'll begin by thanking those of you who helped with the Good Friday service and Ivy's art installation. I heard both went well and I wished I could've been here."

I raised my cane and said: "I was under observation at the hospital for a concussion, and getting a cast put on."

Attie said, "And yet you found time to help the Detective Sergeant harass my poor Virgil. Part of why I agreed to attend this unscheduled… gathering was to remind you of your role in this community and what we actually pay you to do."

On the wall behind Attie hung the pen-and-ink drawing of the exterior of Saint Mungo's. It was one of the few pieces we'd left in place when we dismantled her parlour for this meeting.

I said, "Attie, I want what's best for Virgil, and for Kat…"

"Reverend Book, if your concern is genuine you might consider how long you wish to remain as their pastor."

"Attie, I've lost track of how often I've been threatened this week, but I'm about done with it."

She'd reprised the Margaret Thatcher ensemble from the Monday night meeting, with the addition of a boxy black leather handbag. Her fitted jacket was the colour of arctic ice.

"What else have you been doing," Attie said, "on the congregation's time, to expose yourself to threats?"

Betty said, "Reverend Tom was actually meant to be on vacation this week."

I nodded to Betty.

"Thank you for that," I said, "Attie, I doubt I'll be removed from Saint Mungo's so soon after the sudden loss of Reverend Wilder. But even if you do have the clout to get me fired, can we agree it won't happen until after this meeting?"

That felt better than it should have. I needed to rein myself in.

Attie's look was chilling.

"Reverend Tom," Betty said, "will this be an official council meeting?"

Betty looked to her right, where Ivy was poised with her pen over the minute book. They'd both reverted to jeans and white rec department polo shirts.

"No," I said. "I don't think Ivy needs to take notes. But I would like to offer a short reflection, in lieu of an opening prayer."

Eric smiled, and said, "Is this going to be a sermon, Reverend Tom?"

I said, "Yesterday, my daughter reminded me if enough terrible things happen in a person's life, especially if they happen at a young age, that person may lose faith in life."

I rose to my feet and pushed my chair back.

"Maybe this is a kind of sermon. Sorry about that, Eric."

"No, let's hear it," Eric said.

"Whatever other meanings you may attach to Good Friday, Jesus was killed by people with privilege and power. They saw a problem and decided killing him was their solution."

I paused to lower myself back into the chair. My knees had warned me with sharp spikes of pain when I stood and hadn't relented.

"Sorry, thought I could stand."

I took a moment to let the pain in my knees subside.

I said, "I spent a lot of my childhood calming my father down. Trying to keep my brother and mother safe from his drunken rages. I remember asking why don't we just wait 'til he passes out, and press a pillow over his face? You know what my mother said?"

The room was very still. They all looked at me.

"My mother said, this is not the whole story. There's more to him than you are seeing. You don't know why he's like this. You also don't get to decide it's the end of his story."

"Tom…" Betty said. I saw tears in her eyes.

"We didn't… I didn't know that about your family. Your poor mother…"

"Thank you, Betty. But that's not why I am telling you this. On this day of waiting and wondering, between the horror of Good Friday and the hope of Easter Sunday, we need to talk about what happened to Stephen Peretz and Ed Wilder. They each died because someone claimed the right to end their story."

Michael said, "Amen, Tom."

Lawrence looked over at me, then rose to his feet.

"That may be my cue. Let's start with the most recent events. As Mrs. Beacham mentioned, Reverend Book and I have spoken with Virgil Daniels, your current church caretaker. He has been very helpful."

Attie said, "If he's been so helpful, why is still locked up?"

"Aunt Attie! Let him talk, Kat said. "I need to hear about Virgil."

"Mr. Daniels hasn't been arrested, Mrs. Beacham. You might ask his attorney to bring you up to date. Your great-nephew was lawfully detained for psychiatric assessment. We were concerned he was a danger to himself and to others."

Ivy spoke for the first time.

"Virgil's a good boy. He'd never hurt anyone."

Lawrence turned to face Ivy.

"He will not face charges. My team shares the view that

Mr. Daniels has been under extreme duress. This has influenced our approach to this complex situation."

I said, "When we told Virgil about this meeting, he said he wished he could be here."

Lawrence said, "Reliable witnesses have stated, and Virgil has confirmed that he rammed his truck into the driver's side of Reverend Book's car. This occurred while Reverend Book was trapped in the vehicle, and only moments after his daughter Hope escaped."

Lawrence turned to me.

"I was relieved Reverend Book's injuries were not life-threatening."

Lawrence flipped opened his duty book.

"As Mr. Daniel's assault on Reverend Book was interrupted, he is said to have called out, 'I was trying to keep him away from my sister.' He went on to say, 'Auntie Attie warned me you can't trust these ministers!'"

There was a prolonged silence in the parlour.

Heads turned to Attie and her great-niece.

"But Reverend Book was helping me..." Kat began. "Why would Virgil think..."

Lawrence waited.

"Aunt Attie, did you tell Virgil..."

"Tell him what, Kat? That you were spending far too much time around the church? That you'd fallen under the spell of the lonely minister? That you were as vulnerable, as weak as..."

"As who, Aunt Attie? As vulnerable as who?"

Ivy stood up from the table, fists at her hips.

"She's talking about your mother," Ivy said. "She thinks you were vulnerable to being badly used, the way your mother was."

Attie said, "Ivy, this is family business. You stay out of this!"

"No, Ivy," Kat said, "I need you to tell me what you meant about my mother."

Ivy said, "Kat, I've tried to tell you for years. Do you remember when I used to say, be careful, and let me know if anyone tries to touch you? I said if anybody did, tell me and I'd..."

Betty reached out to Ivy, and said, "Dear, you need to sit, and to breathe."

Now Kat was out of her chair, and she began to shout.

"You, and everybody else in my life. Aunt Attie asking so many questions. I could never bring anybody home. And Virgil. Always watching, snooping. Hanging over me."

Attie said, "Your mother made Virgil promise to keep you safe. So it wouldn't happen to you, like it did to her..."

Attie stood up. She pointed at me, her stiff arm straight as a rifle.

"Which is why when I saw you, in my own house, cozying up to him..."

The blood left my face. I felt dizzy and was grateful I was seated.

Lawrence had warned it could go this way. Her accusation still hit like a kick in the gut.

I said, "Attie, Kat's just a few years older than my Hope. I could never..."

Michael reached over to put a hand on mine. He shot a warning look at Attie.

"Mrs. Beacham, I'd like you to lower your hand, and return to your seat. Pause a moment. Think about Tom Book as you have known him."

"Michael Powers, I don't care if you were a hot shot detective. You don't know them the way I do. You can't trust these ministers. They're all the same."

"No," Kat said in a child-like voice. "Aunt Attie. You have it wrong. Tom... Reverend Book has been nothing but kind to me. Even when I was a bitch."

Attie said, "Kat! Language!"

At his end of the table, Eric Halliday raised his hand to cover his mouth. Was he stifling a cough, or an embarrassed laugh?

He stood and looked at the door.

The movement caught Michael's eye. He glanced at Eric and gave a warning nod.

Michael mouthed the words, "Just a second."

Eric returned the nod and sat.

Michael said, "I think we should all sit... take a time out."

To their credit, Ivy, Kat and Attie followed Eric's lead, and reclaimed their seats.

After a moment, Kat spoke.

"Really, Aunt Attie. That's what you focus on? That I said bitch? You taught me everything I know about being a bitch. Reverend Book listened to me, and tried to help me with Virgil, with Ed, and with you..."

"Ed? Is that what you called that Edward Wilder? Are you saying..."

"Yes, Aunt Attie. Ed and I were... involved."

"I should have known. He went behind my back trying to sell the church to that Brad Kazinski. And he had his claws into you? I never liked that slick bastard."

Kat said, "Aunt Attie! Language!"

Kat half-smiled, but there was no humour in her eyes.

She said, "Ed was less than I hoped for. But you don't get to call him a bastard. Someone killed him."

Attie said, "I told Virgil about your late-night tryst with the good Reverend Book. I said the minister was headed home and should be warned he was travelling a perilous road."

"Mrs. Beacham," Lawrence said, "You don't have to say anything. You risk incriminating yourself."

"Detective Sergeant Kitchen, you've told us my nephew is helping you. It's likely you already know I sent him after Reverend Book. If you haven't charged him for his actions, I doubt you will pursue me related to the same matter. If you planned to charge me, you'd have already done it."

I thought, not for the first time, that Attie's resemblance to Margaret Thatcher was more than superficial.

"Mrs. Beacham," Lawrence said, "the day isn't over."

From his end of the table, Eric said, "I believe it is for me. If I hear any more, I might never care to set foot in this place again."

Eric rose and made for the door. Michael rose to follow.

Michael turned to me and said, "I'll make sure he has a ride home."

I said, "Thanks Michael. Thanks Eric."

As the door closed after them, I saw the faint outline of a notch dented into the frame. A gouge that had been filled and stained to match the dark oak.

Attie scanned the room, her gaze pausing on each of us with the intensity of a searchlight.

"Well," she said, "Anyone else want to go?"

I rose from the stiff-backed, hard-bottomed stacking chair.

"I just need to stretch," I said. "My legs and everything else feel ancient."

I looked around the table. Betty's eyes shone with tears. The muscles in Ivy's forearms were flexed and rigid. Kat's shoulders were rounded and slumped as if she were leaning into a hard wind. She looked up at me, her clear blue eyes wide, and wet with sadness.

Kat hadn't known all that might emerge when she'd agreed to help.

"I need you to tell me," Kat said. "If Virgil did those things to Reverend Tom, did he also do something to Ed, I mean Reverend Wilder?"

I turned to Lawrence.

"Ms. Daniels," Lawrence said. "Your brother admitted to the assault on Reverend Book. He also admitted he started the fire at the manse. But we believed him when he told us he'd gone to the manse because he felt safe there, and he wanted to talk with Reverend Wilder."

"But... if he started the fire while Reverend Book and Mr. Powers were there... didn't he realize... why would he do that?

"Kat," I said. "We don't think Virgil was trying to hurt me, at least not then. He wanted me out of the manse and improvised an over-the-top way to make that happen."

"That's a different matter," Lawrence said. "We don't need to get into that."

"Detective Kitchen," Attie said. "You've just told us Ed Wilder was already dead, and Virgil was still looking for him. That means Virgil didn't kill Ed. So who did?"

"Mrs. Beacham, my team has devoted considerable time and energy to that question."

"And?"

Lawrence gave me a nod.

I sat down again and tried to not think about the itch I longed to scratch, on the back of my knee. Under the cast. It seemed to get worse as things heated up in the parlour.

I said, "Kat, you told me that when Virgil… interrupted you and Reverend Wilder, he brought out his phone to take photos."

"He did," Kat said. "Virgil was angry. Very angry. He wanted to send them to someone."

Lawrence said, "Who would Virgil send that kind of photo? Do you have any idea?"

"Not really," Kat said.

I said, "You mentioned that after Virgil left and you were helping Ed up from the carpet, his phone was buzzing. Any idea who was trying to reach him?"

"I told you," Kat said. "Ed was very secretive."

Attie said, "That's what they're like."

Kat turned to Attie, narrowing her eyes.

"Aunt Attie," Kat said, "you're not helping."

Lawrence stepped away from the table to give the heavy oak door a sharp knock. The door opened, and a uniformed officer with auburn hair entered. She handed Lawrence a clear plastic evidence bag.

Lawrence spoke in a low voice, and the officer nodded.

She stepped into the parlour and pulled the door closed behind her.

Having noticed the mark on the door frame, it now stood out when I looked in that direction. I wondered if I was seeing Doug's efforts to cover damage Stephen Peretz did in his mad drunken rage, all those years before.

"This is Detective Constable Palmieri," Lawrence said. "She's brought the phone recovered from Virgil's truck after it was impounded."

Lawrence returned to the table and set the bagged phone next to his duty book.

He said, "Ms. Torrance-Martens."

Betty and Ivy both looked up.

"Sorry, I mean, Ms. Ivy Torrance-Martens."

Ivy said, "Yes, Detective."

Her eyes were on the flat black device in the evidence bag.

"What do you think my team found," Lawrence said, "when we went through Virgil's phone?'

"Ivy," Betty said. "What is he talking about?"

Attie said, "Yes, Ivy. What is the homicide detective talking about?"

Ivy shifted as if to stand. Betty placed an arm around her shoulders, pulling her close to offer comfort, but it was Betty who trembled.

Ivy pulled away from Betty and turned in her chair to face Attie. There was tension in her taut, athletic form, and I worried she might leap up at the older woman.

Lawrence and the uniformed officer were both on alert.

Ivy said, "Don't you dare get high and mighty with me, Attie Beacham."

Lawrence said, "Ms. Torrance-Martens. Virgil sent you a photo. You were listed in his phone as Art Lady."

Ivy said, "What photo?"

Lawrence said, "Ivy, it must have upset you to see your

minister, and a young woman you obviously care about…"

"You can't prove I saw anything!"

"Reverend Wilder's phone was in his trouser pocket when his remains were found," Lawrence said. "You forwarded Virgil's photo to him. Do you remember what you texted?"

Ivy's head bowed slightly. Her shoulders sagged.

"I said he was a hypocrite. It wasn't enough he and Kazinski were trying to screw the church over… I asked him if he realized he screwed Kat in the same room where her mother was raped."

I was so intent on Ivy, I almost missed Attie rising from her chair.

"You have no right!" Attie yelled. "You caused all of it. If you hadn't bewitched Wendy, luring him away from her husband, we would have got him sorted. It's your fault Stephen Peretz turned his… attentions to Dido."

"Attie," I said. "I really don't think…"

"No, your kind doesn't make much use of that particular organ."

Good one, Attie. If the setting were different, I might have laughed at her joke. Except I'd glimpsed how dangerous and cruel she could be. With the shrewd instinct of a back-alley brawler Attie had aimed at Ivy's weak spot.

I looked at Ivy. Her head was bowed, as if in prayer. She flexed those strong potter's hands. She'd thrown hundreds of clay vessels over the years.

I could almost see her hands forming the outline of the cup of suffering she crafted over and over again, every year, to share at her installation. I had placed one of her latest efforts on the mantle at home.

"Ivy," I said, "Attie's wrong. You cannot be blamed for what Stephen did…"

"No, Reverend Tom. She's right. I can be blamed. If not for Stephen, then for…"

"Aunt Attie…Ivy," Kat said, "What are you two saying about my mom?"

Attie said, "Kat... dear. When we get home... There are some things it's time you were told. But not like this, and not by... someone like her."

Attie's eyes passed over Ivy to focus on Betty.

"Ms. Torrance-Martens, Betty... it might be time for you to take charge of this... meeting, if only to ask for a motion to adjourn. I see nothing to gain by prolonging..."

Ivy cut her off.

"No, Attie Beacham, you don't get to do that today. You love to control... well, everything... I can't believe, no scratch that, I absolutely can believe you never told Kat and Virgil the truth about Dido, and what she went through. You always find a way to sweep things under some expensive rug."

I fought the urge to look at the Persian carpet we'd propped up in the corner.

Ivy said, "Attie, your pretty parlour used to be Stephen's office. Do you have any idea what went on in here? I'm sure your husband knew. Doug saw it all, cleaned up after everything. But he'd never say a word. He was as bad as you!"

Attie said, "You have no right to speak about Douglas. He gave so much, worked so hard... You can't imagine what he did for this church."

Attie turned towards the drawing of Saint Mungo's on the wall behind her. When she turned to face Ivy again, the light in her eyes had changed. Were those tears?

"This may just be a building to some of you. You would have let that Edward Wilder maneuver you into selling it to Kazinski. Ivy, we agree on this if nothing else... He was, in your words, out to screw us all."

Ivy straightened in her chair, raised her head and met Attie's eyes. They seemed to recognize something in each other.

She said, "Yes... yes, he was."

Attie said, "Men like that. Men like Stephen Peretz. Like Edward Wilder."

Ivy said, "They take what they want. They use people."

Kat said, "Aunt Attie, what happened to my mother?"

Ivy said, "Kat, I... tried to help your mother, after. She did the best she could, but it was so much... too much for her, and her own mother, well..."

Attie said, "Ivy, please..."

Kat, "She needs... I need, her, or someone, to tell me."

Attie said, "Your mother was very unhappy as a child, and things did not improve as she became a young woman. She was... easy prey for a man like Stephen Peretz."

Kat said, "You saw this, and let it... let him..."

Attie said, "No. It wasn't that way... I..."

Ivy said, "You what Attie? You were so focused on how things looked from the outside, you missed what was happening right here in this room."

Attie said, "You and Wendy fawning over each other like addled teens... you made a spectacle of yourselves."

Ivy said, "And worrying about us distracted you from seeing what was happening to Dido? She was the teenager, the tender sad child you should have been concerned about! How could you let him..."

Attie said," We took care of him, don't you worry..."

Lawrence said, "Mrs. Beacham, I should caution you again..."

Attie said, "I'm an old woman Detective Sergeant Kitchen, and we're talking about something that happened..."

Attie reached for Kat's hand. Kat pulled it out of reach.

"...something that happened," Attie said. "A lifetime ago. That... creature deserved what happened to him, and he should have stayed where Douglas buried him."

"Mrs. Beacham," Lawrence said, "I really must advise you..."

"Wait!" Ivy said, "Attie, are you saying what I think you're saying?"

Attie said, "You cannot accuse me of standing by when the honour of my family..."

Kat said, "Honour? Aunt Attie, was Stephen Peretz my father... Virgil's father? Did he..."

Attie said, "He was a beast. A slave to his appetites. And that was his downfall. I knew he wouldn't be able to resist. Douglas did the right thing. He cleaned it all up, and it went away..."

This is terrible, I thought, and we need to stop this. I also thought, we're so close.

Kat said, "Is that why... my mom... why she... did what she did?"

Ivy said, "Your mother loved you, and Virgil, as best she could. I know she did Kat."

Kat said, "But she..."

Ivy said, "She got to a point where all she wanted was to not be sad. She couldn't see a way... She made me promise I'd look out for you. It's why I came back to Saint Mungo's, after all that happened."

"Detective Kitchen," Betty said, "This needs to stop. I want to take Ivy home."

"No Betty, I'm going to finish this. I think Detective Kitchen's figured most of it out if he's gone through Virgil's phone."

Betty said, "Ivy."

She lowered her voice. She reached for Betty's hand.

"I am so sorry. You always see the best in everyone and want us all to get along. I have loved you for that, and so much more... you are the most forgiving, and gracious woman... But I'm sorry. There are some things... some people..."

Betty said, "Ivy, what are you saying?"

Ivy said, "I think Attie may understand, even if no one else here can."

Attie's eyes shifted from Ivy to the tin box, and back again.

Ivy said, "Virgil called me that night, after he found Ed with Kat. He told me what he'd seen, and why he'd sent the photo. He said he'd failed his mom, and his aunt, and hadn't taken care of Kat. He was so upset. I told him to stay where he was, that I'd come right away."

Betty looked up at Ivy, who still held her hand.

Betty said, "I'd have gone with you, if you asked. I didn't know…"

"You were already asleep. We'd spent the day setting up for the open house at the centre, and you were exhausted," Ivy said.

"I jumped in my truck, and raced over to the church, not knowing what I'd do when I got there. When I pulled into the church driveway, I saw that Virgil's truck was gone. I planned to go into the church, and check on you, Kat. But then, I saw him… Ed. Slipping around in the parking lot. He looked like a drunken fool. He looked like Stephen. Something… burst inside me. I stepped hard on the gas and aimed the truck at him."

Kat was sobbing. She said, "Ivy, you're my friend. Mom's friend. How could you?"

"You didn't see what he was, Kat. Your Aunt Attie was right. Not all of them, but some of them are…they need to be… when I make a pot, if it isn't working on the wheel, I need to know when to cut my losses… It wasn't hard. There wasn't much to him. I tossed him into the back of the truck, drove to the edge of the lot, and threw him in the snow. It was coming down pretty heavy by then, and I knew the plow would push more to cover him over. I'm sorry they found him on your video shoot. He could have laid there until the spring melt."

Lawrence stood and nodded to the uniformed officer.

He placed his hand on Ivy's shoulder and said, in a kind voice. "My colleague and I will take you to the police station to be booked. Betty, you may wish to travel with us. We'll arrange for a ride home for you later. Ivy Torrance-Martens, I am arresting you on suspicion in relation to the willful death of Reverend Edward Wilder."

46

"Reverend Tom, I need to show you something," Kat said.

She'd showed up at our door as we were finishing breakfast. Hope invited Kat in, offered her coffee while I made a quick change out of my pyjamas and robe, then ducked downstairs to Gwen's suite.

Kat set up her laptop on my kitchen island. The sun was shining bright through the window over the sink.

She said, "I was up pretty late last night, doing a rough cut with footage from the four cameras."

I said, "Kat, I was there..."

"Yes," she said, "and so was I. But the cameras see more than we do, and they can't lie. That's what I love about them. Just... please, watch."

So I did.

I angled on my stool to block the bright sun and cast a shadow over the MacBook screen.

I watched as Lawrence and the uniformed officer escorted Ivy and Betty out of the parlour. That left Kat and her great aunt squared off and staring at each other, and me off to one side.

I remembered wondering about a tactful way to leave.

On the screen, Attie was gesturing at the four walls and saying, "You will erase the recordings on those devious little cameras. You will tell the detective there was a technical problem."

Kat said, "That's not going to happen, Aunt Attie."

They were in a literal standoff, eyes locked even though Kat stood more than a foot taller in her heeled boots.

Attie said, "My money paid for your education, and likely bought these expensive toys. I read the form you had me sign. Your employer's company name isn't on it. You did this on your own, as Odious Kat Productions. Which means my money paid for all of this. Those cameras and whatever is on them belong to me. I demand that you erase them."

Kat said, "No. Aunt Attie, I won't do that."

I'd stayed out of it until Attie tried recruiting and threatening me all in one breath.

"Reverend Book, surely even you can see the wisdom in what I am saying. The image of Saint Mungo's has suffered enough damage. The future of this congregation, and your future with it, may well depend on…"

"Mrs. Beacham," I broke in. "I asked Kat to make the recording."

This was another moment I enjoyed far too much.

"You… did what?"

"And I gave her the money to rent the equipment she needed."

Icy splinters glinted in Attie's eyes. She swung her Margaret Thatcher handbag and slammed it down on the folding table, with force enough to collapse the legs at her end. I would not have imagined she had the strength.

I relived the sudden shock, and watched myself pull back from the loud crash as one end of the table hit the floor. The scene continued as Attie bent to retrieve her bag. She rose up to glare at us, push past me and steam out the parlour door.

Silence claimed the room until Kat spoke in a subdued voice.

"Reverend Tom, can you take me to see my brother?"

Kat pressed something on her keyboard to pause the video.

I said, "Kat, I am so sorry for what you and Virgil, and your mother have gone through."

Kat said, "I need you to watch this next part."

The video showed Attie bent forward with busy hands,

popping open her purse, scooping up the tin box, and sliding it out of sight. Kat's edit now cut to an angle that showed Attie's face, calm and thoughtful, as if choosing an entrée at her favourite restaurant. As she straightened to her full height her placid features transformed to display the outrage I'd seen on her face as she stormed out.

Kat said, "Look at her, Reverend Tom. She's acting! She is in total control of the moment, which she choreographed to make a grab for Uncle Doug's journal."

I said, "She does seem…"

Kat said, "Remember what she started to admit to Ivy? It was like she was bragging."

Kat touched some keys, and I saw her great aunt's face reappear on the screen.

Kat said, "Look at her eyes when I asked her about Stephen Peretz. I think she lost it a little here, let down her guard."

On the screen, Attie said, "He was a beast. A slave to his appetites. And that was his downfall. I knew he couldn't resist. Douglas did the right thing. He cleaned it all up, and it went away…"

Kat said, "She's talking about killing my biological father."

47

"You don't think they'll swarm us, if I walk into church with you and your daughter on Easter Sunday?"

The humour lit her face as Annika smiled. Her blonde hair fringed out the sides of the furry hood of her bright orange search and rescue parka.

I said, "Well..."

We'd sat on a park bench on the Fisherman's Wharf, our gloved hands cupped around coffees from Taste of Colombia. Steam rising from the cups mingled with the fog of our breath.

I was grateful for the blanket Hope left with us when she took Zeke for a walk towards Bronte Pier. We'd used her backpack to push off the crusted snow before spreading the blanket over the bench.

I'd leaned my shiny new aluminum cane against the hard edge of my cast, so I wouldn't forget it.

Annika said, "At my dad's church it was part of their congregational mission to marry off the unattached pastors. It was a serious occupation, that included tracking who they were seen with."

I remembered the buzz around Saint Mungo's when things started with Carrie. We were an item according to the hive mind well before we knew it for ourselves.

Carrie and I came down to Marina Park for walks that spring. When Hope was a toddler we brought her here for outings with my mom, when we came back to visit Oakville.

When Hope's home, and I'm not hobbled up with a cane, we still like to stroll the pier. The shorter of the two rock breakwater berms that shelter the marina, it is topped with a concrete walkway.

I said, "After this gruesome week, it might be good to give the church folks something less horrible to talk about."

Annika said, "That's a point. I've never actually been to your church without stepping over a corpse... is it too soon to say that?"

She dared another smile.

"No, it's true," I said. "I'm not quite ready to laugh about it, but it helps we've maybe cleared up some of the mystery."

Annika said, "Only some?"

People like to venture out on the pier to greet the Easter dawn. The town's snow crews had cleared the snow and thrown down salt. Signs warned of the sheets of ice that can build up as winter winds spray lake water on the concrete walkway.

"There's layers to everybody's story," I said. "I now have this picture of Stephen drinking heavily, and grooming Dido for his own sick purposes. Ivy said he raped her, and I have no reason to doubt it. But is that who Stephen Peretz was? And Ed... Lawrence pegged him as a sociopath. But that's his opinion, not a diagnosis."

She said, "Because of what they did, I find it hard to grieve their deaths. And I never knew them."

The morning air was crisp. The sun was shrouded by grey cloud and hadn't warmed things up.

By early summer more than a hundred sailboats and pleasure cruisers would be tied up at the floating docks. We could see many of them shrink-wrapped in white plastic and dry-docked amongst the snowdrifts in the yacht club yard.

"I'm not saying I'd have liked Stephen, or that I will actually miss Ed. I've been reminded how little I knew this man I worked with for two years. But whoever they really were, it bothers me no one has come forward to claim their remains. For now, their bodies are laid out in drawers in the cold room at the morgue."

"You worked on arrangements for Stephen," Annika said. "Will you go forward with that?"

"I may ask a friend to do the funeral. I don't know if

he'll agree, but I'd love to see him."

I thought of Paul Bennett. I wondered how much he'd followed, from his quiet corner of the world. When he retired from Saint Mungo's he'd started a retreat centre.

If he'd heard what had happened to Stephen, to Ed. To his mother's house, which he'd given to Saint Mungo's when he retired.

Annika said, "How are Kat and Virgil doing? Did you get her in to see him?"

"Virgil's going to need time. His Form 1 will expire tonight, and he's agreed to sign himself in for further assessment. It was good his sister wanted to see him. The pair of them know they need each other."

"So Virgil has a place to stay," Annika said. "Did Kat go back to her great aunt's home? I can't imagine doing that if I was her, and at that age."

I said, "She phoned Lila Brown, the grandmother who lives in Florida most of the year, and essentially told her she's claiming her condo. It's in the building beside the church. She called while we drove to the hospital, so I couldn't help but over-hear."

"Good for her. It's perhaps the least that woman can do."

I said, "Kat expressed that opinion. She has backbone. I think she's going to need it."

Hope had unclipped Zeke from his lead. He seemed content to stay at her heel.

At a spot about halfway to the end of the pier, Zeke halted, his ears up and alert, and his dark snout pointed up to the sky.

I heard the honking before I saw the flight of Canada Geese descending to land at the Marina Park. They live on the waterfront year-round and fly a regular circuit. Folks in Oakville scatter dried corn by the sack despite strenuous objections by local authorities.

"What will happen to Mrs. Beacham?"

"Lawrence will present what he has to the Crown Attorney's office. He expects they'll advise him to not pursue a cold case no one really cares about."

Annika said, "Would that be the end of it? The story gets buried again?"

I said, "Not if Kat has her way."

I told Annika about Kat's early morning visit.

"After hours editing the video, she stayed up late working on a treatment."

Annika, the nurse said, "I'm guessing that means something different in her world."

"It's a proposal for a screenplay. She'd tell her mother's story, and how it was for her and Virgil to live in the shadow of her mysterious sadness. It would be a cautionary tale of a family that placed such a high value on how things look from the outside, they allowed a young woman to be abused, to end her own life, and leave her children to grow up living in fear.

The movie would follow the story of a lonely assistant pastor who sees dead people, and how the spirit of her great uncle reached out to him, to push him out of his own crypt of grief to claim back his own life and set the record straight.

Those are mostly her words, not mine," I said. "She has a certain flair."

"She could write the narration for that Ghost Toucher show. Speaking of which, what was that about the lonely pastor and a ghost?"

I told her about seeing Doug and smelling his lemon furniture polish. I watched for signs she thought I needed to book a room on the same ward as Virgil.

She said, "There were moments on that first shoot when you stared off into the middle distance. I'd speak to you, and it was like you were somewhere else. I also wondered what would compel you, after what we'd just been through, to rummage through a storage closet."

I said, "You don't think I'm losing it?"

"We all lose a lot along the way. I told you my mom died

when I was young. My dad, a practical-minded old farmer, never stopped talking to her. Another time, I want to hear more about what else, who else you've seen."

Parts of me I didn't know had been holding tight, unclenched.

"Zeke's made a new friend," I said, nodding at Hope and the dog, who were heading back toward our park bench.

Annika had met Zeke as an abused and frightened pup and coaxed him back to life. Along the way he learned to sniff out the dead.

Annika said, "He can be stand-offish, even when he's not working. But he's taken to you, and Hope seems to have a way with him."

"Thanks for listening to the stranger parts of this story and still being here," I said.

Annika said, "Have you talked to others about… the spirits? Is that the right word?"

"Gwen has an aunt who calls them that. She says they show up to nudge us towards things that need to be dealt with."

"Like long hidden corpses, and neglected children."

"I've also talked to Michael."

"Your friend the not-so-retired cop?"

"Michael got there in time to stop the storage room shelves from crashing down on me. He also wanted to know what got into me."

"That's not the only time he's saved you this week," she said. "He stopped Virgil from crushing you in your car."

"He also carried me out of the manse fire. We were in that one together, but still…"

She said, "He's like your guardian angel."

"When he visited me at the hospital, I tried to thank him for repeatedly saving my butt."

"He's a good friend."

"Yes, but apparently there's more to it. When I told him about Doug's ghost, he wasn't at all put off by the idea. He said his mother was from a part of Scotland where certain folks have the 'second sight'."

"Did his mother have it?"

"We only met briefly. She was in hospice at the same time as Carrie. From what he said, maybe she did have the gift."

"What did he tell you?"

"Before she died, she told Michael I was to do her funeral, and he was to get involved at my church, get to know me, and protect me from danger."

When he spoke about his mother, Michael's eyes had been wet with tears.

"And that's what he's done," I said. "When I thanked him again, he did his bad John Wayne thing and said, partner, that's why I'm here."

Annika nodded, and said, "My dad was one of those tough guys who are not really tough, even though they are."

The clouds had lifted. Zeke and Hope were lit up from behind by the glow of morning sun. They picked up their pace, Zeke padding along with casual ease as Hope shifted into her 'let's get going' stride. I guessed she was thinking we needed to get to the church. She's a preacher's kid.

"I have another question," Annika said. "It sounds like there's a lot in Kat's treatment about you. How does she know all that?"

"When Lawrence asked me to recruit Kat, I decided to be honest with her. I told her I was convinced Attie and maybe Lila dosed a bottle of vodka to give to Stephen on a night they arranged to have Dido elsewhere."

"There's a lot of darkness in that family."

"Exactly. I told Kat I'd begun to feel that somehow Doug was nudging me to bring this all to light, but it might not happen if we didn't get Attie talking."

"Do you believe they were trying to kill Reverend Peretz?"

"They might have been trying to teach him a lesson. Doug knew they did a similar thing to Lila's husband. I hold on to the hope they didn't know if you overdose, that stuff can do more than make you vomit."

Annika had her gloves off to work her phone.

She read from the screen.

"They messed with a powerful drug. It does more than interfere with the body's capacity to process alcohol. It's been known to cause dizziness, hallucinations, paranoia, even heart failure."

"Doug described Stephen going wild in his office before cracking his skull on the edge of his desk."

"How did Kat react to all of this?"

"She was very quiet, and then told me it fit with things she picked up over the years. She was keen to read the journal and thought it could hold a lot of answers."

"Why not just give it to her and keep yourself out of it? Not all your parishioners would be keen to have the world know about their ghost-toucher pastor."

"Some won't. But one thing this week has brought home is the danger of burying the truth, for the sake of how things look."

"It could cost you your job."

"I'm okay with that. I'm ready for some changes, and Kat can't tell this story without me. As far as I know I am the only one who's read Doug's journal."

"Oh… because Mrs. Beacham stole it. That's what Kat showed you in her video."

That got a chuckle out of me.

"I placed Doug's tin box in the parlour to provoke Attie, but it was empty."

"That's pretty devious, Reverend Book. Sounds like it worked."

"It did, but there's a problem. When the homicide team searched my car at the impound lot, they found the box jammed tight under my seat, but when they opened it…"

Zeke loped up to our park bench. He eyed Annika, who gave him a nod. Then he sniffed at my cast, knocking over my cane.

Hope reached down to pick it up, and said, "Let's get moving, Dad. It's Easter."

278

279

ABOUT THE AUTHOR

Darrow Woods

 Darrow Woods lives in Canada's southernmost town, where he regularly feeds the neighbour's cat.

PRAISE FOR AUTHOR

Mayhem breaks out at St. Mungo's Church. It's Holy Week and a body falls out of the basement wall during church renovations. Unlike the body of Jesus, this one has been there considerably longer than three days. The stink, "like a butcher's dumpster on a hot day," seeps into the church unmasking the pretense of bucolic congregational life. Long-buried lies and secrets are also unearthed.

The young widower, Rev. Tom Book, risks his life attempting to untangle the lies and secrets with the help of a hidden diary, the local law, and the lovely Annika and Zeke, her cadaver-sniffing dog.

The Book of Answers is Father Brown meets Chief Inspector Armand Gamache, in Oakville. Mystery lovers will delight in the building suspense and the steady disclosure of clues. A Five Star read by Darrow Woods, Crime Writers of Canada Awards of Excellence Finalist.

David Giuliano, former moderator of the United Church of Canada, and author of The Undertaking of Billy Buffone. www.davidgiuliano.ca

ACKNOWLEDGEMENT

I am grateful for the encouragement and tutelage offered by Melodie Campbell, who has been my writing teacher, and a good friend. I have also received valuable advice through the Crime Writers of Canada mentoring program.

A special thanks goes to those who read, and offered critiques and corrections to earlier versions of this book.

I am grateful Jim Potter offered his editor's eyes and pencil to the final manuscript.

Manufactured by Amazon.ca
Bolton, ON